CANTERBURY
TRAILS

Barb Dobson

Grosvenor House
Publishing Limited

This book is published by
Grosvenor House Publishing Ltd
Link House
140 The Broadway, Tolworth, Surrey, KT6 7HT.
www.grosvenorhousepublishing.co.uk

This book is a work of fiction. Any resemblance to
people or events, past or present, is purely coincidental.

A CIP record for this book
is available from the British Library

ISBN 978-1-80381-103-1

For Bill. Thank you for being such a
big part of my life and making it extraordinary.

When April with its sweet showers meant that I had to stay home rather than pop to Canterbury to attend an open-air food festival, I took my frustration out on my computer. That said frustration led to the creation of some characters who lived or spent time in or around Canterbury. In 'Canterbury Trails' (not 'Tales', someone else has nabbed that title) we meet the beautiful Cressida whose attention makes you feel like you are bathed in the glow of a lighthouse, and Jon, the thwarted actor craving fame. Whereas Mac is seen hurtling through life without any awareness of the affect he has on others, Marcy and Fatima learn that no good deed gets away unpunished unless they are extremely quick to rescue the situation. Fingers discovers his past but makes sure it doesn't affect his future while Anna remembers the sixties and, despite everything, has survived and prospered. Clarke and Ivan share a failure while Rod gets enticed into a world he never knew existed and finds the secret of another's success. While Ed and Nell nest, Freya and Philip learn a way to overcome the loneliness in their lives. Isla makes those around her suffer from her personal delusions and Caroline slowly grows to know herself and likes what she has become. Josephine remembers a special lady while Charlotte's resentment of her cousin reaches an unpleasant conclusion. Finally, Trina and Nancy focus on their family values and achieve the happy endings they both deserve.

My pilgrims are not all making their way to Canterbury, but the city has touched each of them in some way. Like the River Stour, my characters meander through time and place. Some of them meet but do not realise they are part of the tale others tell. Others exist alone yet experience the vibe of a city which in some ways has affected their lives.

I hope you enjoy my Canterbury Trails and seeing as you don't have to translate it from Medieval English, rest in the knowledge that this book will never need to be studied for A level English Literature but might be just the thing to read by a pool, on a beach or snuggled under the covers before you put the light out.

Barb x

Character list

Cressida	16.11.83	**Scorpio.**	Appealing. Liable to sting those near them.
Freya	30.03.53	**Aries.**	Kind and generous. Can be spontaneous.
Clarke	29.06.69	**Gemini.**	Scrupulously tidy. Sometimes accident prone.
Ivan	02.05.52	**Taurus.**	Dependable. Will dig deep to help others.
Trina	12.07.50	**Cancer.**	Falls in love too easily. Believes in re-birth.
Rod	04.02.74	**Aquarius.**	Intelligent yet can sometimes end up in the soup.
Ed & Nell	1942 & 1950	**Horse & Tiger.**	Chinese water and gold. Can get in a jam together.
Anna	18.01.49	**Capricorn.**	Quick thinking and clever. Can be ruthless.
Philip	02.03.60	**Pisces.**	Caring and curious. Dislikes sharp things.
Marcy & Fatima	1996	**Chinese Rats.**	Strong sense of justice. Influenced by appearances.
Mac	03.09.52	**Virgo.**	Blindly adventurous yet oblivious to consequences.
Fingers	21.08.74	**Leo.**	Fiercely defensive of family. Will never be caged.
Isla	29.02.56	**Taurus.**	Stubborn. Can suffer from cognitive dissonance.
Caroline	29.03.00	**Aries.**	Highly creative yet often blind to the obvious.
Nancy	19.02.52	**Libra.**	Friendly and balanced. Brings harmony and love.
Jon	03.01.89	**Capricorn.**	Intractable, austere. No belief in Chinese horoscopes.
Josephine	18.12.79	**Sagittarius.**	Joyful, creative. Loves life.
Charlotte	05.06.90	**Gemini.**	Unforgiving. Darkness lurks beneath the surface.

⑰ Sevenoaks

⑱ Maidstone

Canterbury Trails

① Canterbury
② Bluebell Woods
③ Whitstable
④ Herne Bay
⑤ Reculver
⑥ Birchington
⑦ Westgate
⑧ Westbrook
⑨ Margate
⑩ Broadstairs
⑪ Ramsgate

⑫ Manston
⑬ Sturry
⑭ Dover
⑮ Dungeness
⑯ Lydd
⑰ Sevenoaks
⑱ Maidstone
⑲ Ashford
⑳ Chilham
㉑ Old Wives Lees
㉒ Chartham

River Stour

Cressida

16.11.83

Scorpio. Appealing.
Liable to sting those near them.

Cressida had always been beautiful. After nine months in the womb, she was identified as a baby in distress forcing her mother to have an emergency Caesarean section. Cressida's head was never squashed to fit through the birth canal. She arrived with a perfectly formed skull while her mother's abdominal muscles were pulled to the point that she was never able to wear tight fitting skirts again. As soon as she entered the world people crowed over her loveliness. And as her blue eyes turned brown, the doctors and nurses who gave her injections and treated her minor injuries commented on what a gorgeous little girl she was. But, unlike their similar comments to other mothers, in Cressida's case, they really meant it. As she toddled down the street next to her grandmother, strangers would stop and proclaim at how pretty she was, and her grandmother would swell with pride. Cressida soon came to understand that she was special and began, but in a very endearing way, to make the most of it.

With good looks and a naturally slim body, very similar to the one her once glamourous mother had owned, she quickly realised that charm got her a lot further in life than A* exam results. In no way academically bright, on the day she left school with no GCSEs but a pass in childcare and the title of 'Most popular student of the year', she had the good fortune to be included in a photograph taken by the local press. This was to celebrate the leavers who were on their way to university. However, the student gaining entrance to Cambridge one year earlier than from any other school that year was ignored as the reporter concentrated on interviewing Cressida. His article outlined her hopes and dreams for the future, praising her as a student who had even taken a Saturday job working with horses while studying for her childcare CSE and her ambition to work caring for others when she left school. None of the girls who had worked alongside her at the stables mentioned to him that she had spent more time talking to the customers whilst they had mucked out and groomed the horses; but then, they were never interviewed. The photographer took a picture of her by herself as well as of her with the high achievers. The photographs were seen by a model agency and Cressida started her first career. At eighteen she had a good year travelling all over the country for photoshoots. She met and bedded men along the way who were entranced by her and who could further her career. Just like her parents, her teachers, friends and school chums, everyone who met her felt that a lighthouse had shone its beam on them when Cressida gave them any attention. They all wanted her to like them and bathed in a form of reflected glory when they claimed her as a friend. Cressida had a lot of friends.

With a sparkle in her eye and a skip in her step, she adopted an enthusiasm for everything perceived as beneficial to her in any way. It was unfortunate that shortly after her photographic modelling career had begun, haute couture decided that the 'Heroin' look for models was the latest thing, and that prettiness was gauche, passé and only fit for Next catalogues. Luckily, men still preferred their women with bright clear eyes and a positive outlook on anything that was suggested and Cressida, who never shortened her name to Cress as she said it made her sound like a salad, became more and more positive depending on the wealth of the gentleman in question. She positively sat through operas and declared how much she had enjoyed them despite being jolted awake at one point by the high-pitched soprano berating her fate in Madam Butterfly. She positively relished the Formula One races and made no complaint that the petrol fumes had caused her sinuses to erupt with protest to the point that she was even unable to flirt with one of the drivers (to her dismay, younger, wealthier and better looking than her, then, current escort). She attended art galleries and declared to be brilliant works of art that, to her, resembled the kind of thing the children she had observed whilst doing her childcare course had proudly taken home to their mothers. Throughout all these activities Cressida charmed and smiled and networked and nodded.

And then, quite suddenly, after seeing the film 'Mamma Mia', Cressida decided it was time to enter a new phase. She didn't like the idea of flying to Greece or anywhere with a warmer climate like in the film. She didn't like flying at all, something that had been a problem with one of her earlier conquests who had owned his own Cessna and wanted to whisk her away on several occasions. So, she did the next best thing and left her hometown of Canterbury for the sunny climes of Newquay where she decided to explore the concept of being a flower child and a surfer.

Although she had always been conscientious about birth control, the experimentation with different kinds of drugs, in particular magic mushrooms that were rife in Cornwall and a lot cheaper than the lines of coke her upper-class friends normally dabbled in, meant that she was sometimes disorientated and not always aware what day it was. Her birth control regime went out the window and by the end of the summer, Cressida found she was expecting a child. She decided the father must have been Gus, an Australian hunk who rented out surfboards to the teenage masses that collected there. As the leaves began to fall and the rainclouds gathered over Cornwall, Gus announced that he was not used to the cold and was heading for Spain, and did she want to come with him? Cressida hadn't told him that she was pregnant and did some very quick calculations. Gus was tall and bronzed and very good looking but completely without a steady income and Cressida had grown tired of eating mung beans and tofu. She mentally ran through the images of the men she had known before her hippy phase and settled on Stuart, a stockbroker from Kingston who had a similar build and the same-coloured hair, but whose income would mean she could have her every need to be a yummy mummy embraced. She had to get back to London as quickly as she could to pick up where she had left off with him eighteen months previously, so she gave Gus a farewell hug, wished him well and sent him on his way adding his mobile number to her already bulging collection. Just in case.

Stuart was delighted to hear from her when she called him and asked if it was ok for her to come and stay as she had a job interview in London.

"I'm just popping back to my parent's home for a day or so," cooed Cressida down the phone as she watched the train pull into Paddington, "I need to pick up a couple of things. I don't suppose you still have the Lotus?" She was checking her purse. The fare back to Canterbury had left her completely broke and she didn't want to ask her father for money. "It would be so lovely if you could come and get me. Say, at the weekend? You don't work then, do you? Perhaps we could have a little stop over on the way back? It's such a shame that work took me away so suddenly. I've missed you" and Stuart's indignation at not being contacted for such a long time melted away as he remembered the pride he felt with Cressida on his arm when he attended functions and her body as she attended to his every sexual fantasy.

"I'll be there at 11, Saturday morning" he replied. And Cressida heaved a sigh of relief. The rest of her plan would fall into place quite easily. And it did.

Stuart had been surprised at Cressida's refusal of champagne since their reunion but had accepted her explanation that, as she was now a Buddhist, she preferred natural juices and simple food like dry toast. He failed to notice that his old girlfriend had no conscience however over being bought exclusive Italian designed leather handbags, shoes, or jackets or that she was able to eat massive quantities of ice cream at all hours of the day or night. She eventually told him she was pregnant as she gave him a hot stone massage one

Friday evening two months later. She took the opportunity to explain her need to give up her job at the local council run nursery where her co-workers had been so unfriendly towards her. In truth, she had already been dismissed for choosing to flirt on more than one occasion with the more attractive fathers rather than attend to the toileting needs of their offspring. But her energy levels were not as they had been, and she really didn't like the noise the children made so she was glad to be without the job. A wedding was organised speedily, and the radiant bride's photograph appeared in The Tatler alongside some minor member of the Danish Royal family whom she outshone completely. Because of her originally claimed religious beliefs, the wedding breakfast was all organic, terrifically expensive, and mostly uneaten by the guests attending the affair.

Cressida made sure she gained as little weight as possible during her pregnancy, ice cream being the only thing she needed to binge on. That craving left her by the time she was six months pregnant so by nine months, her body was still slim and lithe but looked like she carried a small football in front of her. Stuart, whose sister had resembled a sumo wrestler while carrying his nephew Giles, had no idea that Cressida was at full term when she went into labour, and Hella (which Cressida told Stuart was a Buddhist term for 'victorious and successful' and never to be shortened to Hell for obvious reasons) was born 'prematurely', a healthy six pounds nine ounces, in the local Tigi hair salon, without any complications and in the short space of ninety minutes. The paramedics that came to take Cressida and her daughter to the private hospital into which she had been previously booked were astounded that the baby was so well for a seven-month pregnancy or that such a red faced, unappealing and downright ugly child could be delivered by such a beautiful mother. However, Sergio, who was straightening Cressida's hair at the time, had to call his boyfriend to come and collect him as he was in such a state of shock that the paramedics had advised complete rest for the remainder of the day.

But despite her looks, Stuart doted on the little girl and her love for him was obvious. Although he had engaged a nanny, he woke up for all the night feeds no matter what time he needed to get up in the morning to complete deals with Australia or Singapore. Cressida, who had demanded medication to dry up her milk before she left hospital, told him she was unable to breastfeed, and it was Stuart that checked that their daily help had cleaned and sterilised Hella's bottles properly. He bought a buggy which he could push in front of him when he went for his daily run. He left his London office and set up independently, working from home, organising his time so that he could bathe her and put her to bed as she grew. He was there when she tasted her first solid food and when she took her first steps. He made no objection to Cressida staying at home to be a full-time mum and told her he appreciated she needed some time to herself to get over the trauma of the birth and the subsequent post-natal depression that had put her off sex. She had insisted on having those few stretch marks on her body lasered (she had used the most expensive creams during her pregnancy to ensure the stretch marks had been kept to a minimum) and started to have regular Botox injections as she said the broken sleep she had when Stuart got up to feed the baby had given her lines around her eyes.

To get ready for the baby and to Cressida's dismay, Stuart had sold his bachelor pad in Kingston and bought a new home with good internet access and a large garden in Canterbury so that Cressida would be near her parents and be happy. But she wasn't. Cressida was bored and possibly a little embarrassed by her green-eyed daughter who was probably the most unattractive child she had ever set eyes on. Hella was difficult and whinged a lot when she was with her mother, yet an angel for her father, nanny or her grandparents. Cressida wasn't used to not being adored and it hurt her deeply.

Once back in Canterbury, Cressida had tried to connect with some of her old school friends but found that so many of them were tedious. So many excuses were given. They were working during the day or tied up with their children so that they couldn't go out for lunch or dinner in the evenings. She tried yoga and meditation as one of her London friends had told her that spiritual calmness was the key to contentment, but she was bored by the regime that demanded a form of discipline that Cressida was not keen to endure. Besides which, the ladies in her class – and they were all ladies, another rather boring aspect of the whole thing – insisted that green tea and not Starbucks or a glass of red at a wine bar was more palatable after class and green tea made Cressida feel quite queasy. She decided to do some charity work but told Stuart that she found working in one of the many shops in town distasteful. She left after only one session, saying that she was allergic to handling clothing or other items that had been donated as they must have been washed in certain laundry detergents which did not agree with her. The truth was that she really hated committing to certain hours a week and not being socially visible as a charity worker.

To this end, she took to organising balls in aid of one cause or other and glowed in the new gowns she had to buy and the warmth of approval from that small circle of new friends she was gathering around her from the different groups she tried. At Christmas, she was photographed by the local paper as she took soup to the homeless who were sleeping on the streets. More attention was given to her in a rather fetching bobble hat and the goodly works she told the reporter she was doing than the plight of the people who had nowhere to shelter at night. Even the young man with a pit bull who was sleeping in the doorway of Marks and Spencer and with whom she was photographed was dazzled by her smile as she poured boiling hot oxtail from a flask and, handing it to him, spilled most of it onto his lap and his only dry form of shelter, a sleeping bag and a pile of cardboard boxes thus ensuring that he would have a very damp bed for the night. He said nothing of this discomfort as his dog licked bits of onion from his groin and told the reporter that he had been visited by an angel. The reporter didn't include the remarks from the other men sleeping rough near him about how they would have liked to give her one or that she could lick soup up from that particular area of their body any time she liked. He left it with the headline "Nectar from an Angel". Cressida was delighted and her popularity grew - her Facebook account boasted seven hundred and sixty-three friends.

At Hella's third birthday party (completely put together by Stuart as her mother was too busy organising a Charity event to raise money to send a grandmother with motor neurone disease to Disneyland whether she wanted to go or not), Cressida was welcoming the guests when she saw a face from the past she had long forgotten. Bernie! The man who had worked the deck chairs on the beach at St Ives during the day and played in a band at night. He was not good looking, in fact, it could be said that he was downright ugly, resembling a young Ronnie Wood, but he had a lot of charisma and was gliding in on the arm of Prunella, her arch enemy and the daughter of the owner of Cressida's favourite Hotel in town. Her eyes widened when she saw Bernie. She remembered that she'd had a weird 'thing' for him when she was in Cornwall and going through her rock chick phase. Bernie had played lead guitar and sang in a band, and they'd had a one-night stand which, for some strange reason, Cressida had hoped might have been repeated.

"Darling Cress," gushed Prunella as she air kissed her next to both cheeks, "So lovely to see the little ones having fun! How clever of you to organise all this" and she nodded towards the bouncy castle, magician and face painting that were on offer to Hella and her friends from the Montessori play group. "This is my friend, Bernie. He's part of a fabulous band Daddy's booked for the season. Bernie, this is my very good friend Cress." And Prunella, who was very used to losing men's interest very quickly when Cressida was around, grabbed hold of Bernie in a proprietary way. "You must come and hear him play sometime." Bernie took Cressida's hand and put it to his lips. Prunella quickly pushed the hand away.

"Nice to meet you," he drawled in his lazy way of speaking that she remembered so well. "Lovely gaff you've got here. Which one is your sprog?" and he held out a gift wrapped in Peppa Pig paper with a large pink bow on top.

Cressida breathed a sigh of relief. He had obviously not recognised her and her fury at being called Cress (Prunella knew which buttons to push) diminished when she realised he hadn't twigged what it was short for. Last time he had seen her she had worn little more than a bikini top and cut off shorts which he had removed with such dexterity that it had taken her breathe away. Her hair had been long, to her waist and streaked with gold by the sun and the local hairdresser. He hadn't recognised that this elegant creature with her hair piled on top of her head and her Victoria Beckham cat-suit was the same girl he had shagged behind the beach huts on August Bank Holiday Monday exactly two years and three months ago. She decided it would be wise to pretend she had a cold so that she could disguise her voice a little.

"Why, welcome and thank you so much. Prunella, why don't you take, er…sorry, what's your name again? You must forgive me, I'm afraid this cold has got the better of me," she said in a broken, nasal tone.

"Bernie," scowled Prunella.

"Not to worry," answered Bernie. "Here, have a suck on this" and he produced a packet of Jakemans, offering it to her. "I always have them with me so I can sing. I ought to give up the smokes I suppose, but you know what it's like when you're hooked, don't cha?"

"So long as that's all you have a suck on, Cress" threw in the bitter Prunella. She didn't like the way Bernie was gazing at his hostess. "She's quite a girl is our Cress," she pouted, "But she's very much married." And she practically pulled Bernie away towards the marquee where the children were seated round a trestle table.

"Thanks, I'll give it a try," answered Cressida, ignoring Prunella and unwrapping the sweet, she popped it into her mouth. "Prunella, why don't you take Bernie over to see Hella." She called after them. 'You couldn't get him away quick enough, you bitch' she thought to herself as she spat the sweet out and moved off as fast as her favourite pair of Jimmy Choos would allow, not glancing behind until she reached her kitchen where staff were rushing to and fro delivering the tea party for the little three-year-olds. She shut the door behind her and reached into the fridge for the white wine, pouring herself a very large glass as her heart rate began to regulate.

"Ah, there you are my darling!" It was Stuart. He never ceased to annoy her, always checking up on her and needing to know how her day had been etc. He even wanted them to have another child which meant that she had to sleep with him, something she put off as much as possible as she had no irons in that particular fire. She'd had a coil fitted that he didn't know about and kept the morning after pill in the glove compartment of her car to be on the safe side when she slept with him.

"Hi there, Sweetie," she called, pecking him on the cheek. "I think all the guests are enjoying themselves."

"Yes, and little Hella couldn't be happier. I've taken dozens of photographs so you can choose which one we can get canvas printed for our bedroom. Here look." And he thrust his mobile into her hands and watched as she scrolled through the photos. When she saw the one of Bernie giving his gift to Hella, her heart missed a beat. There could be no mistaking who the little girl took after. They were so alike. Cressida 'accidentally' deleted that photograph before Stuart could see the resemblance too.

"Oops, sorry. Not to worry, you have so many more. Let's look at these properly later shall we Stewie? Do you want some wine, darling?" and she proffered the bottle to him.

"No, not now. You shouldn't either. Come on, the Birthday Girl is waiting to blow out her candles." And he took the glass from his wife, put the bottle back in the fridge, grabbed her by the arm and steered her out the door to where the tables were set up and the children were tucking into the party food with gusto. "Oh. And don't worry about the photos. I've already uploaded them, so they are all safe."

Prunella had Bernie firmly in her grasp and was nibbling at his ear as they lay on one of the picnic rugs set out for the parents to lounge on. Cressida felt a pang of annoyance that Bernie hadn't shown any interest in her. She was completely at a loss as to why she felt attracted to this ugly, unreliable man and why she'd had sex with him on the beach that day when there were so many other, more attractive men to choose from.

It was a beautiful late May afternoon and there had been no need for the marquee that had been set up on the lawn. But after Cressida had watched her daughter blow out her candles and hug her grandparents and her father, just saying a polite, "Thank you" to her mother, she decided to take refuge in it thus keeping as far away from Bernie and the proceedings as she could. She managed to avoid everyone as they were leaving, and Stuart was furious with her when he found her lurking behind a large potted palm plant at six o'clock.

"Where have you been? I've been looking everywhere for you. The guests have all left and were asking after you. How do you think I felt having to tell them that I didn't know where you were?" And on and on he went, accusing her of being unfeeling and selfish. Cressida was dumbstruck. He had never raised his voice at her before. Nobody had ever raised their voice at her. She felt violated.

That night, Stuart slept in the guest bedroom and Cressida, who quite enjoyed having the bed completely to herself, fell into a deep sleep very quickly. But Stuart came into the room at three o'clock and woke her. He got into bed and cuddled up to her, trying to rouse her as he was feeling amorous. "I'm sorry, baby," he whispered in her ear as he stroked her left thigh, pushing her nighty up to her waist, "I didn't mean to shout"

Cressida was half asleep. "Fuck off, Bernie," she mumbled.

Stuart sat bolt upright and snapped on the light.

"Who the hell is Bernie?"

Cressida woke with a start.

"Who is who?" she asked.

"Bernie. You told him to fuck off as I was cuddling you."

"Oh, go to sleep! I must have been dreaming. I don't know who you're talking about. Whoever it was I told him to fuck off, didn't I? So, you have no reason to be worried. I wasn't being unfaithful in my dream, was I?" and Cressida turned over as though nothing had happened although inside, she was praying that Stuart would let it go. She had already tried hacking into his computer to delete that photo from the Cloud, but he had changed his password. It was usually so easy as his passwords always had something to do with Hella, but this time, nothing had worked. The photo that might just give her away was lurking somewhere in the ether.

But he wouldn't go to sleep. He sat upright in bed and poured out his feelings about her. He said she had been cold towards him and disinterested in their daughter. He listed all the things where he felt she hadn't done her part in their marriage. He pointed out all the times he had tried to please her and then asked her if she was happy. Cressida was awake but not up to this kind of confrontation in the middle of the night, so she didn't answer except to emit a very loud snore. The snore infuriated Stuart so much, he nudged her with his elbow.

"Did you hear me?" he shouted, "I know you're not asleep. I know you can hear me"

Cressida jumped out of bed.

"You hit me!" she squawked "You've abused me. I don't have to put up with this." And she pulled on the track pants that she usually wore for her morning jog, hauled Hella out of her bed, grabbed her car keys and left the house leaving Stuart open mouthed at the door.

Cressida was nothing if not a quick thinker. She didn't really want Hella with her, she could move more freely alone. But she knew she needed the sympathy of others if she were to make the transition from married lady to single girl and that single parent status would afford her more benefits in many ways. Stuart would not let that little girl go without anything so with Hella she had her meal ticket from him, and the state could top up her income. More importantly, she wouldn't have to put up with Stuart and his demands. It had all worked out for the best.

She landed on her parent's doorstep at five in the morning with a tear-stained face (Cressida could cry at will) and a very upset Hella. They were appalled to hear that Cressida was a victim of domestic violence and she insisted her father accompany her to her house later that morning to collect all her things. Stuart was completely confused when her father, who was usually so friendly to him, called him a monster and said that he would be looking after his daughter and granddaughter from now on. He went on to say that in view of his violent behaviour he wasn't to have visits with Hella unless accompanied by himself or his wife. Word spread throughout Canterbury society that Stuart was a wife beater. He was snubbed at his gym and at his local pub. His friends were men who were married to Cressida's girlfriends, and they had all had Cressida's version of the break-up poured into their ears, so they greeted him sheepishly and avoided as much contact with him as possible. Stuart went through a phase of drinking himself to oblivion in his large family home every evening as he scrolled through the photos of the last day of his marriage when he was so happy to see his little Hella smiling at him with that funny crooked smile he loved so much, her green eyes lit with happiness and love as she looked at her daddy. He missed his wife, but he missed that little girl even more.

Meanwhile, Cressida knew she couldn't bear living with her parents for too long; their need for regular mealtimes and help with the washing up was exhausting, so she looked around and started networking like mad. She joined a gym and had a fling with her personal trainer but as he was broke, and very married, his muscles alone didn't do it for her. She became a member of the local Conservative party but didn't really like sitting through the meetings and found some of the female members not so easily charmed by her as she would have liked and so many of the men, although wealthy, were stuffy or sleazy and definitely sex mad but only with the help of the little blue pills.

She decided she needed something extra to add zest to her image, so she bought an Irish Wolf Hound, or rather she got Stuart to buy the dog for Hella, claiming that the trauma of the break-up meant that Hella needed something special to help her heal. The dog, Rocko, was huge and eye catching, and Cressida joined a dog walking club which met every Sunday and walked from agreed meeting places to pubs where dogs were catered for. She met a man whom she nicknamed Fido because he practically sat up and begged when Cressida deigned to look at him but she made sure to address him as 'Freedo' in case he took offence. With three dogs and the same number of children, one of whom was the same age as Hella, it was fortunate for her that Fido was wealthy and going through a divorce. He came in handy to look after Hella on those days that Cressida's mother had the nerve to want to go out with her own friends. Fido was completely under Cressida's spell, and she kept his interest with the chance that there just might be a relationship with her one day.

The biggie for her though, was when she returned to the stables where she used to have a Saturday job and found that it had changed hands and was now owned by a very handsome man, some fourteen years older than her. Some of the staff there hadn't changed and for some reason weren't all that friendly towards her. Nevertheless, she got Stuart to buy Hella a pony, insisting that although she was too small for it now, the pony should be a big enough size for her to grow in to and she stabled the pony there and went most days to ride him and chat with Darius, who, she discovered had a range of businesses in the area and who was also very fond of exercising in the hay loft after the staff had gone home.

The breakdown of his marriage had a profound effect on Stuart. His drinking got worse to the point that he continually overslept and no longer made any money on the stock exchange. He ended up having to sell the house and move into a rented flat in a much less salubrious part of Canterbury. Cressida's parents started to feel sorry for the young man who, in their opinion, didn't demonstrate anything other than a deep love for Hella. They saw that when Hella was with him, she was happier than ever, not needing treats or expensive things to make her smile. Stuart took her to Bluebell Woods, and they watched them together, climbing trees and hunting for fairies. It was probably Cressida's biggest mistake letting Stuart and her parents get too close because she came home one day from her dog walking with Rocko to find Stuart, Hella and her parents seated round the table tucking into a Sunday Roast. She felt the colour in her face rise but was shrewd enough not to show any anger.

"Hello Stuart,"

"Hello. Have you had a good day? You look well"

"You too. Off the booze now, are we?"

"Yes."

"Good. You know you're well behind with your maintenance? Hella needs new shoes."

"I've just been talking with your parents about making this separation formal. I've seen a solicitor and will be paying the maintenance through the Social in future seeing as you're on benefits too. I can't keep paying at the rate I have so far. The solicitor told me £250 a week plus all Hella's clothes etc. is too much anyway on my non-income."

"How much?" gasped Cressida's father, "Cressida, you led me to believe you were struggling financially which was why you don't contribute for your keep! I didn't know you were claiming benefits either."

"Not your business really, is it Pa?" Cressida had to think quickly. "Anyway, Stuart should get a job and pay his way. He has a child. He has responsibilities."

"Cressida, darling. You shouldn't talk to your father like that" put in her mother, "And none of this should be discussed over dinner with Hella here. Now. Can I set you a place?"

Cressida turned and went to her room. She phoned Darius.

"Hi there, sweetie. Say no if it's too much, but would it be OK if Hella and I come to stay with you for a bit in your lovely little farmhouse? I promise not to be too much trouble." And she started to pack her bags once again.

But as she returned to the dining room to announce her departure, she found that Stuart had gone, along with her car keys.

"He couldn't afford the payments on the lease, Cressida," said her father. "A Range Rover Evoque is very expensive. He said that you will have to find yourself something in future or use the bus."

So, it was in a taxi that Cressida turned up with a crying, stubborn three-year-old in tow, yowling that she wanted to stay with her Popa and that she didn't like horses or Rocko who was licking the tears off her face and looking very uncomfortable as the taxi driver was giving him evil looks through his mirror. He had initially refused to take the dog until Cressida emerged from the house and begged him so nicely, getting into the passenger seat and patting the seat next to her. She made no attempt to load any of the bags she brought with her and watched as her father helped the driver.

On arrival, she skipped nimbly out of the cab and rushed to Darius, in tears.

"Pay the man please sweetie, and get him to bring everything in. I need to sit down. I'm sooo upset." And she dabbed around her eyes, newly Botoxed, so extra care was needed. "I'll explain all later."

By the time Darius had heard Cressida's tale of woe – how her parents had thrown her out because money had dried up, and how she would be so happy to work in the stables to pay for her keep, Darius had arranged to buy a second-hand Nissan from his friend for her to drive and had phoned another friend who ran a private playschool to have Hella looked after every day. He even organised a housekeeper to come every day instead of twice a week to do the housework and look after Hella's other needs.

All Cressida had to do was to be pretty, be on his arm and in his bed. He was more than happy to shell out for her regular Botox and gym membership. She was his trophy 'bride' in almost every sense of the word. Cressida was more than happy to be spoilt and cosseted again but, to her annoyance, nothing is completely perfect. She had to put up with having to be nice to Darius' son, Alex, from his previous relationship who visited every other weekend. She hated the kid and would tell Darius he had done this or that to Hella, which was not true. If anything, it was Hella who started all the squabbles but Alex, who was twelve years older than Hella, usually gave in to her as he had an easy-going nature and knew she was only a little girl who was obviously missing her father. The other annoyance was having to comply with Stuart's demands to see Hella. He had met another woman who, strangely, looked a little like Cressida but who was also divorced with a child of her own. Hella, who was always sulky and unpleasant when she was with Darius or her mother, blossomed like a flower when her father and Ria arrived to pick her up. It was also annoying that Darius seemed to like Stuart, even to the point that he encouraged Stuart to start investing again, lending him the capital to make that start and that Stuart was beginning to do very well for himself.

Darius also didn't seem to be bothered by the presence of Fido in their lives. He didn't wonder why another man was so often in the company of his lady but encouraged it so that Hella would be allowed to carry on having sleep overs with Fido's children. Fido even took Hella to Rainbows with his own daughter when she started. Cressida enrolled Hella in as many clubs as she could so that the child was out of her hair as much as possible.

But after a year, Cressida began to get bored again. She told Darius that she needed to follow a path of spirituality and that she wanted to do the course to become a life coach that was running at Milton Keynes in June. She also begged him to let her go to Glastonbury the weekend after the course.

"Can't she go to her father three weekends running? She'd love that and I've got a big gymkhana event on.

In fact, I was rather hoping that you would be there too, my darling. You're so good at organising events. If you could do the catering side, I could concentrate on the livestock."

"But you've got Alex, so one more shouldn't really hurt. And I can sort the food bit out beforehand. I can get the caterers to serve it. It's not like I'm abandoning you. I'll get Fido to come along and lend a hand. And as for the following weekend, the Foo Fighters are on at Glastonbury, and you know how much I love them." She didn't mention that she'd heard a rumour that Bernie's band might be booked on one of the lesser stages on the Saturday or that she was hoping to 'bump' into him again.

After many heated words, Darius reluctantly agreed to shell out over £1000 for both activities. Cressida got busy getting Fido to do her part of the bargain and, with Amelia, a new friend, by her side she drove up to Milton Keynes and came home two days later with a certificate proclaiming her ability to listen to the problems of others and help them to heal. The people on the course were entranced by her, shocked to hear her tales of how she had suffered abuse at the hands of her first husband and how she was currently attempting to deal with another difficult man. Amelia confirmed how loving and giving a person Cressida was and how, despite having problems of her own, was relentless in helping others by way of her charities, particularly Shelter for the homeless, and those concerned with abused women.

Darius was looking very tired when she walked through the door waving her certificate and suggesting she open a small shop in the High Street or launch a web site, or maybe even both so that people could contact her for help. He did not answer as she chatted on about how wonderful it was that she could now help others every day and it wasn't until she had helped herself to a large glass of prosecco, said how much she was looking forward to Glastonbury the following weekend and asked what he'd cooked for dinner, that she realised by his expression that he was not happy.

"Are you not curious as to where Hella is?"

"Oh, I expect she's playing somewhere. Or she hasn't got back from Stuart's yet."

"No. She's not at Stuart's"

"Oh. Well never mind. Where's Rocko? Oh, there you are my angel." And the dog launched itself at her. "Have you managed to have lots of walkies today? Have you missed your mummy?"

"She's not here either."

"Well, I expect Fido will bring her back when she's had enough."

"He hasn't got her."

"Well," pushing the dog to one side and beginning to feel angry that she was not receiving the welcome home she felt was warranted, "Are you going to tell me where the fuck she is or are we having guessing games all night? Really, Darius! I think it's really selfish of you to treat me like this. I've had a hell of a drive after a gruelling weekend where I have had to learn to search my soul so that I can help others do the same and you haven't even asked me how it went or anything. One thing I have learned, I can tell you, is how to remain calm in difficult situations and keep my emotions even, so if you think you are going to fucking well wind me up because I've had a teeny-weeny weekend away you can sod off."

"She's in hospital"

"Who is?"

"Hella. She got run over on Saturday. She lost a lot of blood. She's in a coma, but then, you wouldn't know any of this because you turned your mobile off and that stupid retreat type thing you went on refuses to take any calls while its students are 'being empowered'"

"Well, it's important that we keep our chakras open and outside influences interfere with our ability to tune in to our inner selves."

"Is that all you've got to say? What about your daughter? I've only just got back from the hospital. I've been sat there all yesterday and last night. I've been worried sick about her."

"You should have looked after her better, so she didn't get run over in the first place."

"Don't you dare even go there. Don't you fucking dare!"

"Stuart could have sat up with her."

"Oh, Stu was there." Cressida grimaced at the familiarity he had with her ex, "He was asked to give blood. Did you know she has an uncommon blood type, and their stocks were low? But he told the nurses it was no good asking him for blood because he wasn't her biological father"

Cressida looked stunned.

"Oh yes. He told them they'd need to get hold of some bloke who played in a band."

"But how did he know?" she asked wishing to God that she'd managed to delete that photograph.

"Don't you want to know if they found Hella's dad and got him to donate blood then?"

"Oh! Yes. Did they find him?"

"Stuart knew exactly where he was. He found out from Pru. He's back playing at one of her dad's hotels again this summer. Oh, and he's booked to be at Glastonbury next weekend. But you knew that didn't you?"

Cressida was speechless.

"So even Bernie is sitting at her bedside right now and he hardly knows the kid. And his band got the sack from the hotel jobs because they didn't perform last night."

"Oh, he won't mind. Prunella was getting too needy I expect."

Darius glared at her.

"Stu said he'd known that Hella wasn't his as soon as her eyes turned green."

"He what?"

"It wasn't that photo, you know. Although he told me he enjoyed seeing you squirm when he showed it to you and how quickly you deleted it."

"What's it got to do with her eyes? And if he'd known all that time, why didn't he say so?"

"Stuart's not a fool. It's very unlikely that two brown eyed parents will have a green-eyed child. Do you realise that Hella looks nothing like him? One glance of that band bloke and the way you were that day, and he knew who her real dad was. But he loves that little girl, and she loves him. And he's such a decent bloke that blood or no blood, he's going for full custody of her."

"But he can't. She's my daughter."

"It's his name on the birth certificate. A certificate that carries a lot more weight than that scrap of shit you've been waving in my face. And you know what, Cressida?"

"What now?" Cressida was seething and already trying to figure out how she was going to get herself out of this sticky situation.

"I'm going to back him all the way. I'm going to testify as to how neglectful you are of that child, how you foist her off on others and ignore her; how you use her to get things for yourself."

"That's not fair."

"Any other mother would have asked me to take her to the hospital to see her daughter. You haven't even asked which hospital she's at. Or how she's doing."

Cressida was silent. She couldn't defend herself any more.

"Your stuff is all packed. I want you and your bloody dog gone today."

"That's fine. I'll go to my parents' house."

"Afraid not. They are in London."

"Obviously not all that bothered about their grandchild either. Must be a hereditary thing."

"No. They are at Great Ormond Street with Stuart and Bernie. That's where she was air-lifted to. And that's where I'm off to now because I actually care about that little girl. I only came back to pack your things. You can keep the car. Pack it up with all your stuff and leave your house keys in the kitchen" and to Cressida's horror and without a backward glance, Darius picked up the keys to his Jeep and slammed the door behind him.

Cressida sat down on the sofa as her legs felt like jelly. Hella must be alright if she was in hospital and so many people there would probably mean they wouldn't let her have any more visitors, so it was pointless to drive all that way. Besides which, she was very tired. The drive and the row had taken its toll on her. She saw the massive pile of belongings at the foot of the stairs that Darius had left for her to take. And her Glastonbury ticket had been torn up and placed on top of the lot. She scowled! She would have to print another one out later. It would take her ages to put all that in her car. And she was very, very hungry. It was, after all, dinner time.

She turned on her mobile and checked her Facebook, uploading photos of the new friends she had made on her course and adding how lovely they all were. She was more than a little pleased to see photos of herself put up by others with comments such as "Cressida, beautiful inside and out" or "Cressida, my new friend for life." She looked at her phone log and saw that she had 42 missed calls from her parents, Darius, Stuart and an unknown. The unknown would be Bernie, so she added it to her contacts. It would come in handy later.

Finally, she scrolled down her contacts until she found what she wanted.

"Hi there Freedo……have you heard? Yes, it's just awful…..No, I was out of range and the centre refuses calls while we are learning……Yes, such a shock!....Oh, I'm ok, just shaken and exhausted…..I've had such a row with Darius…..How could he let something like that happen?....I trusted him to keep her safe…..Oh,…. No, he didn't tell me that….But she knows not to play in the car park!....Of course you didn't see her, that's completely understandable….You mustn't feel bad, it could have been anyone…..No, no! Freedo, please don't cry…..I really don't blame you. Look, what about if we meet for dinner? …..No Darius isn't here right now…..

Well he shouldn't have hit you, you poor love. I'm so pissed off with him, I blame him entirely, not you.

Look, Freedo, I'm so very cross with Darius that I feel I can't live here with him any longer. Would you mind very much if I came to stay with you for a bit?"

Freya

30.03.53

Aries: Kind and generous.
Can be spontaneous.

She took the Park and Ride bus into the city because she wasn't sure how long she would be. She didn't want to be late, running made her go red in the face, but she also didn't want to be early as that made her look desperate. She had spent the day before planning her journey carefully, listing in her head the shops she could visit just to browse if she got there too soon – she didn't want to be dragging loads of bags with her – so unladylike. She'd made sure to have had an early night so that her eyes sparkled and weren't dragged down by tiredness as well as age. She'd bathed and dressed carefully and with butterflies in her stomach, started her day, dreaming of a future that just might not be so lonely and maybe filled with love.

He drove to the Castle Car Park and parked in the disabled bay displaying his permit and the clock showing 9.30am. Looking in the rear-view mirror, he adjusted his tie, pushed a stray hair from his forehead and breathed on his hand to test his breath. He retrieved his jacket from the hanger behind his seat, slipped it on and checked his diary. 10.30. Costa. Widow. Own house. No kids. (Big thumbs up for that!) He'd wait outside from 10.25 so he looked eager. Picking up the box of Dairy Milk he'd bought from Sainsbury's on the way, he pulled the bright yellow 'Reduced' sticker from the cellophane and slammed the door to his car. It was a beautiful spring day, and he didn't want to spoil it by having to contend with the usual Wednesday rabble the market attracted. He had enough time to take a stroll along the river. 'You never know,' he thought to himself, 'I just might bump into someone more interesting on the way.' And he hummed a little tune as he limped towards the exit and made his way towards the park.

The bus was packed that morning and a young, dishevelled woman with two small boys sat next to her. She watched as the mother held one on her lap and squashed the other between her legs. Both children had runny noses and the one on her lap had what looked like impetigo blooming from the corner of his mouth which housed his fist as he complained loudly that he had dropped his blanket. The blanket, which once might have been blue, had fallen on the floor. The mother was so squashed up she couldn't reach it and so was Freya, so the screams, high and shrill, interspersed with wails and sobs continued for the entire journey. When they reached the terminus, the young mother got up. "Pass us that blanket, would you, please. He won't belt up 'til he's got hold of it." Gingerly, Freya retrieved the cloth, now even dirtier, from the floor of the bus and handed it to her and was appalled as the child pulled his fist out of his mouth, replacing it with the blanket, but not until after his mum had used it to wipe his nose and his tears.

"Come on Tyler, shift yerself!" the young woman yelled at her other son, who had now lodged himself between the edge of the seat and the aisle and she poked him with her elbow resulting in a different type of wail.

"Can't. There's people." But the mum jostled her son into the aisle, ignoring the complaints of the other passengers as she started to pull the dirty, tatty buggy with even grubbier toys hanging from the handles out of its designated area and towards the door, banging into the ankles of those unfortunate enough to be nearby as she manoeuvred her way off the bus. The other passengers glared at Freya, and she even heard someone tell her she should have taught her daughter some manners when she was bringing her up. Freya decided to remain where she was until everyone else had disembarked. She looked down at her lap and was horrified to see the remains of a sticky sweet stuck to the pale pink Cashmere of her coat near the hem where the older child had stood.

John set out at a brisk pace towards the river. He felt pleased with himself. That parking permit had saved him a fortune in charges. He always tried to look slightly frail as he left his car in case any nosey parkers challenged him. If they did and asked to see the picture on the reverse side of the permit, he would say he was collecting his wife whose picture appeared there. He always congratulated himself on receiving that permit just a week before she died. It gave him a whole three years of free parking. He shook his head as he passed the cardboard boxes at the side of the road housing a mangey looking dog and a homeless man who looked older than himself although he was probably a lot younger. The man caught him looking "Can you spare some change for a cup of tea?" John looked away quickly and walked a little faster.

Once she'd got off the bus, Freya examined her coat. Finding a tissue, she peeled the sweet away so only the bright orange stain remained. She checked her watch and decided to go into the nearest Ladies toilets to see if she could sponge the stain before it set and emerged ten minutes later with a damp orangey smudge where the sweet had been. She felt cross. The coat was new and expensive and now, possibly, ruined. All because of her worrying about the time. She had a whole hour before she had to be at Costa and here she was, looking a mess, just because of her silly worrying. She decided to have a look around Fenwick, Marks and Spencer and then Debenhams to pass the time, but she set the alarm on her mobile for 10.25 just in case.

John got to the park and decided to inspect the layout of the flowers. He approved of the colour choice, yellow and purple, very Spring like, but wasn't impressed with a large patch of daffodils that had obviously died but had been left withering for all to see. Three of the City's gardeners were working nearby, planting early summer bedding plants around a statue. He approached them.

"Wouldn't it be a little more sensible to attend to those dead daffodils instead of doing this? They look an absolute mess; they let down this park completely!"

"Well sir, you need to address your concerns to the City Council. We're just doing what we've been told to do." Replied Joss, the chief gardener who was raking through some soil. The other two ignored John and kept on with their work.

But John wasn't going to let it go. "It doesn't take a genius to see that those daffs need sorting. Even tying them down would make them look less neglected. Surely, as a gardener, you don't need an order from on high for you to do that?"

"Tying them down takes time, sir. We will cut them back and re-plant in due course. In the meantime, we must get on. Have a good day." And the gardener turned back to his two workmates, "Pass me that compost, Rick."

"Don't you turn your back on me! I haven't finished yet." But Joss ignored him and kept on working. John was incensed so he tapped the gardener on his shoulder just as he was hauling the heavy bag into a position to scatter it on the ground he had prepared. Because he was moving at the time, the tap was a little harder than John had intended and the surprise of the physical contact made the gardener lose his balance and he fell over sideways onto the ground, banging against the statue as he fell. A loud crack and a yell rang out

"What the fuck? You mad bastard! What's the matter with you?" The gardener was obviously in pain. Rick and Tom, the other two men, dropped what they were doing and went to help him.

"I, I'm sorry…I didn't think…"

"I think he's broken my bloody arm. I landed right on it. He's fucking mad. Attacking me because of some dead daffs."

"I'll phone the police. Who do you think you are coming here and throwing your weight around?" Tom took out his phone and started dialling.

"Just a minute, hang on there," stammered John, putting his hand over the phone, "I didn't mean to hurt him, I was just getting his attention and I must have startled him…"

"You did that alright," said Tom, "Look at him. He's in agony. And you can get your hands off me too. I don't want to be on sick pay for weeks on end with broken bones as well. You're a complete twat."

"Come on Joss, let's get you up," said Rick as he helped his mate to his feet. "Do you want the police or an ambulance?"

"I don't know. Ring the office and tell them what's happened." Joss rubbed his shoulder, "I think I've dislocated something. I shan't be able to work today, and I don't know what the council's policy is of us being physically and verbally abused." He turned to John. "What in God's name did you think you were doing attacking me like that over some dead flowers?"

"I was telling your colleagues, I wasn't attacking you, I was just trying to get your attention and unfortunately you walked into my hand."

"Huh! I've heard it all now! What extension do I need, Joss? Who do I need to speak to?" Tom had got through to the office. "And don't you go anywhere, they will want your details, so they know who to sue, you mad old git", he nodded to John who had taken a step back and was looking as withered as the daffodils.

"What do you mean, sue? It was a complete accident."

"Well that all depends on how you look at things, don't it?" said Tom and he looked meaningfully into the eyes of the assailant as he cupped his hand over the phone.

Freya looked at her watch and deciding it was time to make a move, walked out of Marks and Spencer, turning left towards the meeting point. As she wended her way in between the crowds of tourists, schoolchildren on outings and the general bustle of the market, she saw a crowd of people gathering round something that was emitting a dreadful noise. At first she thought it might be a street act, but her curiosity got the better of her and she moved towards the little gathering to see what was occurring. It was the young mother and little boys from the bus, the smallest of whom was screaming because he had lost his blanket. The mother was trying to take the children back into the clothes shop where, she had told the manager, she thought he had dropped it and the manager was refusing her entry as he suspected she had shoplifted a purse.

"What you doin' leaving them fings right where kids can get them anyway? Whatya fink I need a bloody purse for? I ain't got no bloody money. If he took it, it was because he could reach it. I don't want it; I just want to find his blanket. He can't sleep wivout it." And she tried hard not to cry as the manager took his mobile from his pocket. "Please mister, I don't want the purse. Could I just go in and look for his blanket? I don't want no trouble."

"You should have thought of that before you taught your son to steal. I'm calling the police" and the manager started to dial.

Freya could bear it no longer.

"Excuse me, sir," she touched the manager gently on the elbow.

"I'm a bit busy right now, madam. If you pop inside, I'm sure one of my salespeople would help you."

"Please, sir, just one minute. It's to do with this situation."

Freya looked like a very well-to-do person; not his usual clientele and he hadn't a clue how she could know anything about what was going on. She spoke softly and politely, so it would have been churlish not to give her the time.

"It will have to be quick then," he replied, almost gruffly.

Freya pulled him gently to one side.

"I sat next to that young woman on the bus coming into town this morning."

"Is that all?" said the manager and went to move back to the buggy.

"Please. Wait," Freya caught his arm, "Let me finish."

The manager looked at her hand on his arm and then raised his eyes to her. Freya blushed a deep red and let her hand fall to her side.

"It's just that I know she's telling the truth. The little boy lost his blanket on the bus and all hell broke loose. Let me go inside and find it for him so that the noise stops at least."

The screaming hadn't subsided, and the onlookers were telling the young woman what they thought of her as a mother. It wasn't complimentary.

"OK, go in and find it. But then I need to tackle the shoplifting issue."

Freya dived into the shop which was unlike any she had ever been in since she was a girl. There was music playing loudly and the lights seemed deliberately low. But she looked hard around each display until she caught sight of the beloved rag draped over a pegboard of accessories. She noted that it was right next to a set of purses just like the one carried by the manager. She took the blanket and another purse outside to the manager. There was a loud beeping noise as she exited the shop.

"I found it caught on a hook where these were displayed," she said, waggling the cloth in the air with one hand and the purse in the other. "He must have dropped it when he reached to look at the purse." She returned the blanket to the tear-stained little boy who stopped screaming immediately and started rubbing it softly under his nose.

"I'm not surprised that he wanted to look at the purse. It very sparkly and has a cartoon character on it."

"He didn't mean to take it," said the young woman. "Please believe me."

"It's all dribbled over and unfit for sale now," said the manager, almost in a sulk.

"So then, let me pay for the purse." Said Freya and she fished the £4.00 from her own purse which the sticker on the side of the offending article declared as the price. "It's obvious what's happened, so let's just leave things, OK?" She thrust the money at the manager, grabbed the older child by his hand and pushed the young woman to move away.

"That was very kind of you," said the mother. "You didn't have to do that."

"That's absolutely fine. I think you have enough on your plate right now without being bullied by people like him." Freya threw a backward glance at the shop to see the crowd dispersing and the manager sloping back into his shop.

"Come on, I think we both need a coffee." And Freya walked the little family into Costa where she sat with them in the window after she had ordered two coffees, a chocolate milk, some lemon muffins and two gingerbread men.

"I can't pay you back for this right now," said Tiffany, "But I promise you I will once I can get back to work." She bit hungrily into the lemon muffin. "We only went in the shop to pass a bit of time. I have to get out of the B&B by 9.30 and if I get on the Park and Ride bus it don't cost me nuffink to get into town."

"Is that all you do every day then?" asked Freya.

"It's all I can do right now. Me bloke's done a runner and I got chucked out our flat 'cos I couldn't sort the rent. They put me in the B&B 'til they can find me and the kids a place. But it's hard. Kids need clean clothes and stuff and I do my best but…." Freya patted her hand and Tiffany started to cry. "People look at us and I know they think we're rubbish. I try to keep them clean – I wash our bits out by hand in the bathroom but sometimes it takes ages for them to dry. I haven't got anyone I can leave the boys with so I can try to get a job and even if I could, the only jobs are those zero-hour contracts which don't really work with children."

Freya looked at her watch. It was 10.35 and her date had not turned up. She smiled to herself as she thought that maybe he had seen her with this grubby little family and had done an about turn. If that were the case it would have meant that she hadn't really missed out on anything.

John looked at his watch. It was 10.40 and he was at the cash machine not far from Costa. Joss, Rick and Tom stood either side of him as he tried to shield their view of his pin number from them.

"There's a £300 limit on withdrawals," he pointed out as he keyed in the numbers.

"So, it's good you've got another card for a different bank, isn't it?" replied Joss nodding towards John's wallet. "We agreed £500 would make the injury a little less painful. Don't forget, it was entirely caused by you while I was digging in the compost. But if you would prefer it to be £600…."

"Yeah, £600 is much neater to split three ways," added Rick.

"No, no…..I can….." and John hastily inserted a second card into the machine. He cast a sidelong glance at the coffee shop. There was no-one waiting outside, and he cursed to himself that the whole morning had turned out to be a total disaster. This woman had looked so promising too. A widow who probably had a nice little nest egg, her own house, no kids, obviously lonely and with a tidy pension from her job as a headteacher. She had looked quite attractive for an old gal too and he had been sure he could have charmed her. Instead, he had been conned out of £500 and a box of chocolates. He was breathing heavily when he handed the money over to the gardeners who waved cheerily at him as they went back to the park. He noticed that Joss with the 'dislocated' shoulder had no trouble patting one of his mates on the back as they went on their way. He turned away from the cash machine and as he started to make his way back towards the car park, his mobile rang.

"No, I can't lend you any more money," he barked down the phone at his son. "You need to get your finger out and get yourself sorted. You left one lot and now you're telling me you've got another one pregnant. Well, more fool you. No, I don't want to meet her, no matter how lovely she is. If the last one was anything to go by, your idea of lovely and mine are poles apart. My advice to you is to buy a plane ticket and a pack of condoms and use both." And he hit the end call on his phone and stuffed it into his pocket.

He wasn't aware that the two women with the grubby little boys he stormed past might have had anything to do with him. He noticed the older lady though and thought she seemed somewhat familiar but was so cross with the events of the day that he gave her no further thought. As he fished about in his pockets for his car keys, he dropped the box of chocolates which were kicked by a passer-by into the gutter. He was too cross to be bothered retrieving them and continued speeding his way back to his car where he encountered a traffic warden looking through his windshield at the disabled permit displayed next to the time disc. He had already hit the remote to open the door so could not turn back and pretend to be going to a different car. His eyes met those of the warden and then they both looked back to the dashboard of his car where a picture of his late wife lay gazing up at them.

"I've just had to drop her off at her doctors. I'm coming back to pick her up later," he stammered.

The warden continued writing on a pad. "That makes no difference, sir. This permit has not been displayed correctly with the photograph facing down and the permit's details on view. I am issuing you with an infringement notice and in view of this being a disabled parking bay, I'm afraid the fine will be high reflecting the enormity of this offence. You are at liberty to appeal though," he continued as he pulled the sheet from the pad, "Just get your wife to write to the address on the form and you may find she will be treated with clemency."

"But that's ridiculous! You can see the permit is valid. What kind of a jobsworth are you?" John was furious. Spittle was dribbling down his chin.

"Well, you see sir, we have a lot of people misusing our blue badges. People who take a disabled bay and use these badges so that they don't pay to park their vehicles thus occupying a space needed by a genuinely disabled person. Not that I'm suggesting for a moment that this is the case, sir. But it is the council's policy that any misuse of the blue badge, which includes displaying it incorrectly on a vehicle, must be ticketed. Easy for you to verify that this was a genuine mistake. It could be cleared up today if you simply take your wife personally round to the council offices." And he whistled as he walked off towards the next vehicle.

It did not take Freya very long to make the decision to help the little family. She had no children of her own and after a lifetime of teaching, she missed them. She missed their laughter and their squabbles, their sense of humour and their silliness. Since retiring from her school, she had taken up teaching ICT at the local adult education classes in town one night a week, but it didn't replace the daily interaction she used to have with young people. Most of her students there were elderly, needing to know how to operate a computer from scratch. She had tried to join an amateur dramatic group but had found them all a bit too 'fast' for her. The dating site was witness to her loneliness, but she had a gut feeling that the young woman she had met instead of her date that morning was basically decent and that once she was on her feet, she would be a lifetime friend. After being a headteacher for such a long time, she had learnt to trust her own instincts.

She would love having this little family in her home, helping them to forge a new life for themselves. She could see that Tiffany was emotional and stunned by the kindness of the stranger, but her face showed a certain relief that brought joy to Freya's heart. She felt even more joy at the little boy's delight as he picked up a box of chocolates from the gutter which, although a bit battered, was still completely intact and gave it to his mother.

Tiffany took the chocolates and handed them to Freya.

"I think this is the only way I can thank you right now."

Freya laughed. "My favourite, thank you." She looked at the date on the side.

"I think we'll have to share them as soon as we get home. What do you think boys?"

And the new, strange little group laughed as they made their way to the bus stop.

Clarke

29.06.69

Gemini: Proud. Dislikes litter.
Sometimes accident prone.

I got the job as beach inspector as an in-betweener, if you know what I mean. It didn't pay all that much but as I reckoned all it would involve was a bit of sitting in the sun, making sure kids didn't ride their bikes along the prom, then I could handle it until the autumn. I was certainly fed up with my regular job anyway and hadn't been all that bothered about leaving there although it wasn't as convenient to drive to the coast every day and be there by 8.30 am. I mean Canterbury hospital was just around the corner from my place, but after that incident with the corpse, I thought it a good time to make a change. I'm not a person who takes kindly to being told I was being dismissed; it gave the impression that whoever said that was better than me and I won't have that. I'm as good as the next person.

So, I breezed through the interview, which was with four morons who, if they had made something of their lives, wouldn't be sitting in a draughty hall interviewing a group of individuals, some of whom looked as though they could do with a good wash and others who obviously didn't have much between their ears. I knew they would snap me up. And they did. They waffled on for a bit about what the job entailed and I must admit, there was more to it than I thought; they certainly wanted their money's worth.

They appointed me to Westbrook beach which is larger than most of the others apart from Margate sands itself, but I suppose that's because they could see I had a brain in my head. My start date was in April, a bit early to be sitting in the sun, but that was the time that the beach inspector had to paint and clean all the council owned beach huts. By May I was completely knackered and had blue paint coming out of every pore of my body.

I had this supervisor, Derek Flower. He liked to be called Derek, not because he was friendly, but because too many people mocked him by dropping the 'Mr', referring to him as 'Flower'. He had been on the panel of morons who had interviewed me. He was a snide bugger, and I took an instant dislike to him. He strutted around as though he owned the place and would say something like, "Just coming to inspect your inspections" and then laugh as though he was fit for the Edinburgh Fringe. He had a company van and would drive it down onto the prom to my office where he would go in my desk drawer, without even asking and look at what I had written in my daily log the day before.

"No 't' in 'much', Clarke," he would snigger – I always spelt that word wrong. Habit of a lifetime.

"Have you done today's water readings?"

He knew bloody well, that's the first thing you do when you get to work. It involves going to the sea and filling a small bottle with water from the sea, not right at the edge where the scum and seaweed gathers, but further in where the water is a little clearer. Its bloody cold sometimes wading in up to your knees whatever the weather. I roll up my shorts or the waves catch them and it looks like I've pissed myself. On stormy days, I change into my trunks because I get splashed up to the waist. He turned up one stormy day and accused me of taking a morning dip, followed by bellows of giggles like a girl. Wanker.

"On the shelf." I nodded at the shelf next to the first aid kit, "Where it always is." I couldn't help it. The man was a twat.

"Right," he said. He handed me the results of the previous day's readings. The council wanted all the beachgoers to know how pure the water was. They wanted to keep their blue flag. They were particularly proud of Westbrook beach as its water purity was better than any other beach. That might be down to the fact that I waded in so far to avoid any scum, or it might be down to my adding a tiny drop of tap water to every sample. I wanted my beach to be best, after all.

Oh yes, that jumped up little prick had a sense that he was more important than he really was. I remember at the start of the season, him looking through my log. "I see you have bookings for beach huts as of next week, so I need to check you've prepared them properly." And he waltzed off towards the council huts expecting me to follow him like a little dog. But he could dream on. It was a stormy day, so I was getting out of my wet trunks before I caught my death. And I took my time.

He reappeared five minutes later, visibly annoyed.

"They seem to be in order," he snapped, "But I expect my inspectors to accompany me when I appraise their work."

"You don't want me off with pneumonia, do you?"

"It's company policy for you to be with me so that I can point out defects. It saves time all round."

"Were there any defects?" I asked.

"That's not the point. I need you to adhere to company policy in future."

"Well, if you had told me to accompany you, I would have asked you to wait while I quickly changed out of my wet swimming things and I'd have been happy to go with you. But to be fair, you didn't ask me and I'm still not completely aware of all the company's policies. I've been too busy painting and cleaning the huts and collecting water samples and doing all the other things which I was made aware of when I was given the job. And no reasonable employer asks a man to walk out in a storm like this in wet clothes."

He was completely taken aback. I don't expect anyone had answered him like I had. That coast takes quite a bashing, so the huts were stacked away every winter and then re-erected by a team of other council workers in the spring. That cheapskate council had then got all its inspectors to paint their huts as it would have cost them a lot to employ proper painters and then we had to clean the insides and repair any damages. And the huts themselves were constantly full of mouse droppings as they were never completely sealed. It was an almost impossible task. But I made sure my huts were clean and painted beautifully. No family was going to feel uncomfortable if they rented one of my huts.

He gave me a dirty look although he didn't say anything. Wrote something in his book and then said what he always said.

"Right then, Clarke. I'll be on my way. See you tomorrow; bright and early." And he climbed back into his little white van and reversed the way he had come in.

I was never late for work, which probably pissed Derek off as he was the sort of person who would love to point out the bloody obvious. The drive to Thanet from Canterbury was easy at that time of the morning as most people were travelling to the city to work so I got to see the same cars pass by on Monday to Friday. There were also a few regulars that were doing a similar journey to me. The weather wasn't the best that year so I had to use the windscreen wipers more than I should have that summer. Typical miserable British weather. I hated it. I remember, as a boy, living in Kenya with my family, playing barefoot with my brothers in the sun, playing tricks on the houseboys who worked for us. I almost got dad sent back to England when a couple of my tricks went a bit wrong. I mixed some cement powder in with the ugali meal that they ate all the time. One boy ate it and was very ill, but it was the time I added a little something to the water supply that caused all the fuss. Dad was told to get his boys under control. It was the only time he shouted at me – he assumed it was me and not my brothers and he usually left it to my mum to sort me out – so I suppose it made me pull my head in a bit. The Foreign Office sent us to live in Vienna after a while and the weather was brilliant there too. Red hot summers and winters with proper snow so you could toboggan and ski. Those boyhood experiences made me want to live anywhere but here in

Britain with its grey, dull skies in June and its constant drizzle and damp in the winter. I wanted more than that for my kids too.

I suppose you could say that it was the weather that split my marriage up. I wanted to emigrate to Australia, but she wouldn't leave her poxy mother. Too many rows sent her back to live with the old bat and I had to sell the house and give her half. Which is why I've ended up living in a flat in Canterbury while she took her half and married the first loser to come along who took it for a deposit on a house in Wigan. I only see my kids twice a year when she brings them back to Canterbury to visit her mother. They'll forget who I am before long. She's coming for the summer holidays, so I'll be able to bring them to the beach with me with any luck. Which is why I've been getting the office as cheerful as possible. Derek's only comments when he saw that I'd painted the inside of the office a sunshine yellow was, "Did you get permission to do that? It's tantamount to defacing company property."

"Didn't think for a moment that a lick of paint over the graffiti on the walls of the beach inspector's office would need permission Derek. You must admit, it looked pretty awful."

"Well, you should have asked first. I hope that you didn't do it on our time."

"Of course not. I stayed late after work last night. And before you ask, I bought the paint myself. I thought I would get some posters of people playing on the beach and put them up. The room looked like a prison cell before."

Didn't like people using their initiative, did Derek, so he just grunted and shuffled off into the rain with his water samples.

It was the World Cup that year, so I brought a little portable television to the beach and managed to rig up an aerial so that I could get some reception. Of course, when Derek came by, I made sure it was concealed under a pile of beach towels that had got handed to me as lost property practically every day. Always left a particularly gross one sitting on top of the pile which ensured he never went near it. But it soon got around the locals that the Cup could be watched at my office and a couple of them would turn up to watch England play which was great. So, all in all, once the summer got into full swing, my little beach job was working out nicely for me. When it finally deigned to appear in the sky, I stripped off and sat on a deckchair outside my office, soaking up the sun so that by June I had a nice tan and was on good terms with the locals that came to the beach regularly. I had my own kettle and tea making stuff, but I always took a leisurely stroll up to the cafe at around 4 o'clock as there was an old girl who worked there that obviously admired me and who would make me a very nice cappuccino and bung in a little cake or something on the side all for nothing but a broad smile and a little bit of a chat up.

Life was good and I was quite pleased that the labels at the hospital had got a bit muddled as I would have been stuck there and missed the beach.

Well, true to form, once things were going well for me, something came along to cause me stress and bother. And things had never been better. The three men who came to watch the matches with me and who owned their own beach huts further along the bay towards Margate would take it in turns to have an evening barbecue and on those days, I always made it my business to check on their litter bins. The smell of the coals was enough to tell me it was barbecue night. They would hail me and tell me to come over and have a bite to eat with them. There was always steak on offer as Jake Cohen wouldn't eat sausages or ribs and Sarah, his wife made a lovely salad. The Browns, their neighbours, bought their sausages from the German delicatessen and they were really tasty, and the Duncans were very fond of lamb. There was usually plenty of different things to choose from. I usually took some nuts and crisps but always refused the alcohol. Didn't want to be drinking before I drove home. They were such a friendly bunch and there most days as they had retired. One evening in mid-July, I wandered over and joined them for supper and the conversation turned to dog poo.

The Duncans had a little terrier called Scotty who came to the beach with them but who usually sat in their hut out of the sun as he was getting on a bit. He was a nice old dog, and I would see Mrs Duncan take Scotty up the slope to the grass above to do his business at least three or four times a day and she would always take a bag with her to pick up any mess he might make. The council were very strict about dogs on the beach. They were only allowed in certain areas which ensured that the beach was kept clear of any possible dog faeces and there was a hefty fine for anyone who ignored the signs. I hated dog shit and was red hot on watching out for it. One of my kids had fallen face first into a pile of it once when he was a toddler. Poor little thing, I was up the doctors to have him checked out straight away. I don't like shit of any kind and I certainly don't like it on a beach where children should be able to play safely.

Scotty really enjoyed barbecue nights as the odd scrap often found its way to him. Anyway, one evening, we were sitting outside their huts enjoying the company and the hamburgers when a woman came steaming over to me. She had a high pitched over the top posh voice and she looked at me as though I were a piece of dirt.

"Call yourself a beach inspector?" she yelled, "Look at you. Stuffing your face with the very people whose dog muck my little Tabitha has just trodden in. You should be ashamed of yourself!"

"I beg your pardon," retorted Mrs Duncan before I could finish chewing what was in my mouth to reply, "But I'll have you know my dog never does his business on the beach. I always walk him elsewhere AND I bag his poo and put it in the bins. Which is more than can be said for you and your blasted horses. I see you in the morning, bringing them down here and letting them drop their poo all over the sands. I don't see you stopping to pick that up. It either washes into the sea or some poor little kid steps in it."

At that I took a good look at the woman who had abused me. Sure enough, it was the same snooty woman who came from the riding school nearby with other riders. She came first thing in the morning and let the horses canter over the sands before the visitors arrived. Then she would take off their saddles and walk them into the water for a swim. It was nice to watch, but when I hailed her and asked her to collect the horse poo, she had told me to get lost. She was a rude self-centred nasty piece of work. But this quarrel had been taken right out of my hands.

"I think you'd better leave," said Jake and he pulled himself up from his chair. He was a big man and an ex-company director, so he was used to handling people. "We're very sorry to hear that your daughter has had this accident, but just because we have a dog here, it doesn't follow that he is the culprit. I can vouch for my friend here. She religiously walks her dog four times a day and ensures he never leaves his calling card for anyone to step in."

"I second that," said Mr Brown. "It's quite unfair of you to accuse Scotty here of that particular misdemeanour."

Everyone looked at Scotty, who was fast asleep in the shade of the hut having just consumed a chicken breast but who let out the most enormous fart just as everyone's attention was on him.

The woman had no option but to leave. But her parting shot was aimed directly at me.

"I'm going to report you for hob-knobbing with these people instead of doing your job," she snarled. "Don't think you've got away with this. I'll sort you out, you see if I don't."

"It's 6.30pm. I clocked off thirty minutes ago, love." I answered, "So go right ahead. I have my witnesses to the time. Do you?"

It was the beginning of the end. From the next morning on, that woman would deliberately wait on the beach until her horses had defecated and then ride off leaving the piles of poo along the shoreline. At first, there had been only two horses at a time that she brought down, but as July progressed, she obviously arranged for young riders to accompany her and one day, ten horses were cantering up and down the sands. Every day I would go down with the left behind buckets and spades that were handed in to my office and collect the poo.

At first, I shoved it into the rubbish bins but after a bit, I bagged it and gave it to the locals who I knew were keen gardeners. The day of the ten horses was too much for me though and I decided enough was enough.

"Oi!" I called to her, "You didn't like it when your little precious trod in shit did you? But you're quite happy to let other children get your horses' muck between their toes, aren't you?"

"How dare you talk to me like that? Do you have any idea who I am? And do you realise that horses don't eat meat so their poo, unlike your friends disgusting dog, is organic and wouldn't harm anyone. So, fuck off and get a life."

I was seething. I chased after her without a hope of catching her on her horse. But I shouted that I did know who she was and that I would be collecting the poo to return it to her and her bastard horses the next day.

"At least you'll be taking it home with you in one way or another."

The next morning, I was ready earlier than usual. The tide was way out so after collecting my water samples, I waited near the water's edge.

And I waited.

Sure enough, at 8.30 on the dot she appeared with a group of riders and they started cantering up and down the sand. After they'd had their little run, dropping turds here and there as they went, the horses were stripped of their saddles and were led into the water. I waited until the riders were waist deep and walked slowly towards the saddles opening the bag that I had in my hand as I approached them.

"Hi there!" I called to them. They continued to ignore me as I knew she had probably instructed them all to do. "It's alright. I don't expect you to pick up today's shit. I'll do that. But I've got yesterday's here for you to take back with you. Ooops!"

I 'tripped' as I got next to the pile of saddles, laid out so carefully on a rug so as not to get sand on the expensive leather. As I tripped, the horse shit in the bag emptied all over the saddles. I moved it about as it fell so each one got a liberal covering.

"Oh no!" I cried, "I think I've twisted my ankle. And I've trodden in some of your horse poo. It's a good job it's organic."

Just after lunch, Derek arrived with a look of triumph on his ugly face.

"So, Clarke. What's all this I hear? You've been attacking people, have you? You do realise that's a sackable offence?"

"What are you talking about?"

"Don't act the innocent with me Clarke. You attacked Mrs Houghton-Smythe this morning and, she tells us, made threats that you intended doing it."

"Sorry? Mrs Houghton-Smythe? I don't have anyone with that name on my books and I haven't attacked anybody."

"I haven't got time for this. Get your stuff together and get out of here. You're sacked."

"Now just hold on a minute there, Derek. You can't sack me on the say so of someone I don't even know and take it as gospel that Mrs Whoever is telling the truth. I'm telling YOU I didn't attack anyone."

"Do you deny that you threw horses droppings at her this morning?"

"Oh, that's who you are talking about. Yes, I absolutely deny it."

"She says you did."

"Did she now? Well, I didn't. And I went on to tell him how I had asked her not to let her horses foul the beach, a request she refused to comply with, and that I collected the dung every day after she had visited and after being told by the council gardeners how valuable as manure horse poo was, had been in the process of returning a large bag of it to her for her to sell when I tripped over one of the stirrups and accidentally it got tipped onto her saddles.

"So, you see, saying I threw it at her is a complete exaggeration. And as for a threat..." I shrugged my shoulders, "I simply told her I would collect it and return it to her the next day."

"Do you honestly think I would take the word of a feckless individual such as you against that of an upstanding businesswoman like Mrs Houghton-Smythe? And she's a close personal friend of the mayor. Did you know that? No, I expect you don't have a clue how decent people live. Dream on Clarke and get your shit together." answered Derek (I had to suppress a snigger at that pun). "Here's your cards and here's your pay up to yesterday. I'm to wait while you clear your things and then I want the keys from you. Now get a move on." And he folded his arms and waited as he watched me collect my posters, pots of paint, television, (his eyebrows shot up when he saw that!) my towels beach umbrella, sunglasses, kettle, mug, tea bags... The list was endless.

As I started collecting my things, I noticed that Mr Duncan had stopped outside my office. He had overheard what Derek had said and was obviously interested in what was occurring. He was wearing bright green bathing shorts. He had a bottle of Ambre Solaire tucked into his pocket, a sun visor, sunglasses and had today's newspaper under his arm.

"Hi there, Clarkie," he called, "Coming over for a barbecue later? Having a bit of trouble with today's crossword."

"No, Mr Clarke won't be here later. He's just been sacked." replied Derek, who was tapping impatiently on my desk with a pen. As he did it, I remembered it was my pen and held out my hand for it, at which he pulled a face and gave it to me to pack in my bag.

"What?" said Mr Duncan, "How can that be? He's the best beach inspector we've ever had at this beach and my wife and I have had a hut here for the last twelve years."

"I'm not prepared to answer any questions of the public. I am only here to carry out the council's orders."

"Is that right? Well, Clarkie, let me give you a hand with all that stuff and we'll take it to my hut for now so you can have a sit in the sun and tell me all about it," said Mr Duncan. "It all sounds very fishy to me, and you don't have to take any notice of him. He can't tell you what you can and can't do in your own time"

It was obvious that Derek wasn't too happy that I wasn't about to leave the beach under a dark cloud. It irritated him even more when Jake Cohen turned up to lend a hand. It's amazing how much stuff I seemed to have accumulated there, but between us, we carried my bits and pieces to their huts. Derek tried to regain his authority by making a big show of taking the keys off me and locking the office behind me so that I couldn't get back in. As if I would.

The Browns were surprised to see the three of us turn up with the lead of the television trailing behind me. They had the kettle on, and it wasn't long before I had sat down and told them my sorry tale.

"You were a bit naughty dropping all that horse poo on those saddles though," giggled Sarah as she passed me a home-made cupcake to go with my tea.

"You heard him. He tripped over one of their stirrups," said her husband. "And anyway, he's right. Why should she get away with what she's doing? Organic or not, it's not nice for people to have to dodge crap of any kind when they are at the seaside. Nor should his boss talk to him like that. Feckless is a harsh description."

"Slander," said Mrs Brown.

"If dog owners have to clear their pet's droppings, then why shouldn't she pick up after her horses" said Mrs Duncan, fondling Scotty's ears.

"Well," said Mr Brown, "If what you have just told me is accurate and that combined with the conversation you had with Mr Flower which I overheard, then I feel you have a case for unfair dismissal against your company and a possible suit against Mrs Houghton-Smythe. I saw how aggressive she was when we were barbecuing that time. She threatened you then. We all heard her. There's an obvious abuse of power too. Friend of the mayor indeed! So am I as it happens but that doesn't mean I expect a free hand in the way I conduct myself. I'm hoping that this Smythe woman could end up with a hefty fine for breaking a by-law. I'll look into it." And he sipped his tea as he gazed out towards the horizon with a wistful look on his face.

"Oh, he so misses his cases." Said Mrs Brown, massaging her husband's neck. "He has such an active brain; he's found it hard to settle into retirement. He misses the cut and thrust of the law courts."

"Law courts?" I repeated, "What law courts?"

"Francis was a top barrister until he retired," she answered. "Specialising in Company law. That's how we know The Cohens. And Russel here was their accountant, weren't you Russ?" And she grinned at her friends.

My mouth dropped open. I had no idea that they had worked together before in one capacity or another. It dropped further when the men got together and started to concoct a plan to get me compensation for what had happened to me. Nobody had ever fought on my side in my life. Ever. The ladies left them to it and simply carried on chatting about dogs and horses, stopping now and again to point out a sandcastle here and a baby there, oohing and ahhing at the kite surfers that they could see in the distance who were taking advantage of the wind that day.

I stayed at their hut until evening and watched the activity on the beach. No-one came to open the inspector's office and people who wanted to return hut keys or hand in lost property didn't know what to do. A kiddie who'd cut his foot and another that had been stung by a jellyfish had no-one to ask for help. The café owner got very cross with having to deal with people who wanted to hire beach huts or make a complaint about something so he put up a notice in one of his windows that he was not the beach inspector and that they should phone the council. He even added the council's phone number and which extension they should ask for. The rubbish bags weren't removed or replaced, cyclists rode along the prom willy-nilly, one almost ran over an old lady as she hobbled along, and a whole crowd of teenagers had a dance party with very loud music, drinking beer and leaving a whole pile of empties on the sand. A group of young mothers who were sitting near them almost ended up in a fist fight over the noise they were making which was disturbing their babies. Yet I noticed, when they themselves left, there was a pile of dirty nappies and baby wipes left behind. One of the locals called out to them to pick them up and got a lot of verbal abuse.

I couldn't help it. Once the crowds thinned out, I grabbed some bags and went onto the beach retrieving as much rubbish as possible so that it didn't get washed out to sea. It didn't take too long, and I left the bags stacked up against the overflowing bin near the stairs.

On my return to the hut, the smell of barbecue steak had my mouth watering. My friends welcomed me back and gestured for me to sit. I was handed a paper plate with a large portion of steak and salad and told of their plan. I was absolutely confounded at their brilliance and went home feeling almost euphoric that the day had turned out the way that it had.

Three months later, I met them outside the Industrial Tribunal Court in Ashford. I hadn't had to prepare anything for this hearing. Francis had compiled a comprehensive claim against the council. He had collected witnesses from the beach who had seen me picking up litter even after I had been dismissed. He had statements from all the regulars about my efficiency in the job and how well the beach had been kept while I had been the inspector and how dirty it became once I left. Even copies of the water purity's decline had been produced.

The statements about the overheard conversation and the use of the word 'feckless' to describe me was the evidence that nailed it and I was awarded the top amount for wrongful dismissal that the court was able to award.

A month later, I met them outside another court in Canterbury. This time, it was a civil case and the woman with the horse was accused of slander. It was pointed out to her that while there are no laws about removing horse dung from beaches, given that dog owners are requested to pick up their dog faeces, many councils including her own kindly request that horse owners either remove their dung, or at least move it away from the shore area as a courtesy to other beach users. She had not done any of that and had therefore allowed others to have their enjoyment of the beach tainted. It was also flagged up that she had used her friendship with the mayor to intimidate me. She had told council departments and the mayor himself that I had threatened and attacked her, thereby damaging my reputation to the extent that I was wrongfully dismissed from my job.

The woman had no evidence to produce to prove that I had not tripped with the bag of poo. She could not claim she hadn't threatened me though as I had six witnesses to the event. She was ordered to pay me a considerable amount to cover the damage to my reputation, the inconvenience of having to look for another job with said damaged reputation and the further inconvenience of having to prove that she had actively acted against me.

Outside the court, she saw me and glared. I smiled back at her and tugged my forelock.

"Thanks for the cruise I'm going to go on this winter. I'll think of you and your horses while I down a few beers. Oh. By the way, if you run short of some readies after you've paid me out, you can always bag and sell your horse's shit. It's organic don't you know! Highly desirable."

Good old Francis. He'd had so much fun compiling the case and covering every loophole that he and the others insisted on taking me with them when they booked their winter cruise, so I didn't even have to pay for it. But I didn't want her to know that. And I've got a lovely job now as a caretaker in a private school near Canterbury of which my three friends and their wives are governors. I keep the place beautiful. I even tend the garden so that it looks a riot of colour every season. The parents always exclaim at how good it looks. I keep it well fertilised you see. I know just the sort of stuff to use. And the boys there wouldn't dare drop any litter.

Ivan

02.05.52

Taurus: Dependable.
Will dig the whole six feet deep to help others.

It's been so interesting doing this computer course at college. You meet people from all walks of life, and they all have their stories to tell. I've met firemen, builders, retired people who want to go on Facebook because they're lonely and have heard that you get lots of friends on there. I ask them what they do for a living and then I tell them what I do. Lots of people gape at me when I tell them. They shudder and say, "Sooner you than me!" or "That would give me the heebie-jeebies." or something equally facile. And then, more often than you would think, they move away from me as though death is catching. But I find working with the dead – well, no other way to describe it – it's peaceful. And peace and quiet is something I treasure.

I never thought I would end up doing this though. I started off as a merchant seaman, something I loved. It took me to Australia, America, Scandinavia, oh places too many to mention. I was even shipwrecked off the coast of Scotland once. It was a great life, an adventure, but not a life to share with a wife. So, it was love that made me leave it behind and, without any particular skill, I got a job in a hotel as a gardener come handyman's assistant. The handyman taught me how to paint and wallpaper and this gave me a trade of sorts. It was a very posh hotel, part of a chain, near Canterbury where celebrities would often stay or the very rich would take their mistresses for the weekend. The tips were good; they would have been even better if I had taken up some of the offers of the more mature single ladies! I was not bad looking and quite well built in my twenties, with the charisma that went along with youth. But I was also very much in love with my wife and I took my vows very seriously.

My first brush with death came while I was working at that hotel. I was having my break in the staff room one morning when a chambermaid rushed in crying. She was very distressed and between sobs was able to tell us that she had found Mr Gervis in room twenty-four, dead in the ensuite.

"I couldn't open the door as he was blocking the way. I kept pushing and pushing. I didn't know he was there and then I saw a bit of his hand…."

It had been a real shock to her. She had reported it to the hotel manager who, as she was speaking, followed her into the staff room.

"Jim, could you take Ivan with you and go to room twenty- four. Take the bathroom door off. I've phoned the doctor."

"I don't think he can do any good sir," sobbed the chambermaid. "His hand looked blue."

Jim and I went up to the room and after removing the door, found Mr Gervis still in his dinner clothes with his pants down around his ankles sprawled across the floor.

"Often happens, Ivan," said Jim. "It's the heart you see. Can't cope with pumping the blood as the bowel is pumping the shit." And to my astonishment, he laughed.

I had never seen a dead body before and I was a little shocked. I could understand why the chambermaid was so upset.

"Right. You get that end and I'll get this. Lay him out on the bed and then we'll hitch his trousers up."

"Don't you think we should leave him where we found him?"

"Not very dignified for the old bloke though, is it? It's obvious what's happened so no big deal." And he started yanking at Mr Gervis which looked awful, so I grabbed his feet.

Once we'd pulled up his pants, Jim started going through his pockets.

"He won't need them anymore," he said, pocketing a packet of cigarettes and a very smart looking lighter, "And here, there's half of this for you." He was holding up some ten-pound notes.

"You can't do that," I stammered, "It's wrong."

"Well, I'm leaving a tenner in his wallet. No-one would know he had more than that, so they won't suspect anything and he's hardly going to object. Sooner we had it than the bloody undertaker."

I didn't take the money, but I didn't tell on Jim. My wife said that I had done the right thing but that it might have come in handy as she had some very good news for me. My first death and soon my first birth. Life goes in cycles, doesn't it?

The hotel closed for refurbishment so obviously I needed to find more work, but Jim told the boss that I was actually very good at decorating, and I became part of the team. After that I was offered work with a big company and it wasn't long before I was heading a team of painter and decorators that travelled all over the country refurbishing hotels. I loved that job, but I didn't like being away from my little family. We had managed to buy a small mid-terraced house in Sturry, not far from the train station. It suited us very well, though it was in a bit of a state when we bought it; not that that bothered me as it didn't take long for me to fix it up. We were very happy there but for the old couple that lived next door who were crotchety and constantly complaining; the kids crying in the night (chicken pox – very uncomfortable for the twins), me parking my van one inch in front of their house, my wife singing as she hung out the washing. The list was long and nit-picky, and they never passed the time of day to simply chat or exchange pleasantries. It made me cross, but Sally would tell me not to take any notice as she reckoned they were lonely and upset as their son, who only lived the other side of Canterbury, never visited them.

I'd just got back from Northampton one Friday night, dog tired and pissed off as I'd wanted to tuck the twins up in bed and by the time I'd got home they were both fast asleep. I hadn't seen them since Monday. They were growing and changing so fast. Each time I got back I noticed this little thing or that. I missed their first steps and their first teeth. They were at nursery now for a few hours each week and Sally had a little job at the local shop while they went there. We were slowly finding our feet and had decided that we could afford a slightly bigger place. Sally was showing me the house details she'd picked up from the estate agent that day when there was a mad rapping at the door. It was old Mrs Johnson.

"Oh! Why don't you ever open the door quickly?" She wailed, "Its Bertie."

"Calm down," soothed Sally, "Just calm down and tell us what's wrong."

"It's Bertie. He's dead. Come quickly." And she turned and half ran back to her house.

"You wait here," I said to Sally," I'll go." And I followed her into her house.

"Where's your wife? Why isn't she here? I want her, not you."

"She can't leave our children."

"You young people are so selfish. Oh!" And she started to cry again.

"Where is he?" I asked.

Bertie was sprawled halfway down the stairs with a very surprised look on his face. I felt his neck. No pulse.

"I'm sorry but I think he's passed." I said to her, "We need to phone a doctor. Why don't you go back to our house and sit with Sally? I'll wait here for the doctor and the undertaker." And to my surprise, she headed up the stairs towards me and, treading all over the body of her dead husband, started going through his pockets until she found his wallet and then started trying to yank the ring off his finger. I was astounded.

"Those thieving bastards aren't having this," she said pocketing his wallet. "Or that watch. I bought it for him for our fiftieth anniversary. Get his ring off his finger, why don't you? How long before they get here?" She almost trod on his face. I had to pull her off.

"Calm down. You're in shock."

"They'll have anything they can lay their hands on. I don't trust them."

I managed to get her to go back to our house and sat at the bottom of the stairs while I waited for the doctor. I'd told him there was no pulse but that the wife was acting strangely so could he get things moving as quickly as possible. He said he'd phone the undertakers but not to let them move him if they got there before him. I waited for about an hour after the doctor had left before the black van arrived. Sal told me the old lady was up at the window as soon as she heard it pull up. I'm so glad she stayed at our house. The undertakers took a copy of the doctor's confirmation of death, zipped old Bertie into a body bag and bumped him down the stairs.

"Sorry mate, but he's a dead weight, literally. And he's in such an awkward position; these stairs are so narrow. It's the only way we can get him out of here."

I nodded but felt a little affronted on his behalf.

"Oh, and the doc mentioned the old girl is doolally so if you want to get some disinfectant and clean up the – you know," and he nodded towards the discoloured damp patch on the carpet, "It might alleviate some of her discomfort, if you know what I mean."

I mumbled that I would.

"So, we'll be off then. Can you give her our card? She can give us a ring in the morning or when she's ready. OK?" and they loaded him into the back of the van and left.

I phoned Sally and told her I had to clean up a bit, but I was caught scrubbing the carpet when Mrs Johnson came in. She seemed a lot calmer and walked up to me.

She took the brush and said, "You go home now. I'll finish up here. I'll be fine. My son is on his way."

"Do you want me to wait with you?"

"No. Thanks. He won't be long. He only lives in Canterbury. I'll be fine."

I saw her son turn up thirty minutes later. It was the first time I had ever seen him. I only saw him twice in all the time I lived there. The second time was five months later when he came to identify his mother's body.

The whole incident reminded me of Mr Gervis, and I realised that the dead sometimes have no-one to stick up for them. Some of them are at their most vulnerable, robbed and their bodies abused. There seemed to me to be no such thing as dignity in death. I went home and told Sally all about it.

"I can't help it, Sal, I feel that it's horrible. Imagine if that were my dad or yours. One minute you're a person and the next you're a lump of meat."

She rubbed my back, "It's really upset you, hasn't it?"

I shrugged.

"Well, have you thought of doing something about it?"

"Like what?"

She pushed the local paper towards me. It was open on the Situations Vacant page. She pointed to an ad.

"An undertaker's assistant? Why on earth..?"

"I'm fed up with you never being at home, Ivan. I think you would be great in this job. You're kind and considerate; you're strong and you're good with people. What more could they ask for?"

"Being away from home means more money. It's the only way we'll ever afford that new house."

"I'd sooner see more of you than have a new house that's empty of you," she said.

I gave it a lot of thought and the following day I rang the undertakers and asked to be shown around. They were a very professional outfit and the boss showed me every aspect of the business from selling pre-paid funerals to the embalming area. I accompanied him to a funeral and watched how his staff made every aspect of the service as stress free and as palatable to the bereaved as possible. When he asked me if I would like the job, I had no hesitation in saying that I would.

I spent thirty years with that firm, ending up as a branch manager so that I was eventually able to buy Sally a bigger house in Chilham. I was very good at the job, but as my sixtieth birthday approached, I noticed that occasionally I got a little muddled. It was all this computerisation you see. I could cope with the basics – it's amazing how you pick up bits and pieces - but when certificates and permits started flying at me through the emails, I found myself more and more out of my depth. The wind was finally taken out of my sails when I realised I couldn't arrange a funeral for my lovely Sally. The blackness of death seemed to overcome me and I couldn't even get out of bed. The twins were amazing and a great comfort to me, but death had parted us and all I wanted to do was be with her. Not a good attitude to comfort the other newly bereaved so I took early retirement.

After a course of anti-depressants and grief counselling, I took a cruise to jolt me back into life. We landed in Madeira, The Canaries and Portugal. It was bittersweet to visit these places alone, remembering the last time Sally and I had been there. But as I boarded the ship in Las Palmas, I noticed a white van parked near the gangplank. 'Crematorio' means death in any language. I followed the official who had got out of that van up the gangplank where he was greeted by the Ship's Captain. I couldn't help overhearing.

"Is the body in the morgue?"

"No sir. I'm afraid that's completely full. He is still in his cabin. Please follow me."

And I followed them. They meandered through the corridors to a cabin two doors from mine. I didn't stay to witness the removal of the chap who had been in that cabin; the chap I had shared a few drinks with the night before. Nice bloke. He'd been looking forward to seeing Lisbon.

Helicopters came and lifted bodies off that cruise in the middle of the night. I counted five lifts that had been unescorted. Obviously, if someone was ill, the helicopter lowered a nurse to accompany the patient as he or she was hoisted up, but unaccompanied meant that no-one needed to be calmed down or reassured as they were hoisted up on a stretcher into a noisy, whirling aircraft. When the ship berthed at Dover, I was one of the last to leave it. We had to walk to a hanger to collect our luggage from dedicated areas. I was amazed at the area for 'cases to remain uncollected' as it was considerable. Obviously, this cruise had been a favourite for elderly people. At least they had enjoyed their last few days.

Once home, I rattled around our house and it wasn't long before I decided I needed a job again. I was lucky to see that Canterbury hospital was advertising for a mortuary assistant and even luckier when my years and experience as an undertaker was considered proof enough that I was perfect for the job. So, things settled down quite quickly for me.

I worked with a nice bunch at the hospital. I was the main mortuary attendant and in slack times, I helped out as a porter, wheeling patients from one place to another. But I was always called for body removal and for laying out the corpse for identification or family viewing. It was my responsibility to make sure that the corpse had the correct label once it was taken down to the morgue and this was the only part of my job that I didn't feel confident about. Oh, I could place the label in its plastic holder easily, I could attach the label to the corpse perfectly. It was the printing out of the label from the computer that worried me. I mean, there are some things I can do on the computer, like send an email. But fiddling about with printing especially on special label paper confused me a lot.

There was this porter there, Warren. Funny sort of bloke. Had a real thing about litter. Went absolutely ape at some of the young 'uns there who dropped sweet papers or left drink cartons laying around. When he was on duty, the cleaners would tell me they had a much easier shift. He wouldn't even take any nonsense from doctors. I saw him ask one if she had forgotten something and the look on that doctor's face was priceless when he handed her the Styrofoam cup from which she had been drinking her coffee. She looked stunned when he pointed out the rubbish bin in the room. I mentioned I had seen the whole thing.

"The hospital has quite enough to do without picking up after lazy sods" was all he said, "Now, let me show you how to print those labels again." And he made his way with me to the morgue where he spent twenty minutes going through the process.

"Oh, thank you, Warren. I hope you won't get into trouble for disappearing down here like this."

"Don't you fret Ivan. I clocked off at two this afternoon. I was just grabbing some lunch before I headed home. I figure you do a very important job here. It's no problem for me to show you how to print."

"But I didn't expect you to do this in your own time. Haven't you got a wife and family waiting for you at home?"

It was a sad tale he told and it explained how angry he came across at times. I told him all about my Sally and the twins and how I managed to stumble into working with the dead.

"You have a very special way about you, Ivan, you are so important here. People need your type of kindness when they are grieving. I have a great deal of respect for you," he looked around the morgue, "And you keep this place immaculate."

I went red with his praise. Despite our age difference, he and I became the best of friends. We would often meet at The Phoenix for a catch up. I still see him now and again. He works at a private school nearby. He is always on my conscience, but he just tells me not to worry; that I did him a favour.

You see, it was the label thing that caused all the trouble. We had such a strange occurrence that's never been known before. We had two deaths that day. One was an elderly man called Barry Mitchell and another, a dead-on-arrival road accident; a young man called Mitchell Barry. I printed the labels up just like Warren had taught me and attached them, as I thought, correctly. When the family of the road accident came to view the body of their much-loved son, they were horrified when I presented them with an octogenarian with no teeth. They made a huge fuss and couldn't be placated, suggesting that had they not been asked to identify the body, they would have buried a complete stranger. Even when the chief administrator at the hospital explained the way the mix up had occurred, they were baying for my blood or a great deal of compensation.

Warren came to hear of my dilemma and asked to speak to the chief. He told him he had taught me my computer skills and that it was not my fault but his that this mix-up had occurred.

"I told him that I was the one who had laid the printed labels on the trolleys where the corpses lay and that, seeing as the names were so similar, you hadn't realised I'd done it wrong. I told him to sack me and to tell the Barry family that I had been dismissed."

"But why? You had nothing to do with it at all." I asked.

"Well, I see it like this. I've got a life ahead of me and I don't really want to spend it in this place. I can easily find something else to do. But you. You are gifted. Just a touch on a shoulder and you comfort a widow or a grief-stricken father. You make the dead look as though they are asleep and carefree. This hospital needs you. You are kind and gentle to everyone and you never leave litter lying around!" He laughed at the last bit. "So don't give it a second thought. Warren Clarke will be just fine. And I'll still want to catch up for a drink and a game of cards at The Phoenix every Thursday."

And that's why I'm doing this computer course, see? I'm getting so good at it that I'm thinking of writing a blog about how to cope with bereavement. I can surf the net, print, I can even fight Trojans. And the course is much improved by the teacher. She's a rather nice widow, a couple of years younger than me but still very pretty and dimply. No kids of her own but she spends a lot of time with some young woman and her boys who seem to think a lot of her. Always showing me photos of them on her phone. I've got myself one of those smart phones too now. We swap boasts about our grandchildren, that's how she talks about the boys, and I often message her to meet up for coffee or dinner.

It's right what Warren said. There really is life after death.

Trina

12.07.50

Cancer: Falls in love too easily.
Believes in re-birth.

As she signalled to turn towards Birchington at the St Nicholas roundabout, she was surprised to see a faint glow lighting up the sky. Images from the Sci-Fi film she had just seen on the long flight over flooded her head until the greenhouses came into view and put paid to the dread of an impending apocalypse. She shook her head and told herself she needed to sleep. Things wouldn't be that bad. Things would be OK.

"See you're booked in for two nights. I hope you enjoy your stay. Have you got anything nice planned?" The receptionist gave her the key to her room and indicated the lift.

"Oh, just catching up with my past I guess," she smiled and took the key.

"Not been here before? I detect a bit of an accent there."

"I was born here. Lived here when I was a child. I've always loved the place. I've already seen quite a few changes. But then I wouldn't expect not to."

"Well, I hope they're all for the better. Have a good night." And he turned to the next traveller that approached the desk.

Her room was the usual motel type set up; just what she needed. A hot shower, a clean bed and a good night's sleep after such a long journey. All the way over her mind had been racing about coming back. But as soon as she had seen the statue of the lifeboatman looking out to sea, her thoughts returned to being a teenager again.

The summer of 1966. She was fifteen and life was exciting. The weather hadn't been all that great but music from The Lovin' Spoonful and the Mamas and Papas helped her imagine she was living in California and that she was part of a youth movement that was changing the world. All week she travelled from Birchington on two buses to go to school in Ramsgate where she was crammed for O levels, spending each evening churning through her homework. On Saturdays, she worked at Woolworths happily weighing out the pick and mix to earn the money to go to a dance at Dreamland Ballroom or trail around the amusement park with her friends. All the time, looking forward to the summer break.

Because Margate in the summer was an exciting place, a hive of tourists. Girls from Northern factories walking around the town with their hair in curlers so that it would look good in the evening. Mods and rockers roaming the streets half hoping to recreate that 1964 Bank Holiday fight on the sand but knowing they didn't quite have the numbers. The music from the amusement arcades that could be heard even from the beach, outdone now and then when the occasional announcement about a lost child played out over the loudspeaker from the St John's Ambulance hut. The beach was packed with holidaymakers on red and white striped deckchairs, enjoying the feel of the soft sand through their toes and the sea was alive with bathers splashing and squealing and revelling in the salt water. The smell of candy-floss, beer, ice-cream and chips pervaded the promenade. Coaches would arrive every Saturday with a fresh load of holidaymakers and boarding houses would display "No Vacancies" in their windows. Seven solid weeks where the local people could earn a decent wage, where cafes would have no seating left. Seven weeks when she and her friends felt that there was magic in the air. It was the seven weeks of the school holiday in 1966 that she left that magic behind for good.

She met him at the Rendezvous at Dreamland on the first Sunday evening after she had broken up from school. She was with two other friends and all three of them were dancing away to Sam and Dave until the music changed to a slow Dusty Springfield and she felt a hand on her shoulder. He was just a little taller than her; he was good looking, and he smelt really nice.

"Dance?"

They danced, then sat and had a coke, then danced some more. He was from Essex and down for a week with his family, but he didn't want to spend all week with them. He walked her to the bus stop and kissed her goodnight. He asked if he could see her the next day? Could they meet? She could show him around.

And so it started. Each day was warm and sunny. On the Monday, they explored Canterbury. He had always wanted to see the Cathedral and the old Tudor buildings that he had learned about when he was at school. The funny thing was, she told him, she had been to Canterbury lots of times, but she had never seen it in the same way as a tourist. On the Tuesday, the yellow open topped bus took them around the coast, giving him a glimpse of the different beaches. He loved the quaint streets of Broadstairs and the jetty with the old ship's figurehead outside the boating shed. The boats in Ramsgate harbour intrigued him. So many flags and masts bobbing around in the breeze. They walked through Pegwell village and watched the Hovercraft skitter out across the apron on its way to France. They went to see the Viking ship and then walked miles towards Minster, never feeling tired, exploring the country lanes, looking at St Augustine's Cross and the old Abbey. But it was on the day that they spent at Botany Bay, when he kissed her in the sea, she felt that she was falling in love. She always fell in love far too quickly. The week flew by so fast. By Friday she was no longer a virgin.

He left the next day. Neither of them had a phone so he promised to write. But of course, he didn't. And she didn't know where he lived so she could never tell him she was pregnant. She didn't tell anybody and went back to school hoping that things would be ok; that she was just late. By half term, her sickness in the morning and the small bulge under her school skirt made her mother suspicious. By Christmas, the headteacher informed her parents that she would have to leave.

Her son was born on May 1st. They didn't let her see him; they didn't let her hold him. It had been arranged that the baby was to be adopted and that she and her family were to move to Australia where no one need know about the shame she had brought on them. Mid May found her being sick again. This time on a ship as it rounded the Bay of Biscay.

They settled in Perth, Western Australia and things weren't too bad. They were known affectionately as 'Ten-Pound-Poms' and soon made new friends and settled down. Eventually, she married and started a family of her own. The doctor was the only person who knew she had given birth before. She lived with her husband thirty-seven years before he died, never knowing that his own two children had a half-brother on the other side of the world. But every May-day she went off quietly by herself and wept.

It was early in 2019 that she got the letter. The adoption society had tracked her down on behalf of her son. It meant the chance of a relationship, the chance to say sorry, the chance to be with him for the first time. A whirlwind of letters, of phone calls in the middle of the night followed. She was filled by the excitement of booking a ticket and for the last minute hugs and kisses for her grandchildren at the airport, seeing her safely onto the plane to return to England after so long. But still her children did not know the real reason why.

And now, even after being deprived of sleep for over twenty-four hours, she lay awake imagining how it would be, what she would say, how she would cope, until exhaustion took over and she finally fell asleep.

He had suggested that they should meet at one of the cafes in the arches along the Ramsgate harbourfront at four in the afternoon. He had said that he always liked to look at the boats moored there, and it had a great atmosphere. It was no real surprise that she woke late to the sound of the chambermaid knocking at her door, but she had time to have a look around Margate before she left to meet him. She quickly showered and readied herself for the day, left the car in the carpark and walked down towards the town.

The sundeck had gone and there was no pier stretching out to the horizon. Instead, the Turner gallery stood glistening white in the spring sunshine. She had wanted to visit this as soon as she had read about it and made her way along the front, noticing how there were less arcades or shops selling souvenirs or food and that hoardings hid empty spaces. The Bali Hi had gone and so had the pub on the corner that she'd passed every day on her way to school. Naturally, the shops had all changed, no more Bobby's, no Chelsea Girl not even a Marks and Spencer or Woolworths and there were a lot of empty shops in the High Street that used to be crammed with people. She was delighted though with all the little cafes and art shops in the old town and the buzz of people in that area. The Turner gave her even more pleasure, but it was the massive window looking out to sea that took her breathe away. And the figure emerging from the sea by Anthony Gormley, mirroring that other, ancient statue at the other end of the town that made her like the new Margate as much as she had loved the old one.

She had brunch in one of the little cafes in the marketplace and then returned to the hotel to get her car. She decided to take the route of the 52 'bus that she used to catch every day to school to get to Ramsgate. And again, instead of finding Pearce Signs and the Bowkett's Bakery on the way, she encountered the shopping centre that might have helped shut the shops in the town. Coming from a country where there were no little shops, just shopping malls, this place held no attraction for her, and she was grateful to leave it behind and head for the oldness that Ramsgate offered.

It didn't take her very long to find the Arch café. She sat and ordered a coffee and enjoyed watching the activity on the boats, the people walking by and the seagulls swooping at any food they carried. She loved doing that in Fremantle as well. Those birds got up to the usual tricks the world over, she thought, limping around for sympathy, holding one leg up and squawking, before they went in for the kill. She'd once seen a cheeky seagull actually lift a child's ice cream out of his hand. It was as she was watching she saw a young girl walking by, laughing at the bird too. For a moment she thought she was looking at her fifteen-year-old self. The likeness was uncanny. The way she held her head, the smile, the hair. A terrible sadness came over her. Where had all those years gone? Her own blonde hair was streaked with silver and her shoulders stooped a little now. Almost seventy but she still felt a teenager inside her head.

"Excuse me? You are Trina aren't you?" She looked up into the eyes of a middle-aged man who was holding out his hand, "I'm Richard."

She stuffed her fist into her mouth to stop herself from crying out.

"You seemed miles away. I hope I haven't shocked you."

She stood up and gazed at him. Slowly, she put her hands either side of his face. The face that resembled that boy from Essex in so many ways. Her eyes searched it, taking in how handsome he was, how lovely his voice sounded, how beautiful he smelt.

"They never let me see you, "she whispered, "They never let me hold you."

"Well," he put both arms out to her, "You've seen me now. So why don't you hold me?" and he gathered her to him in a warm hug.

The girl she had seen before was her granddaughter. She was sixteen and full of dreams for the future and questions about Australia. Trina thought about her family back in Perth. She thought about how much she loved them. And after spending just two hours with her son, she thought about how lucky she was to have found him again, and how much she liked him. She knew she would love him and his daughter before too long. She fell in love very easily.

Rod

04.02.74

Aquarius: Academically intelligent yet can sometimes end up in the soup.

This mess all started with a bet.

I had everything I needed in life at the time. I'd graduated from university with an excellent science degree and had taken a once in a lifetime job in the USA in a research laboratory for a top pharmaceutical firm. I'd met and was dating a beautiful girl who had a very rich father in the film industry. I drove a classic convertible car, lived in a breath-taking house in Santa Monica, had already put my name to several drug breakthroughs and was set to make yet another discovery on the treatment of depression.

And then I went to a barbecue where I bumped into an old associate from my university days. I say associate rather than friend. Funnily enough, he never seemed to have any friends; but he was always around when things were going on, in the middle of stuff, if you know what I mean. If someone had a party, he was there. If you went to the student bar, he was there, sometimes even serving, but he was always alone. As I said, I was doing a science degree and I know he was doing business, yet on more than one occasion I bumped into him in one of the labs. He seemed to hang around there a lot.

Anyway, I was at this pool party, friends of Sacha's parents, looking at all the rich and beautiful people getting off their famous faces and having a really good time when he tapped me on the shoulder.

"It's been a while!"

At first, I wasn't sure who he was. The face seemed familiar, yet…

"It's Alan. You know. University?"

And with that the memories came flooding back. Not bad memories really, just ones that left me feeling a little unsettled.

"Oh, Al. Of course. How are you?"

"Gee. You two guys know each other?" Sacha's father was passing by and heard us, "Who woulda thought it?"

"Amazing, isn't it?" replied Alan. "It must be," he looked at me with his head on one side," What is it now? Fifteen years? And you haven't changed all that much, Rod." He turned to my prospective father-in-law and laughed, "Rod was a real live one on campus. Always at the parties, always wherever it was happening. Yet charged through his finals with the ease of a thoroughbred. I knew from the very start he would do well."

"Well, he sure has done that! He's landed himself the prettiest little gal this side of the Atlantic," and he slapped me on the back, "Well, I'm gonna leave you two to catch up." And thankfully, he continued on his way to chat to his friends sitting by the pool.

"So, Rod," said Alan, touching me under the arm and guiding me towards some seats in the shade, "Tell me about yourself."

I could have sworn his eyes glazed over as I told him of my girl, my house and my research although he did make the appropriate noises at the right time. When I asked about what he was up to he was almost vague.

"I'm doing OK. Got a place back in Canterbury."

"Oh yes, I remember, that's where you came from."

"Still live there – at weekends – have to spend the week in London." Al gazed at the swimmers in the pool as he spoke, "Last time I heard anything about him," he said pointing to one of Hollywood's latest discoveries, "He was delivering pizza in Mulholland Drive." And he laughed.

"I didn't know you were in films," I said. "I thought you were doing business studies. Talk about breezing through exams, I seem to remember you getting a prize of some sort."

"No, I'm not in films but I suppose you could say I support them quite a bit in one way or another. I'm in banking. Not the sort of thing to set the world alight. Not like you. Finding cures for this or that."

"It's not really cures right now, I'm afraid. More like treatments to help people cope with their lives."

"Funny that," said Alan, "Because I've got a little side-line going doing exactly the same thing. And I was hoping that you could help me with it. It brings in a lot of rewards."

Just then, a very wet and drunk Sacha came over in the skimpiest of bikinis and plonked herself down on my lap. Kissing my ear, she giggled, "Who's your friend, Honey?"

Al held out his hand to her, "I'm Al, how are you? I know Rod from Uni." And the conversation took an entirely different route, so I never had the opportunity to find out what he was doing in America.

Soon after, Sacha's father asked me to take her home before she embarrassed him in front of his friends, so I had to say a quick goodbye to Alan.

"Give me your phone," he said.

"What?" I was a little startled at that.

"I'll ring mine from yours, so I have your number and you'll have mine," he explained as though I were a complete idiot. "I'll get in touch as I want to share a little business proposal with you. Mind you, Rod, you're so set up here and it's so cosy that I bet you won't want to know." And he looked at me with an expression that I took to be patronising.

And there it was. I shouldn't have bristled when he said that. It wasn't the words. It was the implication that I was cossetted and boring and set in my ways.

The call came six days later. Again, the tone of his voice irritated me far more than the words he spoke. He almost challenged me to meet him for a drink that afternoon, "If you can get away from Sacha. Or her dad?"

"I'll meet you." I told him the name of a bar that I could walk to so that I didn't have to explain to Sacha why I was using the car. Her behaviour recently was all over the place and for the slightest reason, she'd started getting more than a bit jealous.

His suggestion to me was outrageous. I didn't know how to react.

"Why me? Why have you come to me?"

"I've come a long way to find you, Rod. I want you because you are the best. If anyone could invent and manufacture the high quality my customers demand it would be you."

"But what you're doing is completely illegal and unethical."

"And very, very profitable. Just think. You could be your own man."

"What do you mean by that?" I bristled at the implication. At that very moment not only did my phone vibrate but the ringtone, "Oh baby, baby..." Britney Spears' coquettish voice resounded in the quiet of the bar. I felt flustered. "Just a second. Sorry. Sacha's been playing with my ring tone again."

He looked away but I could swear his shoulders were moving. He was laughing at me.

"Hi Honey, what's up?...No, not long...I'm by myself...Of course I'm by myself...I'll be back soon... Just needed to clear my head, you know how these headaches get to me.... No, I absolutely will not take any of those painkillers. You know how I hate drugs."

He quickly turned his face back to me when I said that. There it was again, that half smile that seemed to be mocking me.

"No, I shouldn't be much longer...When it's gone, that's when!...Sorry, I'm sorry...No I didn't mean to shout...Baby, I wasn't shouting, I just need a little time to myself...Look, I'll be back soon...Yes soon... Bye... Yes, I love you too." I coughed and put my phone down on the bar.

He picked it up and turned it off.

"Look, I'll be straight with you. I came over here to go to Mexico. I have some contacts there; I needed to see if they could supply what I need. But the quality is poor, and the shipment would involve too many bribes and risks. What I need is something new and that can be manufactured anywhere. I already have contacts in Europe and a distribution system in place that I trust there. You are my back up plan; the Mexicans are not interested in being, well let's say, creative."

I moved to get up, but he put his hand on my arm.

"I want you to come and work for me. I want you to set up a safe laboratory and overlook the invention and manufacture of a product to be marketed worldwide. But I want it to be the best, the elite if you like, as what I already supply is known and trusted by the rich and famous.

But my customers want new ways to achieve the thrills they need. They want them safe and without side effects that can be detected in their appearance or the way they behave once the high has gone. My customers include politicians, celebrities, even royalty. I want you to do what you do best. I want you to research and create a new type of drug that will save people's lives because that's the way I want you to think about it. They want their thrills but want to retain the esteem in which they are held and still have the life to which they are accustomed. And they want them safe.

I have had many enquiries made and I have been fully assured you are the best research chemist in this field. You will be able to give me what I want."

He picked up his drink and just looked at me. I was stunned. My mind was racing. I didn't know what to say.

It felt like two minutes of silence, which he didn't break.

"I have everything I need right here. Right now. Give me one good reason why I should give up the great set up I have in California to do what you are suggesting? It's ridiculous. I think you are completely mad, and I've got a good mind to go to the police and tell them what you've said."

He just took another sip of his drink. I noticed he was drinking orange juice. He was completely sober. I, on the other hand, had ordered a double scotch on the rocks and my glass was empty.

"Rod, you can do what you want. We have no witnesses, and I am here on legitimate banking business as far as the authorities are concerned. But I'll give you more than one good reason to take my offer."

I stood up, "You are insane. I'm going."

He said, "The current firm you work for is soon to be sued because of the side effects of a drug of which you were instrumental in the creation. It's for the treatment of anxiety. I know that you hardly had any input in this drug, but nevertheless, your name appears on the team. The lawsuit will get massive attention and your name along with the others will be plastered all over the media. You will be asked to resign and no other pharmaceutical company over here will want you. The bank will foreclose on your house and the bailiffs will claim your car to cover your debts. Your prospective father-in-law will not want you, a man with no money or prospects, to be part of his cosy family and the lovely Sacha will eventually do whatever daddy asks her to do. Let's face it, Rod, she's a looker but has the intellectual capacity of a Teletubby.

I'm offering you a position that allows you to leave before any litigation starts, that pays you more than you are currently earning and the opportunity to work completely alone on a new drug that will improve the quality of recreation for a lot of people. To assuage your conscience, you can console yourself that it will also mean they will not be using substances that are eventually harmful to their lives. You will never be nominated for a Nobel Prize, but your work will ultimately benefit mankind. Do you want another drink?"

I was stunned. Of course, I had heard the rumble of a few small complaints about Disprinzin. I'd joined the team working on that drug when I first came to America and hadn't really had that much to do with it. But I knew that, like most pharmaceutical firms, the one that employed me was ruthless when it came to any mistakes. If what he said was true, my future chances to be employed as a research chemist were zilch. I slumped back into my seat.

"Same again?" asked Alan. He signalled to the waiter.

"I'll leave that with you, Rod. You think about it and let me know what you decide. Should you want to take me up on my offer, I will pay all your expenses to relocate and provide you with accommodation in Canterbury. You will also be given a car of your own choice and your salary will be paid directly into a bank account that I will set up for you in Switzerland. I leave tomorrow at midday which gives you about," he looked at his watch; I saw it was a Cartier. "Oh, just less than twenty-four hours to make your decision. But should you require further details, I shall have breakfast here tomorrow at 6.30 am and would be happy should you choose to join me."

And with that, he left $50 on the table for the drinks and left.

I sat there for ages thinking about what he had said and was taken by surprise when Sacha came storming into the bar.

"What are you doing, Roddy? I've been calling you and calling you! I knew you weren't walking because I've tracked your phone. Have you been with another woman? What's going on? Where is she?"

I looked at my phone. I had 23 missed calls, all from Sacha or her father.

"You tracked my phone?"

"Honey, you can't just take off on a Saturday when we're due to spend the afternoon with my parents without me being worried about you."

"You tracked my phone!"

His words came back to me: "Rod, you're so set up here and so cosy that I bet you won't want to know."

I collected my thoughts and went with Sacha who was babbling on about the afternoon and what she was to wear. I really had a headache by the time we got to her parents who commented on how quiet I was. I sat under the pergola and Googled Disprinzin. Sure enough, there had already a growing number of people complaining of unexpected side effects who thought it might be attributed to the drug. I checked my emails. I had one from my manager telling me to attend an urgent meeting on Monday morning. It didn't have to specify the subject.

Sacha's father came to find me.

"Son, you seem troubled. Anything I can help you with?"

"No Jimmy, I'm just not feeling the best today. I think I need to go home and lie down. Can you tell Sacha to stay and enjoy herself? I really need time alone and she gets all stressed if I'm by myself. She just won't accept that sometimes I need to be quiet. She thinks I'm out shagging women constantly."

"OK. She's taking that stuff for her anxiety; you know how she is. She's always thought people wanted to know her because of her money and her family connections and not for herself which is nuts. But nowadays she fixates on things, and she told me she thinks you have another woman. She has even asked me to get a tracker fixed to your car for God's sake! I told her not to be silly. I'm right, aren't I, Rod?"

I couldn't cope with much more of this.

"She's imagining things," I said, "I'm just not feeling too good." I picked up my car keys. "Get her a taxi, Jimmy. Tell her to have fun. I'll see her tonight." And I left.

I drove to a car lot and sold my car.

I bought a new phone and destroyed the Sim card out of my old one which I binned.

I walked to the Real Estate Agent and signed instructions to sell the house and dispose of the contents.

I walked home and made a pile of the things I wanted to keep. I phoned a courier company who came round, packed them up and took them away.

I shut the door to my house and booked into a Days Inn.

I had breakfast the next morning with Al and flew back to the UK with him that Sunday at midday. First class.

He took me to meet his mother who had an impressive house just outside Canterbury. Al seemed to have a lot of time for her. She certainly was a lovely lady. She'd obviously missed her son who I gathered usually spent every weekend with her and who had been away for over a week.

"He works so hard; he needs a little holiday now and again. It's so nice he's met up with an old friend. What did you say you do, Rod?"

I looked at Alan.

"He's selling Real Estate at the moment, aren't you Rod?"

I soon discovered Alan never told lies. He just didn't disclose the whole truth.

While staying with his mother, Alan enlightened me on how his operation worked. Canterbury was in a prime position for his needs. From there he had quick and easy access to Lydd airfield, the Channel crossing and London. It is a university town with ample supplies of young people in need of his products or able to assist in the distribution process were they in need of money. He had a team of trusted motorbike couriers who liaised on his behalf with his more affluent clients, usually in London. His banking business provided him not only with a good cover but also with new clients wishing to avail themselves of different ways to pass the time. Despite being the brains behind this large network, he had arranged it so that nothing actually touched him.

He showed me the property he had acquired for the laboratory two days later with instructions to carry out his wishes exactly as he had outlined in California. I couldn't pretend not to enjoy that aspect of my work. Setting up the lab (which was housed in the basement of an old house near Chilham) with massive extractor fans and ventilation units was a dream. It wasn't long before I was able to manufacture the goods required and the quality as promised was top notch. The difficulty in obtaining the ingredients for the drug was handled by another branch of Alan's enterprise. I was able to recruit two young scientists who assisted in the grass root manufacture of the existing drug. This freed me to experiment with finding a new type of drug to give a high without the user having the tell-tale signs of an addict. I enjoyed this part of my job the most. Al was keen to develop this rather than continue with the production of the other drugs. The Russians were making heavy noises which he wanted to avoid, so money to develop the new drug was lavish.

I had a bright, modern apartment in Canterbury, and I drove another vintage car, a 1934 Singer Airstream; I loved it. I had girlfriends but avoided them if they became too clingy and all in all, was, as promised, my own man. Life was good. My Swiss bank account was healthy. The only thing I missed about California was the weather. I certainly did not miss the adverse publicity about Disprinzin that had been plastered all over the news and was glad of the anonymity Alan had provided me with. After over a month of knowing nothing about Sacha, I was surprised to read the headline,

"Film producer's daughter in house attack."

I clicked on the link and was appalled to discover that my old girlfriend had gone berserk in Santa Monica. She had attacked and maimed a woman who was about to show a couple around a house there. I read further that her parents had previously reported her missing and that all attempts to find her had failed. When arrested, Sacha was described as a juddering wreck who could not communicate verbally. She had been hiding in the house next door to my place, waiting and watching for women to enter it. The real estate agent had gone to the house ahead of the prospective buyers to prepare it for a viewing and had encountered Sacha in the kitchen.

"She came at me with her eyes rolling. I swear she was foaming at the mouth. She started hitting me with a coffee maker. All she said was 'Bitch, where is he?'"

I began to appreciate Alan had done me quite a favour.

It took me a few months to come up with what he wanted. I called it Sharp. I tested it in the usual ways, but it wasn't before long I needed human guinea pigs. I recruited some students from Canterbury University who needed to earn some extra cash but who had used other drugs such as cannabis, cocaine, and ecstasy. They all reported excellent results and were eager to buy Sharp on the market as they said it left them clear headed to face their lectures the next day. I tested and retested for two more months and then told Alan I thought it was ready for distribution.

Sharp hit the streets with a whimper because nobody knew anyone else was taking it. There were no dark circles under the eyes or loss of weight; there were no more ruined nasal septum or tell-tale tramlines up the arms of the users. Newspapers reported with wonder at how some footballers were dancing all night and scoring winning goals the following day. Politicians who I knew were customers were sitting in Parliament, holding clinics in their own constituencies, jetting off for meetings all over the world and still turning up the following day looking refreshed and invigorated. The demand for the product was incredible and I had to recruit more staff. Alan ceased production of any other product, thus making peace with the Russians. Having the monopoly on Sharp was enough for him.

I can't exactly pin down when the increase in violence started. Originally, I had attributed it to the discontent that had been stirred up by Brexit. But after a while, I had a sneaking suspicion that it might be more than that.

When I joined the Disprinzin team they were having trouble achieving the universal effect they wanted for most users. The drug was almost complete, and it wasn't until I did an experiment and added a modicum of an extra ingredient (obviously, I can't be specific here) that it reached the accepted level to treat the condition with least side effects. I had used a small amount of that same ingredient in Sharp.

It was when an Arabian Prince, I can't mention his name but let's just say that his wealth far exceeds my imaginings, attacked the husband of a famous singer, that I began to have some doubts. He was rambling incoherently when he was returned to his London home, and it was reported that police investigations revealed that pictures of the singer were displayed, framed in every room. His obsession and behaviour pattern seemed very similar to other attacks that had started happening amongst the rich and famous. A cabinet minister had laid in wait for the chauffeur to the Prime Minister. He had knocked him out and tried to conceal his body in the boot of the PM's car and then drove that same car at an alarming rate through London rush hour traffic, resulting in a collision with a tourist bus. Luckily the chauffeur only received superficial injuries, but the minister was taken away, unable to explain his actions. 'I love him, I love him. I am keeping him safe from the advances of the PM' was not seen as a coherent excuse. Of course, he lost his place in the cabinet and it caused a complete reshuffle. The PM was quick to reassure the public that he was completely heterosexual making sure he was photographed with his wife at his side at every given opportunity, denying any rumours that he had dabbled in homosexual practices whilst at Eton. He went on further to comment that he found homosexuality to be ungodly thus causing massive protests from the LGBT community and a great deal of embarrassment all round. A newsreader was seen by millions, getting up from her desk, walking over to the weatherman and lunging at him, grabbing him in a passionate embrace, demanding he leave his wife that very day and make babies with her. It had over ten million hits on YouTube.

In the streets of Mayfair, outside clubs and exclusive restaurants there were reports of violence. The papers were awash with it, one leading with the catchy headline "Very High Caught Judges". Three high court judges had been involved in a skirmish at a gentleman's club and had been arrested. It seems they had all developed a strong attachment to the same Barrister who had in turn fallen for one of the criminals he was defending.

Alan appeared in my laboratory within a day of that last headline.

"We need to talk."

He took me to Starbucks, bought me a latte and then dismissed me. He was angry as the reputation of his products had been ruined over Sharp and despite all the precautions he had in place to protect his involvement in the business, he had almost been implicated.

"My energy is now concentrated on extricating myself from this whole situation. The laboratory is being shut down as we speak, and I have had your belongings packed up in your flat. Give me your car keys." And he held out his hand.

"But there is no mention of Sharp in the news. How can anyone prove that this violence is caused by Sharp?"

"No-one has to prove anything to me. I *know* this is the cause and I will be destroying all supplies of the stuff. The obsessive behaviour of these individuals that we read about is causing the violence and for every high-profile name in the news being violent, there are hundreds of others reacting in the same way. Have you seen the rioting in Sevenoaks? And Tunbridge Wells? It's never been known before; the rioters are normally quiet middle-class people. They have had to close the Conservative club in Maidstone to repair the damage. It has taken six months for whatever you included in the drug to build up in their bodies to the level that it now affects their behaviour."

"But what can I do?"

"Nothing. You can do nothing except collect your belongings and disappear." He got up and started for the door.

"Alan, wait. Have you thought, we could sell the stuff as a love potion?" but he was gone.

When I went online to my Swiss bank account, I found that it, too, had disappeared. I had nothing but what remained from the sale of my house in California. And after repaying the mortgage, I could only just scrape the money together for a few nights in a Travelodge. Somehow word had got around that I was not employable as a scientist, nor any other job that I applied for.

So, you see, that's why I'm sleeping rough in the doorway of Marks and Spencer in Canterbury High Street. Its bloody cold. Christmas is approaching and

I never seem to make enough to get myself a bed for the night as my guitar playing isn't the best and my vocal range is poor. How a person's life can just turn round like mine did! The only friend I have right now is Bruno, a one-eyed pit bull that I inherited from another homeless guy who died last week from a drug overdose. Bloody drugs. I hate the things. I have a miserable life nowadays because of them. There was only one bright point which happened yesterday when this gorgeous looking girl came and gave me some soup. She managed to get most of it all over my sleeping bag and Bruno got more of a feed in the end than I did as he licked up the spillage from my crotch. Some reporter was with her, and he took our photo which I see is in the newspaper that old Charles (wino, forty-three, looks sixty-six) has got draped over his cardboard box. You can't see much of my face thank God; I wouldn't want that Alan to see me in this state. He already knows he's won again, but I don't want him to be able to gloat. And I know he's just fine because he still comes to Canterbury every weekend and gets driven around in a limo when he's here.

Last time I saw him he had a bloke with him who I did my science degree alongside. He was good but not as good as me. I know he was working at Pfizers near Sandwich when I moved to the US, but that's all finished now, and that site has become a sort of business centre. No more science there. They were deep in conversation as they were getting into the Rolls. I caught a snatch of what Alan was saying before they disappeared behind the tinted windows of the car.

"Teaching at the university? You're so set up there and it's so cosy that I bet you won't want to know."

Ed & Nell

1942 & 1950

Horse and Tiger: Water and gold.
Secretive yet compatible.
Can get in a jam together.

Ed put the roof down on the car and brushed some breadcrumbs off the leather seat before they fell down the tear along one of the seams. She was always munching strawberry jam sandwiches, had a real thing for them. It had been Granny Smiths with her last pregnancy which were much healthier, but this time it was just carbs and she'd put on so much more weight. Like a small elephant. He put the buggy into the boot and then topped up the water in the radiator. Wiping his hands on his jeans, he walked through the door and yelled up the stairs.

"What are you doing? Get a move on! Someone else will get it."

At the bottom of the stairs was a bag bulging with… God knows what. He poked it with his toe.

"And what's all this crap for?"

"A change of clothes and nappies, some snacks, a drink, all the things you need for a toddler. I should have thought by now you'd know I can't just walk out the door like you can. It wouldn't have hurt you to have given me a hand rather than farting about down there. He's just pooed too. I had to change him, or would you have preferred it if I left him in it all day?"

She was cross and six months pregnant, scowling as she waddled down the stairs trying to keep hold of her son's hand and hold up her bump at the same time. He just shrugged and turned back to the car letting her bend down and carry the bag as their little son climbed behind the seat that he had tilted forward.

"Bike car, Daddy" said Andrew, pointing to the fact that the roof had disappeared. "Beach today!"

"No, not today. Shopping today. Canterbury today."

Neither Ed nor his son looked all that happy about shopping. But today was the first day of the sale and he knew that if he lost that chair, he would regret it just as much as Nell, so he put the old Triumph Herald into reverse and pulled out onto the road. Andrew put his hands up in the air like he always did and chattered away to them and himself as he enjoyed the feeling of the wind in his face. Once they left the village and were able to pick up some speed along the main road, Ed stopped feeling so bad tempered and squeezed his wife's knee.

"It'll be nice to have two," he said.

"Yes, but that's it then. I hate being pregnant. Especially in this heat."

Ed felt a bit of a prick. He hadn't meant his new baby, so he thought it best to say no more.

He remembered the time he had seen the first chair. He and Nell had just moved to their house after they had married in January 1974 and, apart from their bed, they had no furniture. Her sister had given them a very nice but tiny couch which they both really liked but they hadn't bought anything else. He absolutely refused to have any form of credit apart from the mortgage. His first marriage had failed and left him with debts for furniture he had abandoned or was being used by another man. Nell and he had had plenty of rows about sitting on the floor or a packing case, but he wouldn't budge, and they had saved up for everything they had so far and bought it outright. They had lots of squabbles, but the one thing he and Nell always agreed on was their taste in furniture. Neither liked the mundane suites offered by the big chain stores. They both liked things that were a little different which was probably why they liked each other.

A few months after moving in, they had met up with his friend Bev in Canterbury and were having a drink in the square outside The Bunch of Grapes. A few wooden tables and chairs had been put outside for people to sit and enjoy the spring sunshine as they drank.

"Congratulations! New house, new baby!" Bev had toasted them with his brown and mild, "When's it due?"

And there followed the usual conversation about the mine where they both worked, the scabby deputies, the near misses when the tunnels collapsed and the talk of strikes. Nell was interested but as she didn't know the men they were speaking about, her attention wandered. She watched the people going by and she listened to the busker playing by the war memorial. Canterbury had always attracted lots of tourists, but now there seemed to be more and more day trippers since the hovercraft meant the crossing from Calais was down to just over half an hour. She reckoned she could spot the French because they seemed to carry their clothes with just a little more panache. She watched one group walk towards the Cathedral gates and as she did, she noticed a sign in the window of a new shop right next to them.

'Opening Soon! All Swedish imports!'

The shop was called Treyndan Fayre and it had pieces of furniture that were completely unique. "Not a three-piece suite in sight," Nell had said after she'd gone over to peer through the window, "What joy!"

They fell in love with the chair as soon as they saw it. It was called a Nomad Chair. It was like a big deck chair that didn't fold up with a black oak bent frame and one large brown corduroy cushion that sat upon the black fabric strung between. The shop had two chairs but at £70 each, more than a week's wages at the time, they knew it was an extravagance and that they couldn't really afford even one. They left the shop and drifted back to the pub where they finished their drinks and gazed across at the chair in the window of the shop opposite.

Ed lit up a cigarette.

"You know, "he said, "If we both gave up this silly habit, we'd be much better off. I worked it out once; it costs us five shillings a day, times seven. That's one pound fifteen shillings a week. Have you got a pen?" He reached for a beer mat while she fished in her bag. "That's…. Oh my God." He threw the pen down on the table. "It's only going to go up too. It's the first thing the buggers raise the tax on. And I read somewhere that women who are pregnant shouldn't smoke, so you shouldn't light that one up now." And he took the cigarette from her and put it back in the box. Bev looked at her and they both smiled.

"We are stopping smoking and we are going to get that chair." He stood up, gave Bev the packet of cigarettes, said he'd catch up later and walked straight back to the shop.

"Here we go again," shrugged Nell, "See you later, Bev," as she kissed him on the cheek.

"You take care," he replied and gave her a hug, slipping the cigarettes back into her bag.

The chair was a great success although her mother baulked at how much they had paid for it. Her father loved it and always fell asleep when he sat in it. It stood out in the room next to the little sofa which Nell's mother had covered with some blue fabric that matched the blue cord carpet that had already been down when they moved in. One window stretched across the width of the room and was hung with long blue curtains from ceiling to floor. Because of the chair, the room had that new 'Swedish' look.

Ed did lots of extra shifts and it wasn't long before Treyndan Fayre delivered a round, teak dining table that extended when they invited the family for dinner, with matching chairs that had woven seats. It was a lovely table although, when it was extended, the person sitting at the far end of the table had to climb over the other chairs to reach it as there wasn't that much room in the kitchen diner.

She gave up work in the September of that year and was grateful for the chair as when she sat in it, like her father, she was able to fall asleep. Her back didn't ache quite so much, and the baby calmed down too. She would have loved to have been able to smoke a cigarette as she sat there sometimes, but she always made sure she went outside so the room didn't smell of smoke when Ed came home. They had got rid of all the ashtrays and he wouldn't even let his brother and his wife smoke indoors when they came round. Her smoking had decreased but hadn't stopped and she felt guilty as she thought Ed no longer smoked. She used to worry that she would get found out because in the evenings she would tell him she had forgotten to get something and had to nip to the corner shop, or that she needed to pop round to see a friend. She'd been lucky though, as Ed worked late a lot and when he was at home he seemed to spend a lot of time in the evening going in and out to the garage to fiddle with the car.

"We need me to do the overtime now you're lying around at home doing bugger all," or, "That old banger of ours needs a lot of upkeep" he would say as he disappeared, sometimes for the third time that night and she took that opportunity to go up to the spare bedroom and smoke out the window.

Andrew was born in the November and his first Christmas was spent in their new home with his half-brother and sister who always spent Christmas with their dad, making a huge fuss of him. He seemed very content when his grandfather visited and cradled him as he sat in the chair. Despite the noise of the washing up and after dinner games, Nell's dad fell asleep on Christmas day with the baby in his arms. They were both snoring softly.

Treyndan Fayre soon became the focus of their visits to Canterbury. A black oak coffee table to match the chair was coveted and then finally purchased along with some tablemats and a lamp. But a second chair never appeared, and the shop said they couldn't order any more. They had been devastated when they had last visited Canterbury as the shop was displaying a sign, 'Closing Down Sale starts 10am May 4th Everything must go'. By pressing their faces to the window, they could just make out various shapes of some of the stuff they'd seen in the shop on previous visits.

And then Ed saw another chair.

He pulled Nell to him and had to pick her up to see over the sign. "Can you see it? It's the same, isn't it?"

She wasn't completely sure, but it certainly appeared to be the same.

"But why are they closing? They are the only shop which is a little different from all the rest?"

"Well, whatever happens, we just must make sure we are here at the start of that sale. I don't want to miss that chair," said Ed.

And here he was, speeding along the road to buy it no matter what it cost.

They were among the first to arrive at the shop and Ed looked about him wildly for the chair. They had to fold up the buggy and carry it as there wasn't enough room to move between the assortment of furniture piled up around the shop floor. They saw a table like theirs but half the price they had paid. There were chairs which were very attractive but the wrong colour and style. There was a display shelving unit that would have looked good in their lounge, but no chair. Nell decided that her feet hurt too much to stand around and she was being jostled by the other shoppers, so she sat down on a pile of rugs and ran her fingers through the wool. There a stack of prints leaning against the rugs and some linen tableware piled on top of what she thought was a table. But then she looked again and saw it was the chair. She called to Ed who clambered over everything in search of a price-tag. She crossed her fingers that it would be reduced.

"Can I help you, Sir?"

The sales assistant was the snooty one who always looked down on them, despite them having been one of their regular customers.

"I'm interested in that chair," said Ed. "We bought one just like it from you two years ago and we'd like another."

Andrew started to moan. He was bored and thirsty. Nell fished his feeding cup with blackcurrant juice out of the bag and gave him a biscuit.

"Ah, the Nomad Chair...yes," the assistant sighed. "Unfortunately, sir, that is not for sale."

"Is it already sold?"

"In a way, yes. One of our best customers reserved it over the telephone last week. She can't get in until eleven o'clock today, so we have moved it back here, so it doesn't get damaged. It's been in our storeroom for quite a time now, but she's offered the original price on it, so you see we have no other option than to accept. Can I interest you in anything else Sir?"

"You've had it all this time? In your storeroom? I've been in here loads of times asking you about those chairs and you said you hadn't got any and couldn't get hold of any others!"

The assistant laughed. "Yes, it had been taken apart and as it folds down to practically nothing but a large cushion, we weren't aware it was there. But never mind. Can I interest you in perhaps this chair," and he indicated a lime green monstrosity which made Nell's stomach lurch as the baby kicked her, probably in disgust. She hugged Andrew to her as he had started to clamber over the rugs too, receiving a scowl from the salesman.

"So, you've sold this chair to someone who just phoned up. Not to a person who made the effort to come in to buy it?" Ed was seething. He towered above the salesman who decided not to keep scowling at the little boy who was dropping biscuit crumbs on the pile of rugs. Nell took the biscuit from him and gave him a sandwich to nibble on instead.

"Well not me personally you understand. But it is sold to Mrs Bennet, the wife of our local councillor. She's very particular about her furniture and wants a second Nomad as they are so comfortable. It's sold and I'm afraid that's that."

"Let me speak to the manager," demanded Ed, who strode off with the salesman scurrying behind saying, "But sir…"

Five minutes later, Ed, Nell and Andrew left the shop. Ed was cross and disgruntled and wanted to go straight home but she persuaded him to stay for a bit. They wandered around the streets of the city, had lunch and bought a few other things they needed for Andrew and the new baby before heading back towards the cathedral wall car park. On the way they passed Treyndan Fayre. The shop had obviously sold a lot of products that day. The window display had changed and there, in the front, was the chair.

Ed went inside straight away with Nell and Andrew close behind.

"Ah, hello again Sir," the same salesman greeted Ed, a little nervously.

"So, is it for sale or not?" asked Ed, nodding at the chair.

"Happily, for you sir, yes it is. Our customer changed her mind." He replied.

"I'm not surprised," piped up Nell. "Look at the state of it!"

Now that the linen and prints had been moved away from it, the chair was in clear view. The brown cushion had dark stains along the seat and there was what looked like red mould on the wood that rested on the floor. She looked at the price-tag. "And you have the nerve to ask £75.00 for it?"

"No, no, that was its original price. You can have it for £60.00." He smiled again and Nell was reminded of a shark.

"Come on Nell, they can stick that chair...." Ed had already started for the door.

"I'll give you £30, and my husband will dismantle it and we shall take it away with us now." Said Nell. "It will cost me at least another £30 to have the wood treated and to make a new cover for it, so I think that's very fair, particularly when your company had mucked us about so much and not valued our custom as you should have. It's not a wonder you are having to close down."

The salesman went off to speak to the manager.

"What are you playing at?" demanded Ed.

"Trust me, I know what I'm doing"

Nell paid the £30 and took Andrew to get the car whilst Ed dismantled the chair. She pulled up outside the shop and waited for him to load it into the boot.

They drove off with the roof down and Andrew waving his little hands in the air.

"I don't know what that stuff on the wood is, Nell, but it was bloody sticky, and it came off all over my hands. And that cushion was sopping wet. Whatever possessed you to give the buggers thirty quid?"

"Oh, I water Andy's Ribena down so much he thinks he's got blackcurrant but it's really only tinted water," she replied, "He's always dripping his cup over our old one at home but its fine once I've sponged it. That'll dry without a stain, don't worry." She signalled as she turned the car back onto the main road. "Would you like a jam sandwich?" she asked, "There's still one left I think" and she nodded towards the bag by his feet. "Or would you prefer a cigarette?" He stared at her incredulously.

"No? Maybe keep that for when you have to fix the car?" she gazed at him instead of the road. "No, keep to a sandwich while I'm around, eh? But be careful, the jam is very runny. It's such a hot day, who would ever think it could just sort of drip off like that? It just gets everywhere. It looks awful on black wood."

And she smiled sweetly, put the car into top gear and started singing 'The wheels on the 'bus' to her little son as he snuggled down for a nap.

Anna

18.01.49

*Capricorn: Quick thinking and clever.
Can be ruthless.*

She sat down at one of the tables along the pavement outside Debenhams and stirred the cream into her coffee. It should have been skimmed milk but at least she'd resisted the cakes that the people in the table next to her were shovelling down. It was June, the sun was out and the street outside the Cathedral was teaming with tourists. She pushed her purchases further under her chair, you couldn't be too careful nowadays, and watched a flock of Japanese people jostle their way past as they followed an umbrella with a Union Jack attached to the top making its way to the Cathedral gate. The group took no notice of the sole busker sitting at the foot of the war memorial. He played a guitar accompanied by a soundtrack from his phone attached to speakers so they must have heard him although the younger members of the group were wearing headphones and were tuned into what looked like another world. Superdry had done a roaring trade by the look of most of the youngsters, but one girl had discovered Primark and was yanking a lacy vest from a paper bag and pulling it on over her tee shirt as she tried to keep up. It went beautifully with her flowery skirt.

"Jeez, that was beaut'. I reckon I could go another slice!"

She didn't know if it was that broad Sydney accent, the girl, the location or the sound of the busker's 'Mr Tambourine Man' that whisked her back almost fifty years. But suddenly she was fifteen again and in that square.

"For fucks sake, Jude, why in God's name did you wear *that* and why are you so late?"

Jude didn't even bother trying to answer as Anna strode off towards The Bunch of Grapes assuming she would follow her through the crowd that had spilled out of the pub into the square. Jude had never gone in there before. It was the kind of pub that was the place to go for university students who all seemed to know one another. She'd daydreamed about being one of that crowd, able to talk cleverly about politics and other stuff that university students talked about. And perhaps be held and kissed by a boy who looked like Mick Jagger.

"Get a move on, Jude. Don't forget what I said. Just keep cool and we'll have a good time. OK?"

It took a while for Jude's eyes to adjust themselves from the brightness of the day to the dark inside the pub. The smell of the place got heavier as she followed Anna further inside and made her eyes water. It was overpowering; a cloying mixture of beer, patchouli oil and a sweet smokiness that wafted underneath. It made her feel a bit nauseous and she made a quick bargain with God for her please not to vomit and show herself up. She'd figure out what she'd do for her side of the transaction later, but in the meantime, please would He keep her lunch in her stomach.

It seemed like an age before Anna got served. She'd had to push her way through to the bar, so Jude shrank back to a table covered in spilt drink, empty glasses and an overflowing ashtray. She looked around her, trying to act unconcerned, placing one hand across her stomach, holding her chin with the other. Eventually, for something to do, she took a packet of No6 out of her bag and a box of matches. Her hand was shaking as she lit up.

"Ah now, you don't see so many of those around here," said a voice behind her. "Can you spare one?"

Startled, Jude turned and took in the greasy hair and glasses. He was not good looking in any way, but he had a confidence about him that made him attractive. He was lanky and thin, dressed in Levis and a grey tee shirt with a leather satchel slung across his chest. Jude wasn't used to seeing men carrying any kind of bag, but he carried it in a way that made it look like it was something all men should do.

"But the place is full of smoke" she pointed out.

"Yes, just not the usual kind. You with Anna?" he asked, helping himself to a cigarette, lighting it from her own.

"How did you know?"

He chuckled and blew the smoke towards the bar.

"I've met a few of her friends. You go to the same school?"

"You know we go to school?"

"Ah, don't worry. It's cool. No-one cares." He lifted his eyebrows at another boy who was pushing his way towards the bar and took a sip from his drink.

"I'm Adam, what's your name then?"

"Jude."

"Well, Jude, how do you do?" he laughed again. "Pleased to meet you"

He put out his hand, so she had to offer her own and was surprised when he pulled her towards him and kissed her cheek. Jude blushed and then blushed even deeper at her own embarrassment at being so thrilled.

"Hi Adam." Anna was making her way back from the bar. She had two glasses of cider and was using her elbows to make a path, slopping the drink onto the floor as she moved.

"Steady now," he answered, "There'll be none left at that rate, and you'll have to start all over again." He put his arm round her neck and kissed her on the mouth.

"You found Jude then?"

"How could I not?" smiled Adam, the eyes behind his glasses rolled slowly over Jude which made her blush yet again. She felt torn between wanting to get away from the pub and the trouble she felt she could be in and staying in the company of this boy and Anna who were obviously so easily part of the whole scene. If she left, she would seem like a baby and Anna would tell the girls at school so everyone would laugh at her. If she stayed, she might show herself up as someone who did not fit in. She was so out of her depth and began to wish she had never come. She looked around her. She was probably the only person not wearing denim and she felt conspicuous in the flowery skirt her mother had made her and the little lacy vest top. She had thought she looked pretty in that outfit, and she did. But she thought she didn't look *cool*. Adam and Anna were deep in a conversation and although she tried to join in, she didn't have a clue who the people were that they were talking about, and her thoughts drifted away as she watched the things going on around her. She wondered what Van Gogh would have made of this place, or Degas. The lighting, the people.....

So deep was she in her thoughts that she didn't hear Anna.

"Get your drink down you, Jude, We're off."

Never had Jude felt more surprised; they had hardly been there. But the smell of the place was really getting to her, so she finished the cider and followed Adam and Anna out into the glorious sunshine. There was a boy with a guitar by the war memorial strumming and singing. He had been doing a Bob Dylan number when she had first met Anna but was now singing The Byrds "Mr Tambourine Man". He was good and had a throng of students round him singing along. He nodded to Adam as the trio walked past. They stopped just outside Lefevres.

"I've got to go now, Jude" said Anna.

"But I've hardly been here. I thought we were going to have a look around the shops."

Anna shot a quick look at Adam who turned his back and waved to a girl standing by the busker.

"I know...But... It's just I've been invited to a party and there's no room in the car for you, sorry."

Jude felt like she had been punched in the stomach. She'd taken the day off her Saturday job to meet her friend, her only source of income while she was at school and the bus fare hadn't been cheap. It was OK for Anna. She didn't have to have a job at the weekends, and it probably didn't occur to her that anyone else did. She told herself not to let the others see her hurt. They would think she was a baby. It wouldn't be cool.

"The thing is," said Anna, "Could you take my bag home with you? I've put my money in my pocket, but I don't want to take my bag to the party as it could get nicked." She nodded her head conspiratorially towards the crowd but, without waiting for an answer, she kissed Jude on the cheek and slipped her bag onto her friend's shoulder. "Thanks Jude. You're a babe. I'll drop round tomorrow sometime to pick it up, OK? Bye." And she ran back into the crowd outside the pub leaving her alone.

Jude stood there for a minute, listening to the music and breathing the fresh air with the sun on her face. She still felt a bit nauseous. The cider Anna had bought her had been warm and sickly and she'd gulped it down too fast. She needed a coffee and somewhere just to sit for a bit, but all around her the places were selling tourist junk or furniture. But there was Lefevre's, the old department store that had a cafe with windows looking out onto the street. "They need to put some seating outside," she thought to herself as she sat and drank coffee, watching the students in the street milling about making it hard for cars to pass. "And they need to make these narrow streets pedestrian only."

The police cars came about five minutes later, without sirens or fuss. She watched as the students melted away into the surrounding streets. She felt a silent shiver of thanks that she hadn't been in The Bunch of Grapes when they had arrived. Drinking cider. Underage.

"Drug bust again I expect," said the disgruntled woman who was clearing the tables, giving them a half-hearted wipe as she went. "Ought to shut the bloody place down, all that bloody noise and types hangin' around all the time. Disgusting. They need to bring back National Service I reckon, that'd sort the lot of them out. You finished, dear?" She stopped and waited, looking at Jude who got bullied into finishing her coffee and leaving.

Anna came round and collected her bag the next afternoon. She was wearing the same clothes as she'd worn the day before and her eyes looked red and heavy as though she hadn't slept. It was obvious that she hadn't been home. How on earth did she manage to get away with that? Her parents would go crazy at her if she didn't go home every night. Anna ignored her questions, grabbed her bag and left, not bothering to ask her friend how her afternoon had gone or telling her about the party she'd been to. Jude watched her get into an old Ford Prefect with a door that was a different colour to the rest of the body. There was no sign of Adam; there were three other boys in the car. She felt more than a bit pissed off at her friend but was also a little amazed that such a cool person had chosen to be her friend. She forgot Anna and went back to her studies. It was the start of the GCE exams the following day and she was in the middle of revising, so perhaps it was good that Anna hadn't stopped to gossip.

Anna had turned up from Australia just after Christmas. Her lazy drawl and easy way with people, her tales of life in a big city like Sydney instantly made her popular amongst everyone in her year. She had the latest in clothes and wore real Dr Scholes, not the copies so many of the other girls made do with. She was also very clever, probably inheriting her father's brains; he was lecturing at Canterbury University on secondment from Sydney for three years.

"Maybe that's how she knows so many university students?" mused Jude.

Anna was quickly accepted as one of the 'in' girls. She smoked and hung out with the others that were 'on the edge', all wealthy and self-assured with the confidence that wealth and a private primary education can bring. The school was the only grammar school for miles and hard to get into unless you passed an exam. Many of the girls had come from private schools where small classes ensured that exam pass. They were used to privilege, but Jude was a scholarship girl from a council house. The only thing that made her semi-accepted by the 'edgy' girls was the fact that she was brilliant at art. She didn't dress in shop bought clothes. She designed her own and got her mother to make things for her and it made her a little different and therefore OK. She was an oddity at that school, but she worked hard and was taking nine O 'levels, including Art, something she'd had to fight for as this school wanted their girls to head for Oxford or Cambridge, not Art School.

The next time Jude saw Anna was at the History exam the following Wednesday which was set to start at 9.15am. Anna was late to school and only just made it to her seat before it started. It wasn't too bad, but Jude was glad she'd revised. She finished early and was checking through her paper when Anna signalled to her. She looked awful. Jude didn't want to respond and get seen by the invigilator, so she looked back at her paper. Five minutes later, the girls left the exam room. Jude waited for Anna to come out.

"What's up?"

"I've got a problem. I need your help." Anna looked as though she had dropped half a stone. Her face was pale and drawn.

"My God, you look awful. What's the matter?"

"I need you to look after something for me."

Jude was naïve but being round Anna and after what she had experienced that Saturday, she had suddenly grown up.

"What's going on, Anna?"

Anna took Jude by the arm.

"We can't talk here. Have you got an exam this afternoon? "

Jude shook her head.

"Good. Let's go to the coffee shop." And Anna pulled her towards the school gate.

"No. Hang on. Just tell me." Jude sat down on a bench under a tree in the school ground. "Just tell me."

So, Anna explained that she had in her school bag some cannabis that Adam had given her to sell that Saturday. She'd been tipped off that one of their contacts had given the police her name and that they would probably raid her home very soon.

"I couldn't leave it at home in case they came while I was at school. My folks will go mad. My dad's visa could get cancelled. I'd be in deep shit."

Jude listened and thought.

"Was cannabis in your handbag that day in Canterbury when you gave it to me, when I took it back to my house?"

"Yes, I couldn't keep it on me. I had a lot that day 'cos I have customers. That's why I had to get out quick. But anyway, you can take it now; after all, you've already done it once haven't you? Bury it in your back garden. Nobody knows you so you'll be fine."

Jude thought of her parents. Her dad's back garden was neatly laid out to vegetables. He came in from work every day and did a little gardening every evening. Her mother worked at a dry-cleaners every morning and then took in sewing in the afternoon. They both worked hard so that they could have holidays, run a car, and have no debt.

"So, you let me take that stuff back to my home and risked me being in all kinds of trouble?"

Anna looked at her friend. "What you didn't know couldn't hurt you."

Jude got up and walked away.

Anna missed all her exams the rest of that week. The headmistress addressed the school the following Monday. She told them that one of the girls' names would be in the paper in association with a criminal offence and she directed the girls not to talk to any reporters that might be hanging around the school gates. Staff were on constant duty at those gates after that and parents even started picking up their daughters at the end of the school day. Somehow, the students doing their O' level exams got through them but the gossip amongst them was rife. What had happened to Anna? They all knew it was her.

Anna came back to the school the following January to sit the rest of her O levels. She was quiet and subdued and kept separate from the other girls. She just sat her exams and then was taken away again. Rumours went round that she was with some kind of carer. Nobody at the school heard any more from her.

"Managed to get my exams though" she thought as she drained her coffee. "Aced them, got to uni and now I'm treading in dear old dad's shoes. Despite getting no help from that girl Jude. Spineless. If she'd only helped me out that once, things would have been so different. Well, maybe not that different. But certainly, much easier."

She picked up her bags of shopping from under her chair, you couldn't trust crowds nowadays, and walked off through the square.

Philip

02.03.60

Pisces: Caring and curious.
Dislikes sharp things.

After Jen died, I found it increasingly difficult to go back to the house. All the pleasure of going through the door was gone. The house was like me; cold, empty and devoid of any joy and I did everything I could think of to avoid being there. We'd had a few good friends who tried their best to help me through it all. Deliveries of casseroles, lasagnes and other ready to heat up dishes were left for me on the doorstep with little notes, "Will pick the dish up at the weekend." Or "Made too much so thought this would save you bothering." The food was stuffed into my freezer or left in the kitchen to spoil. I hated eating in the dining room alone. It made things feel even more final. And the friends, well they ended up irritating rather than comforting me. They were all couples, you see, and the very fact that they came to me in pairs made me feel more alone than ever and I felt angry and resentful that they had each other.

Jack, whom I used to think of as an overbearing philanderer, became my closest friend. He had just come through a messy divorce. He wasn't part of a couple, so his company was slightly more bearable apart from his constant demands to hit the town in what he called his pussy wagon. He didn't seem to get it; that you don't replace a wife like you would a broken toy. He accused me of wallowing in self-pity. In the end, he gave up. People do.

Soon after, I started to suffer from acute headaches. They came on regularly at 5.30pm. So, I went to see my doctor.

"Phil," I remember him saying, "You've got to face up to the fact that although she's gone, that life must go on......" and he droned on with some other sickly platitudes as he wrote a prescription for something which I threw in the bin as I left the surgery. But the one thing I took in from the whole episode was the words he muttered as I left his room, "...so you don't have to be like your mate, Jack, but you should try to get out more – join a club or do a class – have supper out occasionally after work to take the stress out of going home. Phone up your friends, talk to people – you'll soon feel like starting anew."

Starting anew! Hadn't the silly old sod listened to a word I'd said? Starting anew? A new life, perhaps with someone else? Not with Jenny? He didn't have a clue.

We'd met at a friend's wedding five years ago and within a week we were living together. We'd been so intense – our feelings had never lapsed into habit. She'd had three miscarriages. "Nothing to worry about, you're young and healthy" the all-knowing medics had told her. Except they didn't see the cause until she was racked in pain, and it was too late to do anything for her. It took just two weeks and suddenly there was no more Jenny. Just me, a home that should have been teeming with our kids, laughter, and a future. It had all suddenly been cancelled.

I took his last piece of advice though and started going to different restaurants after work. There was certainly lots of them to choose from in Canterbury. I ate Mexican, Chinese, Indian, Burgers; it wasn't the food that interested me, it was whether I felt comfortable. After a bit, I finally found this little place which suited me. The waitress didn't scowl when I asked for a table for one and she got me a small table near the window where I could watch the evening life of the city begin to come alive; students gathering at a nearby pub, people hurrying to a performance at The Marlowe, couples meeting, embracing, and wandering away together. She seemed to sense I needed time to just sit and be, so she left me alone so I could do just that. I always left her a good tip.

It must have been on my third visit that I noticed something – a man. He was sitting by the drinking fountain at the park gates opposite the restaurant. It was the rose in his hand that caught my eye. A single blood red rose, not in a plastic tube like those sold at the florists or hawked around restaurants on Saturday nights, but one carried simply by the stem. I remember thinking he must have pulled the thorns off the stem as he was holding it tightly. He was constantly looking about him, and half got up once or twice when a single woman walked by. It was obvious he was waiting for a lady whom he had not met before, but I never saw her arrive as my main course was brought to me and my attention turned to my meal.

I saw him the following week, again on a Friday. This time he was standing under a large black umbrella, sheltering from the rain. He was taller than I'd imagined him to be. He wore a hat and an overcoat which appeared to be too big for him. He waited in the rain, not seated on the wet wall by the fountain but standing, shifting his weight from one foot to the other, the red rose a brilliant blush of colour against the darkness of the day. I made sure to keep my eyes on him as I gave the waitress my order. Within ten minutes a young woman approached, and they walked off together towards the river, him holding the umbrella over her head to keep her dry.

I'd also taken the doctor's advice and joined a nearby gym. This was completely new to me, but I soon found that I really enjoyed it and in view of my new custom of eating in restaurants, probably a necessity to keep my weight down. My evening headaches were soon replaced by my regular habit of either having a leisurely meal followed by an evening stroll home or a vigorous work-out session followed by a light snack and an early night. Whichever I did, I made sure that every Friday I was at the same restaurant so that I could watch out for 'the man'.

One Friday, I got to the restaurant earlier than usual, and as it had been such a lovely day, instead of going straight in, I took a walk around the park. I'd been avoiding the park up to then as I had found it too stressful to see the places where we had picnicked the year before, or the tree where I had proposed. I even managed to visit the spot where we had posed for our wedding photos and was giving myself an imaginary pat on the back as I made my way back to the exit. So, I was deep in thought when I heard,

"Excuse me, do you have the time please? My watch has stopped."

He'd come from behind me. It was a warm evening, and he wore casual but smart clothes. His hair was dark but thinning and his eyes, behind the glasses, were alert and intelligent. I was surprised to see that he was in his mid-thirties – I'd thought he was older.

I glanced at my watch. "It's six-fifteen"

"Thanks" he said and started to walk towards the park gate. Quickly I made up my mind to follow him.

"Did you grow that yourself?" I asked, "Such a beautiful colour."

The rose was perfect; its petals shades of red too many to count and the fresh, green stem, trimmed of thorns, proudly carried the head of the flower high.

He laughed. "The rose? Well, it's one of my hobbies. They usually give me such pleasure." And he headed straight for his usual seat and sat down to wait.

I hurried over to the restaurant and settled myself into the window seat that the waitress had reserved for me.

Every Friday I watched, and every Friday a different woman arrived. Once, he was left standing there until seven-thirty, and he left, leaving the rose behind him on the seat. I couldn't help but wonder why he had met so many women but that none of them had been seen with him twice. I had counted eight different ladies; surely one of them would have been right for him?

One Friday, he did not appear. I hung on at the restaurant and even ordered a dessert just in case he arrived later than usual. I felt stuffed and uncomfortable the next day, so I decided to go to the gym where I lifted weights and did a heavy exercise program. As a treat to relieve my aching muscles, I booked myself a sauna and massage.

"You new here then?" the girl asked as she slapped lotion onto my back.

"Not really – but this is my first massage."

"Thought so. You get to know your regulars. You're lucky I could squeeze you in."

She was quite pretty, my masseuse, about twenty-five I guess, with streaked blonde hair and big breasts. She chewed on a piece of gum as she spoke and energetically pummelled my body in all the right places.

She seemed faintly familiar.

"Yes. Could only fit you in 'cos of a cancellation from old Mr Perkins. He's got a prostate, see, and can't always lie on his tum."

"Nasty." I replied.

"Mmm. You're *very* tense. You should try and relax more, or you'll die an early death."

I froze as images of Jenny flooded my head.

"OMG! You certainly need my help don't you!" she chatted on, pushing the flesh on my back this way and that as she expertly found my knotted muscles and kneaded them into surrender.

"You should have a massage every week. It does you good, you know. Some of my gents have two. They say I keep them young." She giggled as she squeezed some cream onto the back of my neck.

Her voice was light and soothing. It was strange being spoken to as she worked away. My ideas of a massage had been that it was done in silence. Jack had told me how he once fell asleep during a massage and then laughed as he said he hadn't thought he'd have an actual massage when he'd booked it from the ad he'd found in the paper. Dirty sod.

"It's good you weren't here last Saturday though. It was awful. Police were here and everything. It's nice to get back to normal. Can you turn over please?"

She flipped me over expertly covering me with a towel. The man on the table alongside me said, "What happened to that man then, Trace?"

"Oh, I don't know. I hope they're hanging on to him. I reckon he's too sus' to be let out. He might do it again."

"Seemed a nice ordinary enough bloke at first," said the man.

The suspense was too much for me. "What happened?" I asked.

"Oh. It is a bit of a story really," said Shirley. "But as you're lying here completely in my power I may as well tell you about it," she laughed. She was kneading the ball of my left foot. I closed my eyes and her words, interspersed with the occasional chew of her gum, floated to me from the foot of the massage couch.

"See – it has been about two years now since me and Tom – that's my husband – broke up. We didn't really get along, but that's another story. Anyway, I go out now and then with the girls but – well – I dunno - the blokes I meet, they're all after the same thing. And being blonde and a bit bubbly – if you know what I mean, they think I am too. So, I stopped going to the clubs and stayed home more. I've got a lovely little girl – that's her picture over there."

I opened my eyes she was nodding her head towards her equipment case. On the inside of the lid was taped a photograph of a smaller version of Tracy.

"So, I didn't really mind staying at home. But I get lonely – you know what I mean?"

Yes, I knew exactly what she meant.

"It's nice to be given a cuddle now and then. Or go to the pictures and have someone to talk to afterwards about it and maybe share a bag of chips. You know. Company like. Anyway, I've got this friend, Sue. She pops around from time to time for coffee and a natter. And then I've got my job here and I do a few private massages, so it keeps me busy.

"Well, Sue came round, oh, it must have been almost three months ago now, with this paper with those personal columns in – you know the ones I mean – 'Tall, dark, handsome wishes to meet petite, intelligent red head.'

"We sometimes used to spend the evening looking at those dating columns and have a giggle imagining who they were. I mean, they could have been complete nutters who were married and looking for a bit on the side, or weirdos who could be axe murderers or something, or complete mingers. I just couldn't. Well, I just couldn't if you know what I mean. Those columns are such a waste of time if you seriously want a partner. Anyway, we were looking through it just for a laugh really, but then there was this ad which caught my eye. It was so much bigger than all the rest. The guy had obviously taken a lot of trouble and it must have cost him a fair bit to put it in the paper. I remember the ad well. He was going on about how he wanted a relationship, that he was separated with a little girl the same age as my Tabby, that he liked quiet sort of stuff like I do and that he was a feminist. Well, I don't know too much about all that, but he sounded steady and a bit on the serious side. It said that if you were interested, to write to him care of the newspaper."

She started to rub my chest. I could sense the comforting smell of the detergent she used to wash her clothes mixed with a very faint fragrance of deodorant as she bent over me. I decided that I liked Tracy.

"So, what's that got to do with last Saturday?" I asked.

"Give us a chance; I was just getting to that, but you needed to know what had happened before or it wouldn't make any sense at all." She replied, turning to her trolley, and getting a hot flannel that she put over my face.

"This will help you relax and open your pores. Anyway, after Sue had gone, I wrote to him. He seemed so intelligent from the ad' that I was a bit embarrassed about what to say, but I thought – well – if you don't try, you'll never know. So, I did."

I lifted a corner of the flannel "Isn't that a bit risky – giving your address to a complete stranger?"

"I thought of that, so I only put my phone number on the letter. I reckon I can handle a few funny phone calls" she laughed.

"Did he phone you?"

She pulled the flannel back to cover my eyes.

"Leave that alone and try to relax. Yes, he replied but not for a long time later. I'd almost forgotten I'd ever written! He had a lovely voice and sounded so nice. We arranged to meet the following Friday. He told me where he'd be, and how to recognise him, and I reckoned I'd have a quick preliminary peep at him before I met him in case he looked horrible."

My eyes were wide open now. I pulled the flannel away completely and was looking at Shirley as she pummelled away at my shoulders. When she smiled

– which she did a lot – she had dimples in her cheeks. She wore very little makeup. I felt concerned for her. The man had begun to sound like a threat.

"So, you went?"

"Yep. Turn over again – you're shoulders just won't relax. You've got to try and relax if you want to get the best from a massage."

"Go on with the story."

"Right. Well. We met. He seemed very nice. Very courteous and well mannered. Really different from those guys at the clubs. We went for a walk by the river and then for a meal. He talked a bit about himself and his little girl and then he asked a bit about me. My marriage and my daughter and if I worked. Told me he admired the way I was handling my life – being a good role model to my daughter by working and not just relying on handouts. He asked me where I worked, which I told him – my biggest mistake – but I didn't think at the time."

"You should never let any of the buggers know too much, Tracy," said the man on the next table.

"Well, I realise that now," went on Tracy, "But like I said, He seemed so normal that I didn't feel any need to be careful."

"Go on," I hurried her, "What happened next?" Looking back, I think it was ironic that she was telling me to relax whilst telling me a story that was full of suspense.

"So, anyway, when I told him what I did at the gym, that I was a masseuse, he got all funny. Said I shouldn't do such a subservient job; that a job like that degraded women. I got a bit annoyed I can tell you. I'm not one of those types of masseuses going around giving 'massages'."

I thought of Jack. I knew what she meant.

"I tried to tell him, I wasn't like that, but he didn't seem to understand. He started going on about feminists and the Women's Movement and having pride. I stood up and told him that I was too busy earning a living to be bothered with such things and that I wasn't going to take any insults from the likes of him, a complete stranger. I didn't care if he thought I was the kind of person he thought I was, and I left him at the table. I hadn't even eaten my dessert. I tried my best to walk away with dignity, but it was pretty difficult. The place was crowded, and everyone was looking at me and probably thinking I was one of 'those' girls. I was so cross."

"Did he try to follow you?"

"I don't know. I went straight outside and then ran. Fancy him thinking that I was like that. I tried to tell him I did women too. I went home and had a good cry."

"So, what's that got to do with the next day – here at the gym?"

"Well, like I said, I'd told him where I worked. He only came over here didn't he! I was doing Mr Perkins at the time. He came right in here and tried to tell me I'd got it all wrong and that he'd thought we should have another go. He tried to pull me away from my client and told me he could get me a job as a receptionist at his company. I started to cry, and Mr Perkins told him to push off and some of the other clients tried to get him to leave. But he wouldn't, and in the end, Mr Roberts, our manager, came and tried to throw him out. And there was this terrific fight and Mr Roberts got stabbed."

"Stabbed?"

"Yes, in the arm, with a rusty old pair of secateurs."

"A pair of what?"

"Secateurs. You know – those things you use to prune shrubs and stuff. He had a pair in his jacket pocket, and they'd come unlocked and poked through his pocket as Mr Roberts was trying to manhandle him out of the salon. He'd used them to pick me a rose from the park. That's how I was to recognise him in the first place, by a rose. I thought it was ever so nice of him using a rose for me to know him by and it turned out he had pinched it! The council don't like people pinching their roses."

Tracy told me the massage had done me a lot of good and she hoped I'd book them regularly in future, but not with her. She conceded that it might be the fact that I found it very hard to stop laughing that had released my tension but wasn't happy that I found her story so funny pointing out that having her manager streaming with blood wasn't a laughing matter, but this made me laugh even more. After casting a look of disgust in my direction, she walked away leaving me to cover myself with a sheet and stumble to the changing rooms. Maybe one day I'll tell her why I was laughing if she ever gives me the chance. But after I'd had a shower and managed to calm myself down, I phoned Jack. We are meeting tonight for a drink. We might even go to a club or something. I reckon he'll die when I tell him about the man with the rose.

Marcy & Fatima

1996

Chinese year of the Rat.
Strong sense of justice. Can sometimes
be too influenced by appearances.

From a very early age Marcy had wanted to be famous for something. She dreamed that it could be for writing a book, or having a painting hung in a gallery, or for helping those in need. She just wanted that one day she might hit the headlines so that she wasn't overlooked.

She had grown up in Canterbury and had been overlooked at Daisy Bud's nursery only achieving the role of third sheep in the nativity play. At school she had been overlooked as she had not shone at any particular subject and was never appointed monitor to give out the books or collect the colouring pencils. She was always the last kid chosen to join a sports team because she was not a fast runner and had the tendency to drop whatever she was holding, which was probably why she was not asked to collect or give out anything in class. In year four, she had attended camp with the rest of her year group and was put in the tent with a girl who wet herself at night and another who cried for her mother. She came home to her own mother, bleary eyed through lack of sleep and smelling strongly of urine. Her mother, who loved her dearly but who was struggling with two jobs and an ailing father, relied on Marcy to 'be good' and not cause a fuss. So, Marcy retreated to the tiny box room in the little terraced house and sang to her hairbrush and danced in front of the mirror. She did not mention to her mother that, although she loved writing stories and had always received good marks on her essays, the teacher hadn't credited her with more than a 'D' on her report. She knew this was unfair, but she did as her mother said and didn't make a fuss.

Marcy's hopes were raised when she left her primary school and entered secondary education. She thought the colour of the uniform and the style far more flattering to her dumpy appearance and hoped that a fresh start would give her the opportunity to be seen anew by different teachers and gain some new school chums. But her grades had followed her to this new school, and she was placed in a class with pupils who behaved abominably. They spent the lesson calling out, throwing chairs around and breaking as many school rules as possible. So when her mother asked her what she had learned that day when she came through the front door and Marcy had replied, "Nothing", she really meant it. But she always did her English homework and surprised her teacher who finally had some marking to do from that group. Her teacher was even more surprised at the quality the work she handed in but made no attempt to move Marcy out of the class as it would cause a lot of bother to the school timetable and extra work for the teacher and her colleagues. Besides all that, the teacher enjoyed having a pupil that seemed to grasp everything she was taught. Such a refreshing change that she was reluctant to give up.

In her room, Marcy still sang to her hairbrush, but no longer looked in the mirror so much. Her body hadn't changed; she was not turning into the tall, svelte princess that her celebrity magazines had indicated she should resemble once she reached puberty, and who lots of other girls at her school seemed to have emulated. She was still quite short, plump and had angry, red spots appearing overnight with blackheads peppering her nose. She felt sad that the only friend she had at school was Fatima, a new girl in her year who was spurned by the other kids as she wore a hijab, thick glasses and had something wrong with her which meant that she had to wear a big, custom-made shoe on one foot to compensate for having one leg longer than the other. Fatima was constantly being called a 'curry muncher' and told to 'go home'. The jibes at her ethnicity were harsh and cruel. The taunts came fast and thick. 'Don't go near her when she's carrying a backpack.' 'Don't let her do chemistry sir or we'll need a rebuild.' One lunchtime the nasty, cruel comments culminated in a group of kids backing her into a corner, threatening to stone her because she was a smelly terrorist. Marcy saw that happening and ran to defend the little Muslim girl.

"Go away and leave her alone. She's never done anything to hurt you."

"Ooo, ooo! Listen to pizza face. We'd all better watch out or we'll catch germs off her."

"Clear off, or I'll put this video I've taken of you doing this on the student website." And Marcy held up her phone, snatching it back from Sahara who'd made a grab for it.

"That won't do you any good, I've already emailed it to myself."

Sahara stood back.

"Come on. Leave the pizza and the Pakki alone. We'll get them another time." And with that the crowd dispersed.

Unlike Marcy, the other kids didn't see the glint in Fatima's eye or hear her laughter when neither of them was chosen for sports teams or special duties to represent the school. They were seen as a couple of losers by the girls in their year group who mockingly called the pair "Fat-arsy".

Fatima might have had a slight disability, but she was certainly not stupid. She would say to Marcy, "Look at it this way. We don't get hot and sweaty doing something we aren't good at and being sneered at by everyone else. We have the freedom to do our own thing."

Fatima had moved down to Canterbury when she was in year nine from Blackburn, so her strong northern dialect added to the reason why she wasn't easily accepted by the other kids. But her inability to do sport meant that she had developed her computer skills far beyond her years. She could set up websites and had even taught herself how to hack other computers. Once she discovered her best friend's ability to write, the pair of them hatched a plan to sort out the inequalities at that school. They were going to have fun hacking into the school's network and causing a little bit of chaos of their own.

They started with the bullies. Parents of those students who had been particularly vile to Marcy and

Fatima and some other students were surprised one day when they received an email from the head teacher advising them that their son or daughter's language and behaviour at school was unacceptable and asking them to address this issue as it had caused offence to other pupils. They were to respond to him personally and within a day to confirm that they had spoken to their offspring or face their expulsion. Similarly, they sent emails to the parents of students who they knew had also been bullied, informing them that he was aware that their son/daughter had been a victim and that measures had been put in place to address the situation. The head was inundated with complaints from parents who sprang to defend their little preciouses and others demanding to know why they hadn't been informed before about the plight of their offspring and what were these measures that had been put in place? He couldn't cope with the phone calls, had no idea how the situation had manifested itself but was finally forced to address the issue without delay. In one swoop Marcy and Fatima had halted the verbal bullying by the gobby students not only towards them, but also all the other 'uncool' kids at that school.

"They could have done this ages ago," said Fatima, "But this school is just too lazy. If they are going to claim to have a bullying policy, at least they should follow it through."

"To be fair, Fatima, I never told anyone what those bullies were doing to me, and I don't think anyone else did either as they were too worried it would make them an even bigger target," replied Marcy.

"That's your trouble, Marcy," Fatima logged on to receive the last email, "You're just too fair to everyone except yourself." And she copied the previously prepared email to the parents of Sahara Biggins, an exceptionally nasty princess in their year, thanking them for their co-operation in this issue, looking forward to better behaviour from their daughter and an increase in her grades and attitude to learning.

Once the main bullies had been dealt with, word spread around the school that the head was getting tough on behaviour. It had an instant effect and classes became calmer. Teachers suddenly had their work cut out to do some actual teaching, especially with the lower sets. That was when Fatima and Marcy decided to review the teachers' performance management files. It made very interesting reading as it soon became obvious that the hierarchy at that school wasn't dependent on the skills or ability of each individual teacher. It seemed that there was as much bullying and unfairness amongst the staff as there had been amongst the pupils.

"How on earth can Ms Salt be promoted to Assistant Head above people such as Mr Francis?" An amazed Marcy turned to her friend, "She used to take you for computing didn't she?"

"Yes, she was even made head of computing last year and she didn't know how to log in! I remember one lesson, she was supposed to be teaching us programming," Fatima rolled her eyes, "She didn't have a clue. Freddie had to tell her about some YouTube video which taught us while she did her nails! He even had to show her how to log off. She couldn't answer any questions and I had to help the ones who didn't understand."

"All I know is that when she took us for assembly, she kept calling us 'you guys' and said 'somefink' and 'nuffink'. It made me grit my teeth. She should have been able to speak properly when addressing the school. What are you doing now?" Marcy looked over her friend's shoulder.

"Just having a squint at her personal mail. Oh! So that's why!" and Fatima and Marcy discovered just how Ms Salt had climbed the slippery pole and advanced to Assistant Head with a very poor degree, an almost failed teaching qualification but with some very alluring nude pictures and suggestive emails that had passed between her and the Headteacher.

"I wonder what would happen if Ms Salt 'accidentally' copied in Mrs Headteacher to a couple of these emails she sent to 'Big Boy'?" said Fatima.

"Oh no, Fatty, you can't…" but it was too late.

The girls weren't all that surprised when Ms Salt found another post at a different school very soon after.

"Just call us 'The Caped Computer Crusaders'" remarked Fatima. She had managed to leak enough from the Head's personal files to the local paper to cause a surprise Ofsted inspection at the school and had been very satisfied to see the Headteacher squirm before he resigned.

"We shouldn't have to go to these extreme measures to have some kind of decent education," remarked Fatima as she perused the applicants for the vacant post of Headteacher, deleting those she could see were self-serving career educators, leaving a sole applicant whom the girls decided would do a good and fair job.

Thanks to these changes, the pupils at that school passed the rest of their years far happier than they had ever been. Marcy's English skills were soon recognised, and it was discovered that she was improving daily in all other areas apart from sport. It came as a surprise to her mother that she qualified for university. Her mother was even more surprised when her daughter gained a first-class degree and got a job working for the local newspaper. She covered unimportant local events to begin with, but Marcy told her mother that all the best reporters started this way in small newspapers. She was sure it wouldn't be long before she would be asked to write the main features and then, perhaps, be recruited for a national. She still had her eyes on achieving her childhood dream, to be famous.

Fatima went on to study computer science, graduating as the top student for that subject. After doing a short stint working for an IT company, she set up her own business and had some very lucrative contracts, some of which required her to travel all over the world.

Throughout it all, Marcy and Fatima had remained very close friends, both blossoming not only in their own careers but also in the way they looked. Fatima had undergone eye surgery and no longer had spectacles to obscure her incredibly beautiful brown eyes with long lashes that skimmed her cheeks when she blinked. She had decided to wear a scarf instead of a hijab at university, and now her long dark hair could be seen falling thickly to her shoulders. She still limped but was so successful that she could afford to have stylish shoes made for her making her impediment less noticeable. Marcy had grown taller, shedding weight as she grew so that she could almost be described as skinny. Her complexion was flawless, and although not beautiful, her face had so much character she wasn't easy to overlook.

The friends made a point of having lunch together every Friday in a small bistro near the cathedral. They liked the atmosphere of the place and the friendliness of the staff there who soon saw them as regulars and made sure they got good service. And then, one day, they were astounded to see a face they recognised from the past coming to take their order.

Sahara Biggins.

The woman before them still had long blonde hair and an athletic build, but her once arrogant face now sported a broken nose which gave her a quizzical look. They stared at her until Sahara noticed that her customers were more interested in looking at her than at the menu.

"Sorry ladies, but have you decided? Shall I come back later?"

Sahara was polite and deferential, so unlike her former self.

"Sahara? Sahara Biggins? Is that you?" Fatima was the first to speak.

The waitress was taken back. She blushed.

"Sahara Philpot now."

"No!" Marcy couldn't believe that such an awful boy such as Terry could get anybody to marry him. At school he had always been the source of any trouble, punching and kicking other boys who disagreed with him yet managing to avoid any repercussions. If Sahara had been the female bully in chief, then Terry was the male version. Judging by her bruises, he hadn't changed. Perhaps they deserved each other?

"Sorry, ladies, but how do you know me?"

"You don't recognise us?" asked Marcy, "I'm pizza face and this is Fatima. We are Fat-arsy."

Sahara looked uncomfortable. She shifted from one foot to the other and fiddled with her order pad. Marcy noticed she had a bruise on her left ankle.

"No. I wouldn't ever have recognised either of you. You've changed."

"How long have you been working here Sahara? I haven't seen you here before."

"Oh, I'm always around. I don't do set days, but I help out now and then when its needed. Depending on childcare of course."

"You have children? How lovely. How many?"

Sahara was a little taken aback. After their initial remark about the name she used to call them, she wasn't expecting these women to be pleasant to her. She remembered too well the way she had made their lives a misery while at school and she had no doubts that they remembered it too.

"Sorry, we are very busy today; I don't really have time to chat with the customers," she replied, "I need to do this job. Have you decided what you would like?"

After ordering their food, Fatima and Marcy were quiet, both deep in thought.

"We are so lucky." Said Fatima. She shifted her feet and looked at her shoes. Bright fuchsia boots, custom made and costing over £800.

"I was thinking just that," replied Marcy. She glanced at her phone. She had a message from another friend confirming she had booked their long weekend break to New York. "I bet she wishes she'd spent more time studying and less time pushing other kids around."

"Fancy ending up waitressing. Can't pay all that much. And did you see the bags under her eyes?"

"And those bruises?"

"And the broken nose? I bet that Terry knocks her about!"

"Those poor kids. She said she needs this job. I bet the sod's out gambling his social cheque away. He was always a nasty piece of work."

"I never liked Sahara. I mean, she was vile at school. But we were all kids then. Did you see her face when you told her we were Fat-arsy? I almost felt sorry for her. She was obviously embarrassed"

"She looks like she has a hard life. Let's be kind. After all, if she hadn't been so nasty to either of us, we might never have become friends."

So, when Sahara brought their food she was greeted with genuine smiles, and finally when she brought their bill, she said, "Three."

"Three?" asked Marcy.

"Children. I have three. Two boys and a girl. The boys are twins."

"Oh, how lovely," Sahara looked at Fatima but saw that she wasn't being sarcastic. "Have you got any photos?"

As Sahara reached into her pocket for her phone, they both saw that she had a bruise on her arm. They looked at each other, then looked at the photos. The twins were two and the little girl only three months. Sahara was undoubtedly proud of them, but one look at her face was enough for both girls to see that she was completely exhausted. They assumed she was probably having to work because of money troubles.

When she collected their payment, Sahara was surprised to find that alongside their payment there was a very generous tip and they both called a cheery, "Bye. See you next Friday." As they left the bistro.

She was intrigued; why had they left so much? She had been a nightmare at school and a nasty bully where these two women were concerned. She recalled one time when she had got some friends together and waited for Fatima to walk home through an alley. She and her mates had stolen her backpack and thrown it into the garden of a man who they knew to be a racist and a bigot with a very nasty looking dog. They had laughed after a drama lesson when everyone had to remove their shoes and they had hidden her special shoe so that she had to borrow some from lost property and spent the day limping. And there was the time she had written a note to the Adonis of the school pretending to be Marcy, telling him how much she loved him, and he had made such fun of the girl, embarrassing her so much that she had gone home in tears. There was a whole litany of things that she had done, and she was ashamed. She couldn't even remember why she'd done them. And then she recalled how suddenly it all had to stop because the head had somehow found out and her parents hadn't been impressed.

She discovered from the other staff that these women usually came in every Friday, so she decided it best not to work those days; that avoiding them was a far better and less embarrassing idea. However, two weeks later, she had to fill in for another waitress who was sick. She agreed before she remembered that her old school friends would probably be there again.

"Missed you last week. How are you?" asked Marcy when Sahara came to take their order. She noticed the old bruises were a pale yellow but that there was a new one on the back of her left leg and a mark around her neck that looked suspiciously like a thumb print.

"Have you decided ladies? Can I take your order please?" Sahara looked anxious and embarrassed.

"Sahara, does he hit you?" Fatima was always blunt. "We want to help. You shouldn't have to be hit like that. How will your boys learn how to treat women?"

"What?" Sahara looked confused.

"Let us help you," said Marcy.

"Sahara," the proprietor of the restaurant quietly pulled his waitress to one side. "Excuse me ladies, but I need a quick word with Sahara. Can I get you both an aperitif, on the house?" and he waved across the room to another waitress who came to serve the friends.

They didn't see Sahara again that day but bumped into her in the street as they were walking towards the war memorial the following week. Sahara looked exhausted and stressed. She was pushing a double buggy and had the baby in a sling around her front. When she saw the women, she knew they were going to try to talk to her, so she called out, "Sorry. Can't stop. Have to sort the children. Take care." And she bustled on her way.

"She shouldn't have to work as well as care for all those little ones."

"She must need the money. It's just like that sod Terry to knock her about and keep her short."

Neither women could imagine how awful Sahara's life must be, but the need to protect those who can't help themselves arose again. Even if it could be claimed to be Karma that Sahara was the one now suffering.

It was just a shame that, at that point, Marcy hadn't used her considerable research skills before they decided to go ahead and plan revenge for Sahara. She had just tracked Terry through Facebook and read that he was married with three children and had his own business, when she was phoned by the news desk and told to attend a car crash near the city wall and get the full story from the injured party that hadn't been taken to hospital. She was further distracted by her editor sending her to a local fair to interview the winner of this year's prize marrow, followed by a chat with a young man who had been nominated for teacher of the year at her old school. By the time she returned home after writing up her copy for publication, her phone went. It was Fatima.

"Well? What have you found out?"

"Have had a mad day Fatty. Saturdays are always busy, but I've made a start," and she told her what she'd discovered about Terry so far.

It surprised Fatima as she couldn't imagine Terry having the initiative or drive to be employed, let alone self-employed.

"What does he do?" she asked.

"From what I could gather, he has his own garage in a small industrial complex on the outskirts of Canterbury. He does MOT's and general repairs. From some of the comments on his page, it looks like he works alone. You can have a look for yourself. His account isn't private."

Fatima snorted.

"It wouldn't matter to me if it was, Marcy."

"I haven't had time to do a drive by to check that it was him," she said. "Or ask around about his family. Just to check that it's the same Terry, but his profile pic looks a bit like I remember him looking."

By this time, Fatima had already logged onto Terry's account.

"That's him alright," she said, "He hasn't changed all that much. Still good looking in a cruel sort of way."

"Mmm, but now with long dark hair. Looks like he wears it in a man bun." Had she not known what he was like, Marcy would have fancied him herself. "I should really do a drive by to make sure."

"No, don't worry. I'll do that. I'm free Monday morning. I might even be able to get the ball rolling. Operation save Sahara can start right away."

Terry was surprised the following Monday when a woman in a relatively new vehicle turned up asking him to check a weird noise that was coming from her engine.

"Best you take that back to the dealer," he told her, "It should be covered by them. I can't touch it. If I do that'll cancel the warranty and you'll be up for the cost"

"But perhaps you could just have a listen? I need to feel safe when I drive there."

Terry climbed into the driver seat and after turning on the engine, told the woman that everything sounded just fine.

"Maybe you need to take it round the block? Just to be sure? I heard a kind of grating sound as I drove along. Perhaps take it for a bit of a spin?"

So, Terry obliged and, leaving his office door unlocked, drove the car to the main road and back. He was gone for about ten minutes. It was enough time for Fatima to nip into his office. His computer was already logged on, so all she had to do was download and install the software that would enable her to control his computer remotely. She was standing outside the office when he got back.

"No, it's all good," said Terry as he got out of the car. "No problems at all."

"No clunking or grating?" a wide-eyed Fatima fluttered her very long eyelashes.

"It's a lovely bit of kit. Leased?"

"No other way to have a car nowadays!"

"Unfortunately, true. Doing me out of a job though. All the dealers want to do the repairs. Charge an arm and a leg too."

"Well, thank you anyway. I feel much safer now. How much do I owe you?"

"No, you're alright. I enjoyed the drive. Get fed up with just tinkering with old bangers. I hope you don't mind me saying, but do I know you? You look vaguely familiar."

And after convincing Terry that they had never met before, Fatima went home to log on to her own computer and remotely interfere with Terry's.

The MOT certificates that Terry had completed that day were deleted first, then his orders for parts and direct debit payments to his suppliers were cancelled. After a few days, Terry could not understand why his customers were angry that they couldn't tax their vehicles or had been pulled over for driving vehicles that had no MOT certificates. It was only the original paper copies that had been issued that convinced the police that there had been some sort of computer error. Parts that he ordered for his repairs were not delivered or were completely wrong, so he had irate customers who took their vehicles elsewhere. He had a visit from an Inland Revenue official who claimed he had lodged a fraudulent tax return. The owner of his industrial unit informed him that non-payment of rent would result in his eviction and when he complained to his bank, they informed him that he had himself cancelled all his direct debits. He set about putting things right and emailing to explain that there was a computer error and things started to go smoothly for him for a week or so, but then the chaos started happening again.

Angry emails from his customers started appearing on his Facebook feed and his friends started receiving lewd videos from him on Messenger. He deleted the posts, but not before prospective customers had read them and when they complained, he told his friends he hadn't sent the videos and he thought he'd been hacked. Terry changed his password but within a few days the problems started again. In the end, he deleted his Facebook account completely.

The stress that all this caused Terry made him very bad tempered and ultimately ill. His brother became very concerned about him.

"You need to take some time off, Terry. And perhaps get yourself a new computer as it seems to me that you've got gremlins in that one."

"I can't afford to take time off. And I can't afford a new computer either. Business has never been so bad. Things just seem to keep going wrong all the time. It's been madness off and on for over two months now."

Terry's brother had done very well since leaving catering college. He owned three establishments in Canterbury and his wife persuaded him that they should invite Terry and his wife over for lunch in one of them to cheer him up. The foursome were eating at the bistro that Friday lunchtime when Fatima and Marcy arrived for their regular get together. They were shown to their usual booth, and it wasn't until Fatima heard a familiar voice that she realised Terry was in the booth next to them.

"Let's go," Fatima pulled at Marcy's sleeve. "He might recognise me"

But the waitress appeared to take their order and the conversation from the next booth had developed enough to keep them rivetted to their seat.

"I did what you suggested and had my mate have a look at my computer, but he couldn't find anything wrong with it. It's working fine but then he checked the history…"

"Oh, that's dangerous!" Sahara's giggle was unmistakable. Strangely enough, it didn't sound quite so threatening as it did when they were at school.

"He's got Sahara with him. We should go!" hissed Marcy.

"No. Not yet. I need to know what he's doing with his computer. It's lucky we are here."

"Well, I'm glad he did actually check my history as it clearly shows that all the problems had originated from my computer. He couldn't explain why, but reckons I've definitely been hacked or something." Terry explained.

"Hacked?" another male voice. "Why would anyone hack a garage computer? And how?"

"Well, he said he didn't really know the ins and outs of it. But he's lent me an old laptop to use while he works on mine and he's right. Things have settled down again. So, it *was* my computer."

"Terry has been sick with worry," a different female voice. "He had to get sleeping pills from the doctor and…" There followed a description of Terry's illness due to his business worries.

Fatima and Marcy looked at each other.

Terry's voice again. "I'm determined to get to the bottom of why and how this has happened to me. And when I do…"

"Now, now, Tel," the male interjected, "Best to let it go. Just be thankful things are back to normal. You and Lizzie should take a week off and have a break away. Why don't you use our villa? Sahara and I can't go as she has her operation booked. Its half term soon; the kids will love it and you both can just relax. Swim in the pool and chill."

Marcy froze. "Sahara and him? Not Sahara and Terry?"

"Shh!" Fatima waved her hands at Marcy. "Please be quiet."

"How is the gym going Sahara?" the other female voice enquired. "I don't know how you do it or why you do it! I couldn't. You always look so tired too. Is the baby still not sleeping through the night?"

"Oh, she's getting better. I got five hours uninterrupted last night. And the gym? I love it."

"She loves it so much she hardly helps out at the restaurants."

"That's not true. I've been here quite a bit recently." Sahara laughed.

"Helps out? I thought she said she needed the job?" said Fatima.

"Restaurants? He has more than one?" replied Marcy.

"I've always loved sport and I used to go to play netball or go to the gym every day before I had the children. But since then, things weren't so easy, so Simon bought the gym by the park, and I run it. I've started up lady's kick boxing classes. You should come along, Lizzie. It keeps you fit."

"No thanks. Not if I end up covered in bruises like you, Sahara. And your nose!"

"Oh, I didn't do that at the classes. I'm booked to get that fixed properly soon."

"Wish you'd had it done properly the first time," Simon put in, "You look like you've done a few rounds with Tyson Fury instead of tripping over a train set the boys had left lying around."

"I was breastfeeding. I couldn't go into hospital. She was only a few days old."

"Well, I think that's great. Kick boxing? No-one will be able to mess with you, will they Sahara? Tell you what, when I find out who's done this to me, can I set you on them?" said Terry and the foursome laughed heartily before the conversation changed to children and childcare and the vagaries of the government.

Marcy and Fatima left their untouched lunch and enough money to cover the bill plus a tip and quietly left the bistro never to return. Fatima told Marcy she had to get back to her computer and sever the link between her and the one Terry's mate was tinkering with as soon as possible. She told her that it had something to do with addresses. And her reputation.

Marcy was too stunned to take it all in. All she could think of was how stupid she had been. She might have known that Sahara wouldn't be pushed around by anyone. And the awful thing was, had they not gone for lunch today, they might not have overheard that conversation. And then, the computer hacking would have been discovered.

And traced back to Fatima.

And to her.

And she could imagine the headlines, 'Vile Vengeance of Vicious Vixens' followed by a story outlining their cyber-attack on an innocent man trying to build a legitimate business in difficult times.

She would never have been overlooked then and she would have achieved her childhood dream.

She and Fatima would have been very famous indeed.

Mac

03.09.52

*Virgo: Blindly adventurous
yet oblivious to consequences.*

Mac always said it as he walked under the Westgate Towers.

"See over there," and he looked towards a wall where a person curled up inside an old sleeping bag was sleeping in warmth of the day, "There used to be toilets there. "

The entrance, where the sleeping figure now snuggled had been bricked up completely, but she could remember when there had been public toilets there. In the unexpected heat of that spring day, she fancied she could remember the smell they had exuded, but that probably came from the figure that, as they passed, languidly put out a hand to scratch a fly away from its face. She couldn't tell if it was a man or woman and wondered why whoever it was needed a sleeping bag on such a warm day.

"....and when I went inside my stomach couldn't take the stench. And there in the corner, some filthy dirty bugger had done a turd. It was still steaming, and I swear it was shaped like a Mr Whippy ice cream. It had swirls! All it needed was a chocolate flake. And how they had done it so neatly in the corner, God only knows. They must have got their arse so close it's a wonder it hadn't stained the wall. I wished I'd had a camera with me at the time…." She had already stopped listening. She'd heard the tale so often and knew it word for word.

They walked on past the Army Recruitment office.

"And that's where my dad used to work. It's where I signed up for the second time. It was the same day as the turd…." And on he went with his story about how he had got a medical discharge from the army, the first time, because he had told them that the acne on his back was really a reaction to the army uniform and then signed up for a second stint as he didn't know what to do with his life.

And here you are, ten years on, and you still don't know, thought Viv. Her feet hurt her because they were swollen, and she couldn't afford to buy some new shoes.

"It'll be a waste of money," Mac had said. "It's only because of the heat. Once they cool down, your feet will be back to normal. I don't know why you didn't wear flip flops anyway. You look good in them." And he carried on talking about his army days and how his feet had played him up and that she had no idea what bad feet actually were until she had worn army boots. And so on. And so on.

They never seemed to have any money for things she needed, despite all his shenanigans trying to make it. They had been together almost nine months, and in that time he'd had, and lost, five jobs. She cast her mind back and ticked them off in her head. She had met him when they both worked at a funfair in Margate last July. He was tall and bronzed and had made her laugh because he was so outrageous. He said the things she thought but was too discreet to say out loud, and this made him unforgettable. He worked on the brake on the scenic railway riding around the park with his shirt off, flirting with the girls who queued and then jostled to sit as near to him as they could. He was such a glamorous creature and so far out of her reach that she didn't even bother trying. She was stuck in a kiosk dishing out ice creams, slush puppies and doughnuts all day. She had to wear a uniform and hat that made her look frumpy and the smell of the oil that was used to fry the doughnuts was so pervasive, it seemed to cling to her even after she had bathed and washed her hair.

Perhaps it was her apparent lack of interest that made her attractive to him. He visited her kiosk every day, making her laugh as he conned free ice creams. One day, he persuaded her to come and take a ride on the scenic railway during her break. That was the first time he got the sack. He stopped the ride at the top of one of the hills and came and sat next to her while the queue for the ride stretched away below them, but he wouldn't start the ride again until she agreed to go out that evening after her shift had finished. When the ride got back to the ground, his boss was there, holding his tee shirt in one hand and an envelope with his wages to date in the other.

It didn't seem to bother him too much though. He went straight over to the rifle range and got a job there and turned up at her home with a bunch of flowers that still had the "Reduced for Quick Sale" sticker on the cellophane. They went for a walk along the beach, and he told her all about his life as they watched the moon bob about on the sea. He made her laugh so much that it never occurred to her that he didn't ask her too much about herself.

A few days later, when they were both off, they took the bus to Canterbury and spent the night in a club where they met up with some others from the amusement park and had a great evening. Mac held court most of it, telling his mates how he was earning a nice little bit on the side because he'd nipped out and bought a box of shells of his own. "It's ten shots for a pound, so every third punter gets sold mine! How can they check?" They'd missed the last bus that night and so had walked and thumbed a lift home. She got about four hours sleep before she had to get up to get to the kiosk and had felt very fragile all that day, as the effects of the vodka shots clashed horrendously with the smell of the doughnut oil and the sickliness of the ice cream mix. But he turned up at her counter at lunchtime with a sunny smile and an invitation to lunch on the beach which instantly made her feel better.

The summer at the funfair passed in a blur of laughter. They'd had such fun together. The owner of the rifle range found out about Mac's fiddle over the August Bank holiday when his takings were down, despite the record number of visitors to the park. He didn't manage to get another job in the park, his reputation had spread quickly amongst the stall holders and ride owners, so he decided to try his luck digging up the road for the Water Board. It had been a very hot summer and the autumn didn't appear to be that much cooler. Mac worked without his tee shirt on, just topping up his tan and singing loudly, as he dug away.

He lasted two weeks. He was digging in a road where a lot of bored housewives waited for their husbands to come home from London. One lady kept asking him in for coffee and another offered him afternoon tea. He wasn't where he should have been when his supervisor called by to find out why progress on the road was slow.

"I promise, I resisted all their invitations," said Mac as he nuzzled her neck. "I was only interested in their French Fancies and Victoria sponges" and he kissed her outside the letting agents as they looked in the windows for flats to rent.

He wasn't a bad driver and knew the area well, so his next job was working for a private hire car company. He got his licence easily and she breathed a sigh of relief as she had decided not to go back to college straight after the summer, but to take a job at Tesco so they had at least one regular income to pay the rent on the flat. Working the cabs meant he wasn't around at different times of the day and there were times when she didn't see him; sometimes he left for work as she arrived home from the supermarket. After a short while, she qualified for a reduction in all her purchases and that helped a lot. They sold such a wide range that she was able to buy those little things that made their flat cosy. "You're nesting!" he would say to her when their paths crossed, and she didn't object when he lay down on the little second-hand sofa she had got from an ad in the local paper and put his boots up on the new cushions she had bought from work to cheer it up. He grabbed her and kissed her. "This is nice and cosy. How's about a cup of tea?" and he pinched her bum as he pushed her back off the sofa. "And I'll have one of those cupcakes if there are any left." There weren't. He'd forgotten he had polished them off the night before.

On his days off from driving, he often took the ferry to Calais, just for a day trip. He didn't smoke so she was puzzled at the number of cigarettes and cigars he bought. She came in the door of the flat one day and tripped over a large box on the floor which she couldn't move as it was so heavy. It was a case of Glenfiddich single malt. It was nearing Christmas and the flat was beginning to resemble an off licence. She was tired and footsore. The store had been manic and if she heard another Christmas song she would scream. She had left the flat spotless and tidy and now it looked like a storeroom at a boozer.

"Is that you Honey?" Mac called from the bathroom, and he popped his head round the corner.

"Who were you expecting? Anyone interesting? Are you having a party?"

He came into the room with a towel round his waist, rubbing his hair dry with another which he threw on the floor when he put his arms around her and kissed her.

"Just a little business venture. You see, I pick up so many fares after the pubs have shut who are on their way to a party. I hear them moaning that they can't get their hands on some booze, so I just pull out a bottle and 'voila', problem solved. And I've earned a tenner on top of my outlay." He dropped the other towel and took some pants off the drying rack. "They usually give me a good tip as I've helped them out. I've got some cigars and ciggies inside my jacket if they run out of them too and I'm going over to Belgium next week to get some fancy chocs. There's their last-minute presents sorted. A happy Christmas for everyone. It's all good." And he disappeared into the bedroom to put on the rest of his clothes.

Viv just sat down and looked at the mess in the room. The boxes, the towels and the take-away container with the remains of a curry congealing on the table where he had dropped dollops of the stuff as he rushed to eat his meal. He kissed the top of her head as he made for the door. "It's gonna be a late one tonight Honey. Don't wait up. Love ya!"

Her feet ached as did her head. The sight of the curry made her want to heave. She picked up the towels and went to the bathroom and ran a bath adding the bubble bath she had bought for her mother for Christmas. She felt she needed spoiling, so she lit the candles that came in the set with the bubbles and placed them round the bath. As she bent to swirl the bubbles around, she withdrew her hand with horror. It was stone cold. He'd used all the hot water.

Mac's enterprise continued and thrived right through Christmas. New Year's Eve was a bonanza for him, and he decided that he would continue with his sales just on a Friday and Saturday night up until Easter.

"It was just my bad luck that I picked up that copper and his wife." he told Viv, as he went through the Situations Vacant page of the local two weeks into January. "I suppose I should have been more on the ball about what's going on around here. But how was I to know they were using the Winter Gardens to give that bloke some kind of honour? The place was teaming with coppers. He told me I was lucky that he was off duty as selling alcohol without a licence is a serious offence. Mind you, his snidey wife said she was going to report me to my boss. Cow. Good job I didn't ask him if he needed any cigars!" and he chuckled as he turned the page. "Got a pen?"

He was lucky to land the job with the sign company that month. They were desperate for a driver who could handle a bit of basic fixing, as their usual man had been taken ill suddenly and they had an urgent commitment to meet. They were delighted with Mac as he was so very personable and cheerful and only good reports about him reached the office. Once their regular man came back they offered him a permanent job. The money was good, and the hours meant that he and Viv were able to have some kind of a social life again. She started to feel that life was getting a little better for them both.

But it was now April, and they were on their way to the Job Centre once again because he had lost that job too. Using the work van to run his own man and van business at the weekend was doomed to failure on two accounts. Firstly, his customers were suspicious when the van turned up with 'Bright Neon' emblazoned on the side and secondly, the van was kitted out on both sides with racks stacked with fluorescent tubes and fixings which continually turned up damaged at work on the following Monday. The suspicions of his supervisor were confirmed when he himself booked Mac through the advert he had placed in a local newspaper.

And here they were once more, walking through Canterbury, heading for a two o'clock appointment at the Job Centre. As Mac chattered on, Viv realised she wasn't listening to him. She looked around her at all the other people. There were the usual tourists making their pilgrimage to this lovely city. There were the families enjoying a day out, having lunch, browsing in the shops. There were the students, sitting at the tables placed out in the sun smoking, laughing, talking about the sort of student stuff that she used to talk about this time last year. She felt tears form in her eyes and suddenly stopped. Mac just kept on walking and chattering away, oblivious to the fact that she wasn't next to him. She watched as he went further and further into the distance and made the decision to turn round and follow the tourists into the cathedral.

She loved the grounds and stood quite still as she gazed up to the building, marvelling at the way it had been built without the aid of any modern machinery. Her wonder didn't leave her as she walked slowly through the cathedral, loving the smell that had evolved through almost a thousand years. She touched the stone and felt the firmness, the solidity of it and understood why the cathedral was so important, not only religiously but also psychologically. This place had survived through wars and peace; it had survived intrigue, murder and drama. It just stood calmly in the centre of the city, attracting pilgrims from all over the world who, like her, were probably stunned by its magnificence. She stopped at the font and gazed fondly at it, imagining the number of babies and people who had been christened there. And it was the font and the comforting kick from her own baby within her that gave her the resolve she needed. She turned back to the door and walked out into the spring sunshine.

The street was still congested, but she didn't have to look to see if Mac had noticed she wasn't by his side. And she decided that she didn't really care any more. With the sun on her face, she took off her shoes and turned back towards the train station and the rest of her life.

Fingers

21.08.74

Leo. Fiercely defensive of family.
Will never be caged.

Having been forced to live on his wits since a very early age, Finger's self-preservation had started in the corner shop near his mother's flat in the early seventies. Abandoned by her husband and with very few skills to survive in the workplace, Mrs Fennel had done her best to provide for her son by working cleaning jobs back-to-back through those dark days of the three-day week and power cuts. Unfortunately, the very same power cuts and her very meagre wages had resulted in their poor diet of peanut butter sandwiches which needed no cooking, and which made Fingers quite nauseous. Desperation took him to the Mace at the end of the road and, waiting for the evening dimness to set in, he was able to 'acquire' some milk and two Cornish pasties in his school satchel for their dinner. When she asked where the money for them had come from, he told his mother he had managed to get a little from collecting lemonade bottles that people had thrown out which he had then returned to the shop to claim the deposit. This excuse led Fingers to the idea of doing just that. He started climbing into the yard, taking bottles from the crates stored there and returning them to the shop a few minutes later. Many corner shops existed in those days, so Fingers had the sense to vary this course of action, but it kept him going until he moved on to another ploy.

On reaching secondary school age, Fingers noted how so many of the shopkeepers were wary of letting more than two school aged children into their premises at a time for fear that their shoplifting numbers would increase. He was smart enough to know that should he need essentials he would have to devise a plan more cunning than his contemporaries who were usually after cigarettes or Playboy magazines. His school bag was much larger than most of the other students, but as Fingers was known as a swot, he explained that he liked to carry home as many books as possible to help him with his homework. He did, indeed, get top marks in all his subjects, but the bag was not full of books. He always carried a change of clothes so that, as students entered the shop two at a time, the shopkeeper watched them intently and paid no heed to the smartly dressed young man who went home to his mother with their evening meal and a treat or two to follow. To keep her happy and to allay any whiff of possible criminality, Fingers arose very early in the morning and did a paper round and told her he had used his earnings to buy the food. She loved her son for it. "We are a team." she would tell the ladies in the houses she cleaned. "He will do so well, he's so clever," she told the gentlemen in the solicitor's office where she filed the day's papers and sorted the post. "He will make something of himself."

She told the old lady who she fed and tucked up into bed every night. And he did.

The seventies saw even more difficulties for Fingers and his mother but as the eighties loomed and the recession bit, Mrs Fennel lost most of her cleaning jobs.

"Mr Portland was made redundant," she told her son, "So they can't afford to pay me anymore. And the Browns and the Fosters have let me go too. They said they were having to move to get work. The Taylors are even emigrating to get away from all this."

"What about the solicitors?"

"They have offered me another hour a week, but it's not enough."

By that time the old lady had died.

Fingers had a Saturday job at a butcher's shop as well as his morning paper round and the weekly distribution of a local free newspaper. He scanned the same newspaper before he delivered it so that he could be the first to apply for any casual work he could find advertised. Because of his efforts, he and his mother were able to limp through the decade without having to join that ever-increasing dole queue. Despite all the extra duties he acquired over this period, by the time he was eighteen, he had gained the highest A levels of his cohort and was snapped up by Leeds University where he studied business law.

Fingers did very well at university. Fitting more into his life than simply attending lectures and studying, he got a job in the student bar where he made many friends and another as a courier for a pharmaceutical company where he made just as many contacts. He sent money back to his mother to make sure she had enough to live on and aced his course at the same time. During his vacation periods, he came back to Canterbury and got himself a job as a loadmaster at nearby Manston airport. This meant that he was employed to help load the cargo to be flown overseas. Goods of every description were handled there, even livestock and Fingers made sure that if anything she could benefit from was being flown out, his mother would be the first recipient. It was during this job that he was nicknamed Fingers; the other men working there marvelling at his prowess at removing articles and getting them out of the customs sealed area. Finger's mother had a new kitchen sink fitted that first summer, a suede coat and complete set of Marks and Spencer underwear. She and the old folks who lived near her in Canterbury had fillet steak for their Sunday dinner one week, the meat having been expertly filleted by Fingers (thanks to his days at the butcher's shop) and the fact that some Shah or other had ordered prime refrigerated scotch beef to be flown out to him in the Middle East.

But most of all, the loadmaster job came in very handy for Fingers' own little import/export business that he had managed to set up on the side, custom's control not being as stringent at Manston as perhaps it could have been, and flights to Amsterdam and North Africa being frequent.

When Fingers left University, winning the Dean's prize for top Graduating Student, he was snapped up by a large firm in London where he completed his training to emerge two years later as fully qualified with a speciality in Banking and Finance. He worked very hard for that firm, proving his worth and gaining status within it until, at the age of thirty, despite being the only non-public school educated junior, he was invited to become an associate partner. Years of an ongoing enterprise, thrift and avoiding the drunken reveries and cocaine habit pursued by most of the other young solicitors had enabled Fingers to purchase a small home for himself and his mother in Canterbury and a modest crash pad in London for him to use during the week.

Despite his sober ways and lack of obvious involvement in London club life, the other juniors liked Fingers as he had a very easy manner about him and seemed worldlier than them. He had no problems allowing them to look down on him occasionally and no hesitation in declining their invitations to Mummy or Daddy's estate at the weekends. "I have commitments elsewhere," was all he would say. And he did.

The contacts he had made during his university years and during his everyday business enabled him to make sound financial investments of his own, dealing in cash wherever possible in one aspect of his life and, with the other, avoiding tax wherever a loophole could be found. It wasn't very long before he moved his mother into a larger, more comfortable house in Charing, employing a daily help so that she never had to do housework again. His mother's friends with whom she never lost touch, marvelled at the granite worktop in her spotless kitchen, the gleaming conservatory with its view over a lawn which ran down to a small coppice and the walk-in wardrobe next to the en-suite in her south facing bedroom. Fingers opened an account for his mother at Fenwick's, the local equivalent of John Lewis, and told her to buy herself any clothes she needed there. She was not to make do with Marks and Spencer or Debenhams. He opened accounts for her at the best butcher's shop and local delicatessen. He decided it was too late for her to learn to drive safely so he also had an account with a taxi firm which he told her to use as though it were her own vehicle. She lacked for nothing, and his overseas bank accounts paid all the bills without having to be asked.

Meanwhile, Fingers' business in the South-East thrived to the point that he was able to employ more University students to carry on the delivery and distribution of the goods he handled. He was alert to the benefit that social media could afford him. The internet provided the kind of anonymity that was perfect for his needs. His intellect in operating everything to his advantage assured him that this anonymity could be protected. It was, therefore, to his horror, when he returned to Canterbury one Friday evening in June 2005 to discover his mother sitting on that sweeping lawn chatting to a man who looked as though he needed a wash and a change of clothes.

"Ah, there you are my little love!" called his mother, beckoning him to where they sat." I've just made a fresh pot of tea, or would you like a cold drink?" She nodded at the stranger who was cupping a frosted glass of beer in his grubby hand which he lifted towards Fingers and said, "'Allo Alan. Long-time no see." And he winked, almost conspiratorially.

Fingers said nothing. He did not allow any emotion to show on his face, thanking God for his training and ability to remain poker calm in difficult circumstances.

He put out his hand, "Pleased to meet you. And you are.....?"

"I'm your dad, Al, or should I call you Fingers? Come and give your old man a hug." And he grinned revealing yellow stained teeth like tombstones with wide gaps between where others had fallen or been knocked out.

Not faltering for one second, Fingers quickly took stock of the situation. Somehow, this man had learned the nickname given him by his old workmates at Manston which meant that he knew he had stolen quite a bit in his youth. This meant that Fingers also knew this man had a hold over him as theft did not sit easily with those in his profession. He could tell from the way he was leering at his mother that he was also going to milk the situation for everything he could get, that his interest lay only in his own gratification and that his mother could get hurt by him in more ways than one because she was a kindly soul who had always made excuses for her absent spouse. She instantly forgave anyone who was mean or unkind towards her and in his heart, Fingers knew that she would forgive him. So, it would be useless just to give him money to leave their house because she would let him back in at the earliest opportunity. He did not know how Billy, his long-lost father, had managed to find out that they were sitting pretty but he knew that he wanted to free load off them so he made the quick decision to appear welcoming until he could form a plan to sort this situation out once and for all.

"Dad!" he said, bending and hugging the old man to his Saville Road suit, doing his best at the same time not to breathe in the foul odour of his breath or the smell of his trousers that had some very unpleasant stains.

"I was telling your mother here," replied a slightly disarmed Billy, "That I don't remember what happened to me. I went out to the pub one night when you were a nipper and the next thing I knew I woke up in a hospital in Scotland and there were celebrations going on all around. The Scots love Hogmanay, especially when it's a Millennium. I must have lost twenty years. Me old memory's been a bit patchy ever since, but bits and pieces come back to me now and again like." And he nodded wistfully, casting a rheumy eye sideways at his son, taking in the smartness of his suit and the expensive attaché case that he had dropped on the grass.

"Well, not to worry right now," replied Fingers. "Our guest room is out of action at the moment – leaky radiator or something, so I'll book you a room at The Abbot and maybe we can find you something to wear while we get your clothes cleaned. You're about my size, aren't you?"

"I told you how good my little love is," crooned Fingers' mother. "I told you he would look after you. Heart of Gold, our boy. Heart of Gold." And she gazed lovingly at her son. "It's so nice to be all together again."

At dinner that night Fingers kept up a steady chatter as he took account of the man that said he was his father. After a shave and a long soak in their whirlpool bath and wearing an outfit that Fingers felt made him look smart but casual, Billy Fennel looked passable as a guest at the Hotel into which he had been booked. The three of them inspected his room which Billy described as "proper grand" and left him there to return home with a firm promise to be back the following morning to take him shopping for more clothes. Billy went to bed cleaner and more comfortable than he had been for years, and Fingers sat up all night pondering his position until he had formed a plan that would suit his purpose perfectly.

The weekend was spent shopping and dining, his mother and father telling stories and filling in the gaps that so many years apart had stolen from them. When Fingers left for London on Monday, he kissed his mother goodbye and told her he would be looking into finding a flat for Billy so that he had a place of his own.

"Well, he was mentioning that it would be nice to move back in with me; with us, I mean" blushed his mother." He says he wants to get a job and be his own man. It's hard for someone as proud as he is to keep taking off his son, you know."

Although he had frozen inside, Fingers did not react. He brushed a hair away from his mother's innocent cheek and simply said, "Well, of course that should be the ultimate plan, ma, but I think you need to have some time to get used to each other first. It has, after all, been a very long time. Let's not move too fast, eh?" and he climbed into his Porsche and sped away.

Once back in London, Fingers set to work very quickly. He used his contacts to do a complete background check on Billy Fennel. Life had taught him quite a few tricks, one being that you never used the one source to gather information. Fingers employed different men to find out different parts of Billy's previous life.

Bit by bit, during the course of the week, the details of over thirty years of absence were filled in and Fingers soon realised from where his talent for crime had been inherited. The only difference being that, unlike his son, Billy wasn't quite so clever and had frequented Her Majesty's Prisons on more than three occasions, the most recent being Maidstone. Here he had shared a cell with a man who used to work alongside Fingers at Manston Airport during his university days. Both were serving sentences for burglary and were delighted to find out that they had something else in common.

"I worked with this youngster once with the same surname as Billy and I told him all about the lad. Fingers Fennel we called him; never knew his real name. He was magic when it came to pinching things. He even managed to smuggle a stainless-steel kitchen sink off the base. Said it was for his mum. Loved his mum, did that boy. Looked after her. Said he had to as his old man had done a bunk when he was three…"

The private investigator stopped playing the recording he had taken of his conversation with Billy's old cell mate and looked at Fingers over the top of his glasses. Because he was on a £500 a day retainer, he knew there was a lot of money at stake, so he had decided to hang on to that information for later. He hadn't realised that Fingers had been watching him carefully and had seen a certain look on his face which had spurred him to nip any future dealings with this particular investigator in the bud.

Fingers remained very cool. "By the way. If you are considering for a single moment to use that recording later at some point, think again. I don't believe for one moment the ramblings of a pot head will be considered good reason to investigate any allegations you might choose to make. So, keep it or delete it. It makes no difference to me." And there was something in Fingers' eyes that made that investigator delete the recording straight away and wish he had never heard it.

Another investigator had been pursuing Billy's personal background. There was a Mrs Fennel in Edinburgh, a Mrs Fennel in Newcastle and a woman who refused to marry him as she was already married but who called herself Mrs Fennel and who had borne him two children living in York. Fingers learnt with sadness that five other children had been deserted as Billy made his way up the Pennine Chain. All but the Newcastle wife had been left penniless; she had had the sense to throw him out when she had discovered him stealing from her purse once too often and had since moved in with yet another man who had also let her down.

Fingers got all his information together and then made a few more phone calls and, as he rarely took leave from work, arranged to take a short holiday which he knew would give him plenty of time to put his plan into action. He travelled back to Canterbury the following Friday brandishing tickets for a Mediterranean Cruise for his mother and her best friend Gloria that departed that Sunday.

"But I can't go my little love. Billy and I were just getting acquainted again."

"He'll still be here when you get back. Look, mum, I won these tickets; they were part of a deal I pulled off. And you know how busy I am. I just can't take the time to go right now. It would be such a shame to waste them, and Gloria has been so poorly; it will do her good. I've even paid to get the insurance for you both. Billy won't mind."

"We were going to do all sorts of things next week. He'll be so disappointed."

"I tell you what, Ma, I'll take him back to London with me and we can spend a bit of man time together. How's that?"

"Well…"

"I mean, I think if he's going to be a permanent fixture round here, it would be so much better for both of us if I spent some *proper* time with him, wouldn't it?"

On Sunday morning, a taxi picked up a very delighted Gloria and Mrs Fennel to ferry them to Gatwick and Billy and Fingers settled down to morning coffee on the patio where, without Mrs Fennel being present, Billy was able to pump Fingers mercilessly for information about his job, his assets, his love life and his future plans. Fingers was delighted at how easy it was to let slip the kind of information that made Billy's greedy little eyes shine with pleasure.

"So, how come you made so much dosh in such a short time Al?"

"Well, it's knowing the law and knowing certain people and sort of bending them towards each other so to speak." Replied Fingers watching Billy helping himself to another biscotti which he dunked unceremoniously into his expresso.

"Isn't that a bit risky?" asked Billy, pushing away his cup and leaning towards his son, "I mean," and he looked around him to check they were alone," I mean, isn't there always a paper trail with that sort of thing? It can all be tracked back to you, can't it?"

"Oh yes. But that's where Trusts in different names or overseas accounts which get moved about here and there come in handy. It's good odds that it will slip under the radar. And if anything does emerge, it'll be difficult to prove."

"So, what kind of deal are we talking about?"

"Last time I cleared fifty in a week"

"That's a lot of trouble for fifty pounds," scoffed Billy. "I could get that on the three thirty from

Doncaster." He almost fell off his seat when he learned his son was talking thousands.

"I tell you what dad, I think I could help you out a bit here. I mean, if I lent you the money and handled the deals for you, you could come out with a nice little profit too. You could be your own man like you keep telling mum you want to be. Make your own fortune. Then you could even treat mum and me a bit, to make up for all those years you missed. What do you say?"

"What kind of money are you talking about, then?" enquired Billy who was now sitting on the edge of his seat.

"Well, as I've just acquired access to that £50,000 I was telling you about, I'd be willing to invest that for you and give you a leg up, if you know what I mean. You could pay me back once you've made a profit, and I'm talking about a probable one hundred percent profit if we get in quick on the ground floor. Or, if you prefer, I could give you £10,000 now on the condition that you sign an independently witnessed document that you've accepted the money and then just disappear before mum gets back. If you take the money, there won't be any more though, and I will show mum the document so she can see where your heart really lies."

Fingers watched and saw how Billy was juggling mentally with his propositions. He had judged that his father would be greedy enough to want to take the risk and his instincts proved right. It was arranged that he accompany his son to London that Sunday night when Billy was, once again, astounded at the small 'crash pad' which Fingers had told him about. It was a luxurious suite overlooking the Thames on Canary Wharf with access to a rooftop swimming pool and communal gym.

After their evening meal, Fingers made a dramatic gesture of downloading and getting his father to sign three forms.

"These are giving me the right to open three accounts on your behalf," explained Fingers. "You sign them, and I'll fill in the names once I get to work. We have a bank of names we use."

"Where do you get these names from then?" asked Billy.

"We have a department that deals with that," said Fingers. "I usually cut in whoever does it for me on my personal deals, so that will come out of the profit, but it's a win-win situation." And he touched his nose and winked as he had seen his father do so many times since his reappearance.

"Well, what happens next then?" asked Billy as he signed the blank forms.

"I will set up these accounts, invest the money and just keep watching the markets until it's time to sell."

"And what can I do?"

"Nothing, dad. You just enjoy the ride."

So, Billy enjoyed the rooftop swimming pool, the Jacuzzi, the endless supply of beer in the fridge, the strip clubs in Soho and the other pleasurable pursuits London life afforded him while his son went to his real flat and worked at what he knew best, coming back to Canary Wharf every night with news that things were looking good.

Fingers knew all the tricks where insider trading was concerned. He had listened very carefully to the talk in the office and had read widely to make sure he could talk about it with authority. His biggest concern was getting rid of his father without upsetting his mother again, and it was this part of his plan that was the trickiest to arrange. But on Friday, he arrived at King's Cross at 5.30 pm in time to meet the train from Waverley station, Edinburgh.

He recognised the three ladies immediately from the photos supplied to him by his private investigator. He stood at the meeting point and let them come to him rather than approaching them first. All three looked younger than his mother but were all blonde and blue eyed, wearing clothes that had probably been bought in Primark or Charity shops and sporting expressions that showed they had very little joy in their lives. Fingers quickly introduced himself and took them to dinner where, after he had introduced each Mrs Fennel to the other and given them time to get over their surprise, he went over again his reasons for bringing them to London and what he hoped would happen. The ladies were a little awe struck by their surroundings at dinner and even more so when they saw the three rooms Fingers had booked them into in a hotel they had only seen in films. His assistant at work had been a little confused when he had asked her to meet him that evening but was happy to take the ladies to Monsoon and get them kitted out for the next day in London.

"I want them to look quietly affluent." He had asked her. Don't forget shoes and a large handbag each." And he had handed her a wad of cash, knowing full well he could trust her implicitly.

He arrived back at Canary Wharf late that evening with the news that his father's investments had done well and that he had sold the stock that afternoon. He explained that after deducting the original investment from the total, the profit was £30,000.

Billy rubbed his hands together in glee. He could hardly wait to get his hands on the money.

"There's just one thing we have to do," said Fingers.

Billy looked at him and stopped smiling. "What's that?" he asked, this time a hint of malice in his voice.

"Oh, do you remember the names we had to put the accounts in? And how I said we would have to give a cut to the people who arranged them?"

"Oh, yes." Billy's relief was audible.

"Well, we are meeting them for lunch and then we can sign everything over to you. After they've taken their cut that is. OK?"

After Billy had finally gone to bed, Fingers made a phone call. Things hadn't been so easy for his business since Manston Airport had closed. The cargo flights there had been useful and his contacts at the airfield had needed to be renewed as people moved on or retired, but contracts still needed organising and shaking on, so weekend trips to Canterbury had been essential. Lydd airfield was still operating but establishing things there had been more difficult than he had imagined. Fingers was a very hard worker, and it wasn't long before his regular imports started happening again and the cash part of his enterprise was relocated to that area. It was an hour before a motorbike pulled up outside and Fingers took possession of what he needed.

The next day, after a morning spent at the bookies where Billy had managed to lose fifty pounds from the money his son had given him, he wandered along to the little bistro where they had arranged to meet. He was humming a tune as he looked through the menu and picking at the garlic bread that had been placed in front of him, squinted his eyes at the price of the beer, deciding that he might switch to spirits. But familiar voices drew his attention to the door. He stopped humming abruptly as his son entered with his three ex-partners two of whom waved gaily at him.

"Wotcha Bills! Long-time no see," said one.

"Look at you!" said another.

"You filthy piece of shit" said a third who walked up to him and whacked him round the head.

Billy just sat there with his mouth open.

The ladies looked at him more closely.

"Hi there, Willy," said an Edinburgh accent.

"Hey Bill, shut your mouth. I don't want to see your food." said the Geordie.

"You bastard." The York lady was still very angry.

Billy tried to swallow the bread, but it stuck in his throat and was causing him to choke.

"Seems you lost your memory quite a few times, dad," put in Fingers. "Anyway, judging by the look of these lovely ladies, it seems all females are a lot better off without you in their lives." And all three women laughed and nodded in agreement.

"Didna' expect us to land on our feet, did ya hen?"

"Thought we'd just pine away with grief after you left?"

"We're all better off without you!" Billy ducked a second whack.

"Let's get a photo," called Fingers, hailing a waiter to the table. "Moments like this need recording." And he handed his phone to the waiter who snapped away happily.

"Give me my money and let me get out of here," complained Billy, trying to shield his face but having his arms held by two different women, was finding that impossible.

"Oh, don't you want to hear about how well your children are doing? After all, you haven't seen them for ages. Did you bring photos ladies?" and Billy was forced to sit through a barrage of happy snaps of his offspring at different ages and the "Oohs" and "Ahhs" of the ladies as they compared the similarities they could see between the half siblings.

"I just want my money," moaned Billy.

"Oh, of course." The ladies each produced a cheque which they gave to Fingers.

"Now, let's see." And he handed all three to Billy.

"What the fuck?" exclaimed Billy. "What do you think you're doing?"

"I'm giving you the residue of the profit after I have given these ladies their cut. They are, after all, the names on the account. They don't actually have to give you anything."

"And I haven't actually signed my cheque," piped up the Geordie.

"Mine's post-dated to 2050" said the Edinburgh accent.

"I think I've made a mistake with the words and figures," said the lady from York. "I've never written a cheque before."

"What's up Billy?" asked Fingers, "I think three lots of £17.00 profit from all the dealings I've done for you is very good. After all, you said you wanted to be your own man and paying something for your children's up bringing is doing just that, isn't it? You haven't even had to lift a finger to earn it."

"I'll have you," steamed Billy, "You see if I don't. I'll report you for dishonest dealings to your firm. I bet they'd like to know all about that insider trading stuff you were talking about. And just you wait 'til I tell your Ma. She'll kick you out. She loves me."

"Go ahead Billy. Do what you want. There was no deal. There were no accounts or insider trading. I just decided that I needed to get rid of dirt like you from my life and invested a bit of cash to let you think you were onto a gravy train. That's not my flat you were lazing in; I borrowed it from a chap at work. The money I was going to pay you to go away, well, I thought to myself, why should a scumbag like you have that when there's three other women and five kids you've left high and dry. And I'll tell you one more thing, Billy," and Fingers stood up, taking his father by the scruff of his neck, "If you think you can crawl back into my mother's life, taking advantage of her good nature, think again." And he shoved Billy towards the door, "Because I have all these lovely photos of your reunion with your other ex-wives to show her and I have their word they will testify in court, and you'll be back in the nick before your feet touch the ground on three counts of bigamy."

"Two," mumbled Billy, "Only two. I never married her, and he nodded towards the lady from York."

"Thank God." She replied, "Now piss off."

Billy sped out of the restaurant as fast as he could. He found his key card no longer worked at the flat at Canary Wharf and he was unable to collect his new clothes. He found the credit card Fingers had given him was declined when he tried to get some cash. He couldn't get the three cheques cashed either because of the discrepancies his ex-wives had spoken about. He sat on a bench on the embankment and realised there was nothing he could do. "I should have taken the cash when he offered it," he thought to himself, "Then I could always have popped back for more and sorted things so she forgave me." He spent his last £10 on a bottle of cheap supermarket vodka and returned to his old life surprisingly easily, but with a tale to tell of his offspring's disloyalty.

Fingers and the three Mrs Fennels enjoyed their lunch immensely. The waiters brought bottles of champagne as Fingers answered their questions about why he had done what he had.

"I knew that if I just bought him off, he'd be back again and again. I watched my poor mum suffering after he left and I know you probably had to scrimp and save to get by with your own children,"

They nodded in unison,

"It was so hard. My mother had to bail me out and babysit my two so I could go to work, and she was poorly herself," said Mrs Newcastle.

"I had twins. He lasted until they were six weeks old and then left without a word." Said Mrs York." I couldn't work 'til they were at school as I had no-one. It was benefits for me and the sneers of the neighbours."

"I only had one child, but that was hard enough," said Mrs Edinburgh. "I love my girl but life as a single parent is hard. So hard."

"Which is why I want you all to have this," said Fingers. He reached into his attaché case and took out three separate envelopes. "You've helped me, so now I'm going to help you. Don't open them now," he told them. "Put them straight into your handbags and open them when you get home tonight."

The envelopes were big and bulging.

"And don't go mad and buy flashy stuff all at once and don't put it into the bank. Just use it on a day-to-day basis to make your life a little easier and to treat the kids."

"Why? You don't have to do that," said York

"We've already had a lovely time." said Edinburgh.

"What's inside?" asked Newcastle, fingering the envelope.

"First, promise me you will do as I ask?" replied Fingers.

Three heads nodded.

"There's ten grand in each envelope for you. I will check on you now and then to make sure you aren't struggling any more, but you mustn't breathe a word of this to anyone or it will all dry up."

"But, how…?" asked Newcastle.

"Don't ask," replied Fingers, "Let's just say I have a little deal going somewhere and you don't need to know any more." And he kissed each lady on their cheek, paid the bill leaving them to enjoy their desserts and coffee.

"You're a lovely boy," they all agreed. "Your mother must be so proud."

And Fingers waved them goodbye with his left hand as he reached his right into his pocket to answer one of his many mobile phones.

Isla

29.02.56

Taurus: Stubborn. Can suffer from cognitive dissonance.

Isla was very pleased with herself. She looked back on her life so far and was smug in the knowledge that she had cracked it. Thanks to her careful planning and the occasional, but rare, bouts of inconvenience, she had arrived at a point in her life where she had always wanted to be. She thought about her lovely little detached property in an acceptable suburb of Canterbury which, although previously a council house, was right on the edge of the estate and next to a modest, but obviously privately built bungalow. And as Jack had done all the alterations exactly as she had told him, the façade of her house was such that no-one would have guessed it used to be rented to policemen in the 60's for three pounds a week. She thought about her son, Cameron, her favourite child, at last settled with a woman who, although twelve years older, had managed to become impregnated by him, thus putting paid to those nasty rumours she had heard that he was a mummy's boy, and probably gay. She thought about her other pride and joy, Rachel who looked so like her father and who had, like him, excelled at everything. It was such a shame that they had both chosen to live so far away from her, Cameron in Spain and Rachel in London, but at least she knew they were both leading lives that she would have wanted for them. She thought about the drama club and how she now had ultimate power over what went on there. 'Yes', she thought to herself as she completed her tenth and final length of the swimming pool, her hair still dry as she only did breast-stroke in a very ladylike way with her head elevated above the water; the black looks she had sent to those splashing as they charged past her had done the trick of keeping over enthusiastic swimmers away, 'Everything is perfect. Except for maybe just one small thing.'

She reached the side of the pool and climbed out daintily, adjusting her swimming costume so that it held in her increasing girth and bosom. Reaching for her towel which she hastily wrapped around herself, she flashed the young lifeguard a smile leaving him utterly confused as to what he had done to deserve it and made her way to the shower room.

The gym was the most expensive one in Canterbury; Isla wouldn't dream of being seen at any other establishment. The music was piped at a low and calming volume. The lights in the changing rooms were flattering so that when she looked in the mirrors, Isla saw an attractive woman of 65 who, she believed, looked more than ten years younger.

After having showered, moisturised, dressed and applied make up, Isla made her way to the in-house cafe and ordered a jacket potato with coronation chicken and sweetcorn and was about to start eating when Grace appeared, red faced and panting.

"Hello Grace. Why don't you join me?"

Grace looked around. There were very few vacant tables and much as she wished she could avoid it, there was little she could do but nod and say, 'Thank you' and make her way towards Isla's table.

"You look a bit stressed, Grace."

"Well," puffed Grace. "I got caught up in the Zumba class. Someone fainted and it was a bit of a drama."

Isla sniffed. "I can't do that class. All that jumping about and vulgar music."

"Oh, I love it. It really gets the blood pumping and helps shift a few pounds too. Won't be a mo." And Grace left her bag with Isla and went to the counter to order her lunch.

"So, what's new?" asked Grace as she slipped back into her seat. "How's the production going? It's 'Stepping Out' isn't it? Could be made for you, you've got such good legs."

Isla had a mouthful of food so covered her mouth, chewed, and swallowed it as quickly as she could before answering. "Well, thank you. They are my best feature I suppose. It should be alright now that I've managed to get rid of that stupid woman. The chorus is finally working together just as I like."

"What stupid woman?" asked Grace.

"You know. Phyllis. She thinks she can dance. And sing." Isla rolled her eyes. "She has a voice like an animal in extreme pain. And as for how she looks…"

The waitress delivered Grace's order, a grilled chicken breast with a green salad. Grace thanked her and added low calorie dressing to the meal.

"I always quite liked Phyllis. She has a wicked sense of humour. She made rehearsals at the panto so enjoyable. The cast will miss her." And Grace took a sip of her sparkling water.

"Well, sorry to spoil their enjoyment, I'm sure," retorted Isla, tartly, "But Jack had to look at the big picture and weed out the bad stuff. She had to go. Besides, she was getting fat and it ruined the look of the line-up. All this talk about Phyllis has given me a headache," said Isla, finishing her wine and looking again at the menu. "I wish you hadn't brought her up, Grace."

"I didn't Isla. I just asked you how things were going,"

"Well, I shall have to have a dessert now as you've ruined my good mood." And Isla left the table and went to the counter. Grace continued to eat her meal when her phone rang.

"Oh, hi there, Jo. How are you?"

"Fine thanks. Have you heard about Phyllis?"

"Yes, actually I'm at the gym with Isla now. She told me Jack got rid of her."

"Oh God! You're with Isle the pile. What have you done to deserve that? And it wasn't Jack that got rid of her. It was old misery guts herself that organised the whole thing. Jack just did as he was told – as usual. Weak as piss that one. No, Isla can't bear it if someone shows her up to be the no talent zombie she is when she dances or sings."

"Ooh, Jo! That's a bit harsh."

"Harsh but true. You know it, I know it, everyone knows it. The cow gets everything she wants at the club because she's married to the chairman. *And* she wheedled to get the little runt into that role. He is so under the thumb I almost feel sorry for him. Anyway, enough about her. I was calling to ask you to make up a table with me for a quiz that Phyllis is organizing for Friday. It's in aid of Shelter - a charity do. It should be fun."

"Oh, I love a quiz. Put me and Adam down. Is it BYO?"

"Yes, but there'll be a ploughman's provided and you can bring your own snacks too. Make sure you don't let your gym buddy know about it please. We want a fun evening, not one with her shoving her fucking photos under everyone's noses or complaining about her headaches. Seven o'clock start at the centre. I'll get your tickets and you can pay me later."

"Look forward to it. See you then." And Grace finished the call.

"Who was that?" asked Isla as she plonked herself back down.

"Jo."

"What does she want?" asked Isla.

Grace was taken back by Isla's nosiness.

"Well, it was personal."

"Really? How...personal."

"Very. So I let's leave it, shall we Isla?"

The waitress arrived at the table with a large portion of lemon meringue pie with ice cream. Isla took the dish and waved her away. "There's no need to be rude. I was only showing an interest like friends do. Is she alright? Is Jo OK?"

"Yes, she's fine."

"She's not ill or anything?"

"No, she's well."

"So has she got marriage problems?"

"No."

"Is her family OK?"

Grace looked at Isla.

"I'm not going to tell you. For God's sake let it go."

"Really, Grace. Jo happens to be a friend of mine. It's quite normal for me to be concerned if she has troubles. Goodness only knows, I've had more than my fair share of problems to deal with in my life what with losing Hubert and all, and there's probably no one like me in a better place to give advice."

"Well, if that's the case, if you and she are good buddies, then I'm sure she will contact you in due course and confide in you. But in the meantime, I'd prefer it if I respect her request for discretion and that we leave the subject. How are your grandchildren? Have you seen them lately?" and Grace quickly did her best to change the subject.

"But I can't understand why it was you and not me she called first," continued Isla.

"Are they well? Have you seen the baby yet? How's Rachel?" Grace knew Isla couldn't resist the chance to talk about her family.

"They are fine thank-you. Jack and I are going up to London at the weekend to babysit for Rachel as she and Felix are going to an event. It's his firm's annual dinner dance in some very exclusive venue. They are doing so very well you know. The move to London was the best thing they ever did although they are finding property there a tad expensive. I had to cash in some of the shares Hubert left for me to help them with the deposit on their flat. It would have bought a proper house if they'd stayed in Canterbury."

"So, you'll be staying overnight with them then, seeing it's a late do?"

"Well, we might. It's a bit small, their flat and their sofa isn't all that comfortable. Jack had to sleep on the floor last time we tried it and what with his problems it wasn't the best. I will have a look to see if I can get a late bargain with a voucher code and book into a Travelodge or something so we can spend the day with them on Sunday. I expect they'll be home from the party by twelve, but when we went up for their friend's engagement party it was nearer two o'clock and Jack and I drove home. It was a bit tiring. It all depends on how much the room will cost really. London is so expensive. They need us to look after Leon because Felix's parents live in Enfield and have told them to get a babysitter and Rachel would never leave Leon with a stranger. He's such a lovely little boy." And Isla dug in her bag for her mobile and clicked on her photos.

Grace heaved a sigh of relief. She was a little surprised that Felix's parents, who lived a mere tube trip away couldn't babysit for the young couple but didn't want to pry into that. She didn't comment that it would have been a lot easier for Rachel to get a friend from the fabulous new job Isla was always boasting she had to babysit Leon, or that she and Felix should perhaps give up their bed to the older couple who were doing them a massive favour. She was thankful her own daughter wasn't that inconsiderate as she scrolled through each picture making the usual 'Ooos and Ahhs'. There was nothing more boring than having to look at photographs of other people's grandchildren, something that Grace always bore in mind, never inflicting her happy snaps on her friends. Ever.

"And this is a little boasting book Cameron and Karen put together and posted to me. Our little Jessica! Only three months and on solids already." Isla lay a book in front of Grace, and she had to go through the procedure a second time. "We are going to Spain as soon as we can so that we can see her in the flesh. It's been so hard getting away since she was born. What with Jack being the chairman and needing my support so much since his troubles."

Grace refused to be drawn on the subject of Jack's troubles. Only last week she had been forced to sit through forty minutes of his visits to A&E, his subsequent operation and physiotherapy and follow up visits to consultants. She was surprised the man could walk the way Isla described it. Yet Isla had made his pain seem meaningless in comparison to her own difficulties in having to visit him and support him. "You have no idea the pressure it put on me. I had such a terrible time coping with the worry – it brought on a migraine, and I was bedridden for three days with no-one to make me so much as a cup of tea…" Jack had been forced to get a taxi home and Isla had told Grace how cross she was about that as the bus stopped right outside the hospital and how much cheaper they are than taxis. Rather than go through a repeat of that episode, Grace cut in, "Well, it will be lovely to spend some time with them when you manage to get there. They're near Barcelona, aren't they? And they've got a swimming pool? That will be so nice for you both, a real rest. And their villa is only a short ride to town, isn't it?"

"Yes, but we can't stay with them as Karen's parents will be there at the same time and they only have one spare room. She said she could borrow a couple of camp beds and we could stay in the lounge but I'm not sure Jacks' back is up to camping just yet." And Isla gave a little laugh.

Grace was horrified. To think that both Isla's children treated her and Jack in such a cavalier fashion.

"Well, why don't you postpone the visit until Karen's parents have left?"

"They came just before the baby arrived and Karen wants them to stay for the summer, so it would mean I won't see Jessica until the autumn."

Grace was beginning to feel very sorry for Isla and guilty about not telling her about the quiz.

"Oh, by the way. I don't know if you have heard but there's a quiz on at the centre on Friday night. Seven o'clock. Are you going?"

"No. I hadn't heard. Have you made up a table yet?"

"I have no idea. I was invited to join someone there. It's for the charity Shelter, so I'm sure you can buy tickets on the door, and they will fit you in on a table. Unless, of course, you can get a group together for yourself."

She finished her meal and told Isla she had to go as she had an appointment. Isla suggested that they split the bill. "It makes life so much easier all round then, doesn't it?" and Grace, who noted that this meant she paid a lot more for her lunch than she should but decided it would be petty to comment on it, wished she hadn't had an attack of conscience and had kept her mouth shut about the quiz. They got the bill and Isla gave Grace exactly half, neglecting to add anything for a tip, picked up her bags and left with the parting shot, "I'll let you settle up as I have a headache and need to get home to check my insulin levels. A headache might be more than a headache when you're diabetic. Byeee"

There was a queue at the till and Grace was already running late for her appointment as she made her way to her car. She was fuming when she saw her diabetic friend coming out of a shop munching on a chocolate bar as she leisurely looked in a dress shop's window and then wandered through the door. Had she not been expected somewhere else, Grace would have gone into the shop herself and asked Isla how her insulin levels were, but this small pleasure was denied to her. She hurried on her way and tried to think of a way to tell Jo what she'd done without being permanently removed from her Christmas card list.

The following Friday, Grace arrived early at the hall to give Phyllis a hand to get the food organised. She liked Phyllis who was always cheerful despite having been widowed suddenly the previous year. While they were working, Grace told her about how she had met Isla, the business about Jessica whom she hadn't yet seen and how so very sorry she felt for her that she had ended up telling Isla about the quiz and how furious Jo would be if she knew. Phyllis just laughed.

"Isla is the least of my worries, Grace. I'm just hoping I've bought enough cheese to go around." Phyllis was cutting generous slabs of cheese and adding them to each large basket, already stuffed to overflowing with other delicious tit bits, that was to be placed in the centre of each table at half time. Adam was helping Jo's husband to set up the scoreboard and various other people were putting out tables and chairs and posters displaying the need for Shelter as a charity. Someone had had the forethought to stream some music and that combined with the general hubbub gave the hall a very pleasant atmosphere.

Jo burst into the kitchen area. "Would you believe it? Isle the Pile and that meathead Jack have just turned up at the door. How in God's name did she hear about it?"

Phyllis looked at Grace who had gone very red. She waved her hand. "Oh, don't you worry about them, Jo. I got a message to her. Didn't want her to feel left out. Now, could you two help me cover these baskets over and we'll put them over there in the cool."

Grace's mouth fell open. She marvelled at her friend's generosity. Jo was still muttering when they finally sat down and studied the picture questions that had been left at each table.

The quizmaster that night was Barry, a minor celebrity of Canterbury who had appeared on the TV in a couple of plays. He made a small speech thanking everyone for coming and telling them the rules and how the scores would be awarded. He was an excellent speaker and Grace could tell that he would get everyone to join in the games and buy raffle tickets. Phyllis was so clever to have got him and as she made her way to her table, she passed Isla, who was sitting with some people she hadn't met before, welcomed them all and remarking on how clever Phyllis had been to organise the whole thing. Isla sniffed.

"A quiz is hardly difficult to sort out. And as for that Barry. He's not my cup of tea. He's certainly overrated, and I don't think he's a good role model for people. Don't you remember all that scandal about him and that young chap who was doing work experience backstage at the Marlowe? And then there was that young personal trainer at the gym? Grooming him he was, never mind that he was married at the time. Queer as they come and pretending to be straight. Can't bear two faced liars like that. It's just because he's from Canterbury that you like him. Jack could have done a much better job, wouldn't you Jack?"

Jack mumbled something that no-one could hear. The lady opposite Isla hooted with laughter.

"You've gotta be joking love. Barry's a legend. And he's great at raising money and that's what we're here for, chick."

Isla went pink and hissed at Grace, "Isn't there room on your table? These people are so common and probably thick too. We don't have a chance of winning."

"Sorry, Isla. We are expecting another couple who told us they were running late. Have a good quiz." and she removed herself as quickly as she could.

The first half of the evening went very well. Each table displayed the name of a famous detective. Grace was on the Columbo table. Isla was on Danger Mouse. There was a massive cheer when Barry announced at the end of the first half that those two teams were head-to-head at the top of the table, swiftly followed by Cagney and Lacey, Morse and Inspector Gadget with Poirot, Maigret, Inspector Barnaby, Sherlock, Sexton Blake, Juliette Bravo and Bergerac all trailing behind. Jo and Grace left their tables at half time to distribute the baskets to each table and hand out further picture questions. There was to be a break of forty minutes to give each team time to eat and catch up and then some more games to raise extra money plus a raffle.

On returning to their table, Grace asked Phyllis why she wasn't doing 'Stepping Out'. "I thought you had quite a big part?"

"It was all a bit embarrassing. It seems that unbeknownst to the producer, Isla had asked if she could play that part and had pre-auditioned for it in front of the chairman and been given it. So, they had double booked as it were. And as its first come, first served….."

"Hang on. Didn't you go to the auditions on the day it was advertised as being held?"

"Yes, but Isla couldn't make that date, so she auditioned at her house the day before and told him the part she wanted."

"I see. So, if we were all to have turned up the previous day and made similar requests, we would have been treated on a first come, first served basis too? I don't think so." Grace was fuming.

"Not to worry, Grace, I'm not that bothered. I've found another drama group and I'm keeping myself out of mischief there. We are doing 'An Inspector Calls' and its good fun."

"That's not the point though, is it Phyl? Madam muck is so up her own arse thinking she's something she isn't. And she can't bloody act." seethed Jo.

"She's got good legs - far better than mine – and she's done that part loads of times, so she knows it backwards. Let it go, Jo. It's not worth getting cross about."

At that point, Barry's voice could be heard on the microphone.

"Now folks, don't forget to buy your raffle tickets. We will be drawing them at the end of the quiz, and I must say the prizes are not your usual old clap trap. Thanks to Phyllis, who has obviously worked super hard to persuade our shopkeepers, we have a range of gear. Just look at the table. We have a bottle of Gordon's and some glasses. We have a hamper of goodies in a very nice picnic basket. Two tickets to the Marlowe's fabulous new production starring yours truly…" The audience laughed. "A voucher for afternoon tea at the Patisserie, another for dinner for two by the river, you know, that very posh place. When I take my wife there she knows somethings up." More laughter. Barry went on to list each prize until he came to the very last.

"And the final and most desirable prize of all…. and Phyllis, God only knows how you managed to pull this one off…. oops, that's a bit of a naughty pun. But I know Phyllis is too much of a lady, so I won't go there," more laughter, "A weekend for two to Barcelona."

A great "Oooo!" swept through the room.

"Now folks, now you know why the raffle tickets were £50 a strip. So far, we've kept the holiday a secret, but Skyways have just emailed me and confirmed it. So, get those tickets. You never know your luck. There's a cash machine over the road so feel free to pop out and get your extra money. Don't miss out on this chance, and remember, it's for such a very worthy cause. But be back in ten minutes to play heads or tails!"

And there was a great exodus for the door as the quizzers decided to take that chance.

Phyllis and Jo were kept really busy selling the raffle tickets. There were twelve tables in the room with eight people on each table and everyone seemed to buy at least one strip. Some even bought more than one. While they were selling the tickets, Grace helped to collect the empty baskets and clear away the rubbish from the tables ready for the games and the second round.

"That's a ridiculous price to ask for raffle tickets," sniffed Isla when Grace came to her table. She and Jack were the only ones sitting at it. The rest were queuing for tickets or talking to people on other tables.

"Well, I think you can buy just one for £10. Barry didn't mention that because people usually buy a strip…."

"Oh, it's not that we can't afford it," went on Isla," It's just that I think there are far more worthy causes for that kind of raffle than donating the money to beggars on the street. It would be better given to a worthy cause. "

Grace bristled. She was having a nice evening and didn't need Isla's sourness to spoil it.

"Well, you must do as you see fit, Isla. I did tell you the charity was Shelter when I saw you last. Perhaps you shouldn't have come? On the other hand, you've got a chance for a weekend in Spain. A chance to see you little granddaughter. Think about it." And she collected the basket which was completely empty and the chocolate wrappers and cake boxes that also littered the area around Isla and moved on to the next table.

When Grace staggered back to the kitchen with the baskets, she saw Jo and told her about the conversation she had just had with Isla.

"Miserable old cow. Isle the Pile never changes."

"Why do you call her Isle the Pile, Jo?"

"Because if anyone looks as though they permanently suffer from haemorrhoids, it's her. The look on her face and her constant complaints about this or that which is wrong with her. She's sex starved too."

Grace almost dropped her drink.

"What?" she spluttered, "How do you know that?"

"Old Jacko there," and Jo nodded towards the door, "It's not just his back that's given out. He had to have injections in that to take the pain away. Let's just say that it's not just his back he has to inject when Isla's feeling the need."

Grace choked with laughter and then felt guilty.

"How come you know this?"

"Unfortunate word choice, Grace. Let's just say that a friend of mine who will remain nameless but who works at the doctor's surgery was royally shit on by dear Isla in a play we were doing a few years ago. She got very drunk one night when we were having dinner together and let the cat out of the bag. She had to do the filing in those days – they weren't computerised then. She couldn't help but read his notes."

"Oh, poor Jack. Poor Isla."

"Oh, poor nothing. Colin said that if he had to shag Isla, he'd need more than an injection."

"Jo, you are awful."

"No. She's poison that woman. I'm sure Jack was fine when he first met her. He used to help her out in the garden of the house she had with Hubert who was her second husband, her kid's father. He was a lovely chap and I know her first husband wasn't that bad either. Both dead, but Isla was never widowed; she divorced Hubert when he got motor neurone disease. Said she couldn't cope with an invalid because she hadn't got good health herself. And when he died, and by that time she was married to Jack, anyone would have thought they had never divorced. She acted like she was a widow, wailing and bawling about how the father of her children was dead and how hard she was finding it to cope. Took his money though and made sure that his other kids by his first wife, the one she stole him off, got cut out of his will completely."

At that point, Phyllis walked into the kitchen.

"What are you gossiping about, you two?"

"Bloody Isla, Bluebeard of this parish." Replied Jo.

"Oh, Jo, that's not nice. Come on, she can't help it that all her previous husbands died, can she? Anyway, hubby number one died while he was married to his second wife. You make it sound like she's bumping them off left, right and centre." And Phyllis plonked a large tin onto the table stuffed with ten-pound notes. "Look at this lot. Haven't we done well?"

"Bet Isla didn't buy any though," sulked Jo, feeling slightly ashamed of her vicious outburst but not taking back her words. She really didn't like Isla at all.

"No, not a whole strip. But she did buy one. I sold it to her myself."

"You'd have thought she would have bought a strip," remarked Jo. "After all, her son lives near Barcelona, doesn't he?"

"So did you know Isla's first husband?" asked Grace, "What was his name?"

"Sean. Nice chap. Worked with my Paul, that's how I knew him. He died just before Paul actually. He told us she had a headache the day they were married! Made us all laugh at the time. Anyway, enough of her, we must have raised over four thousand tonight, so I've got to put this somewhere safe and then get back to our table. The second half is due to start." And Phyllis looked around for somewhere she could lock the box away.

The three ladies returned to their table just as Barry was finishing his game of heads and tails. The audience were very merry and eager to get on with the quiz. Phyllis was delighted that the evening had turned out so well even though her table lost the lead and Cagney and

Lacey took home the quiz prize, sharing two cases of sparkling wine between them.

"And now we come to the raffle," Barry's voice echoed once more around the room.

He drew the smaller prizes first. People were so good humoured that if they won two prizes, they put one of them back, so it was quite late by the time he drew the star prize.

There was an audible hush in the room as he announced the winner.

"Green ticket," (moans from those holding pink) "Number 342!"

"Phyllis," Shouted Jo, "Look! It's you!"

Phyllis said she couldn't believe her luck. She never won raffles. Everyone on her table cheered as she went to the rostrum and collected the envelope.

"There you are my lovely," boomed Barry as he placed it in her hands and turned her towards the photographer from the local press who snapped her as she took it from him "In there, vouchers for two airline tickets, names to be confirmed and a room with half board at an H10 in Barcelona. Let's give her a clap, everyone. Phyllis is always helping others, so it's great that she's won this. She deserves it because tonight folks, and mostly down to her efforts, we have managed to raise £5560 for charity."

The room erupted as Phyllis walked back to her seat, red faced, and her table crowded round as she opened the envelope to show them the vouchers.

The rest of the evening was spent clearing away everything so that the hall was empty, ready to be decorated for the wedding reception that was to be held there the following day and everyone went home agreeing that it had been one of the best nights out they'd had in a long time. Everyone that is, except Isla who could be heard muttering that it had been a put-up job and that she expected that not all the takings from the night would reach those beggars on the street corners either.

Two days later, Phyllis rang Grace's mobile.

"Hi Grace. Sorry to bother you, but did you say that Isla's son lives in Spain now? Near Barcelona?"

"Yes. She was telling me about it at the gym last week. He's had a baby and she hasn't seen her yet. Something about there being no room at the inn or something."

"No room at what?" asked Phyllis.

"Never mind. I was being unkind. It seems her son's partner has her parents there so they can't all fit in or something. Why do you ask?"

"Well, my prize is for two and I'm alone now I've lost Paul, so I thought it would be nice to offer her the other ticket so she can see them. We'd have to share a room, I know, but I don't think she'd mind….."

"YOU WHAT?" Grace almost screamed down the phone, "Why in God's name do you want to inflict that on yourself?"

"I just think it would be a nice thing to do. It would mean I have company too. But I don't want to offer it to her if it would offend her. You know what a funny old stick she is."

"Oh, she'd snatch your hand off, don't you worry. But, Phyllis, are you sure? She's not an easy person in small doses, so a whole weekend? I don't think I could bear it."

"I don't expect I'll see much of her once we are there except at night in the hotel room. She'll be with her son. It'll be fine."

Phyllis and Isla jetted off the following weekend. Adam and Grace dropped them to Gatwick as Jack was having trouble with his back. ("Allegedly", Jo was to remark later, "Probably too tight to fork out for the petrol.") Three days later, Jo and Colin picked them up.

Things were strained in the car as it headed back to Canterbury and Jo was more than a little curious as to why.

"So, you had good weather, I can see. Look at your tan!"

"Yes, it was lovely," replied Phyllis," A real treat."

"And did you see all the sights?" continued Jo.

"Oh, I fitted in all I could on the Saturday. I saw the Gaudi Park and the Cathedral. I had lunch on The Ramblas. It was fantastic."

"Didn't you go with Phyllis, Isla?"

Isla didn't answer.

"I don't think Isla's too well, Jo. I should leave her be for now."

"I have a headache." Mumbled Isla and she closed her eyes and held her head to get the point home.

"So, what did Isla do on Saturday if you went by yourself?" Jo was relentless.

"She caught a bus and went to visit her family. It was a chance for her to see her little grandchild."

"Oh, I see. Well, that must have been nice for you Isla."

There was no reply from either of them.

"So, what about Sunday? What did you do on Sunday? Did you get a chance to sit round the pool? I looked at your hotel on the internet. A rooftop pool in Barcelona. How fab!"

"Isla wasn't feeling herself on Sunday. Jo, have you heard anything back from Shelter? Were they pleased with the money we raised?"

Jo turned and looked at Phyllis who was shaking her head and holding a finger over her mouth. She all but said the words to be quiet. Jo got the message and they chattered about other things, the visit to Barcelona now recognised as Taboo.

They dropped Isla home first. Colin helped her out of the car and carried her bag to the door. Isla walked straight past Jack who was standing there with his arms stretched wide to hug his wife. She charged up the stairs and left Colin to face Jack. She didn't say thank you or goodbye to anyone. Both men shrugged their shoulders. Jack thanked him and waved to the ladies in the car. The door shut on them all.

"She's a strange one," said Colin as he eased himself back into the driver's seat. "Right Phyllis. It's your house for a cup of tea? Grace will be there. She said she would pop round with some fresh milk and bread to welcome you home. She wanted to hear all about your weekend too. I'm parched." And he pulled out into the road.

Jo could hardly contain herself.

"Come on Phyl. Give!"

"Wait 'til we have a cuppa. I'm parched too."

So, it was as they were seated in Phyllis' front room with tea and a plate of digestives that the events of the weekend were recounted.

"I feel sorry for her. She's had an awful shock and if I tell you what happened, please promise me it will go no further."

"Oh, for God's sake Phyl, this is Isle the Pile we are talking about. The meanest, most selfish person for miles around. A person who didn't even thank you for thinking of her when you won that prize. All she said that night was that it had probably been rigged."

"Did she think that?" asked Phyllis, surprised.

"Yes. She not only thought it. She said it – quite loudly too. That's why I was so surprised when you offered the other ticket to her of all people."

"Jo was seething. She wanted to go with you!" laughed Grace.

"Oh well, perhaps it would have been better for Isla if she had," sighed Phyllis as she sipped her tea.

Jo looked as though she were about to burst. "Please Phyllis. Tell us."

"First you must promise me."

And Phyllis began her account of the weekend.

"After breakfast on Saturday, as I told you in the car, I set off sightseeing. I decided to get a bus tour, so Isla and I went to the bus station, and she found the bus she needed to get to her son's district. I didn't see her again until when I got back to the hotel at 6 o'clock. I went up to our room and I found her on her bed in floods of tears. Eventually, she told me that she had turned up at her son's house and had been greeted by Karen's parents who were very unfriendly towards her. At first, they wouldn't let her in. She hadn't told anyone she was coming as she had wanted to surprise them."

"Bloody awful surprise if you ask me," cut in Jo.

"Jo, do you want me to go on or….?"

Jo made a zipping sign across her mouth.

"Anyway, once she was let in, they wouldn't let her see the baby and she started to get annoyed.

Cameron was nowhere to be seen, but eventually, Karen appeared, with a fag hanging out of her mouth telling her parents to clear off for a bit so she and Isla could talk."

"I didn't know she smoked," said Grace, "Isla told me they were both health freaks, That Cameron was always at the gym when he lived here. I used to see him. He even had a personal trainer. Nice young chap – what was his name now?"

"Grace!" Boomed Jo, "Shut the fuck up! What does it matter what the blokes name was?"

"Sorry," said Grace. "You don't have to swear at me, Jo. Anyway, I've remembered. It was Karl. Haven't seen him for some time though"

"Yes, it was Karl. I know his mother. She's a lovely woman," said Phyllis

"Go on," said Jo, flapping a hand at Grace. "What happened next?"

"Well, it seems Karen sat Isla down and gave her some brandy or something. Then she took Isla to see the baby. And the baby, Jessica, was not the same baby that had been in that boasting book she tots around all the time. Both Cameron and Karen are blond with blue eyes, and this little girl was …well, let's just say, she was mixed race."

"Get away!" said Colin, who normally wasn't all that interested in his wife's gossipy mates.

"Noooo!" yelled Jo.

Grace's mouth simply dropped open.

"Naturally, Isla was very shocked but then she and Karen had a row because Isla presumed she had been unfaithful to her darling Cameron."

"Well, that does sound plausible" put in Grace.

"She insisted on seeing Cameron and after a bit, Karen managed to get him to come out of his room. He told Isla that he hadn't wanted her to know about this. That he and Karen were going through a divorce quietly and that they wanted to spare her any pain over the whole thing."

"Snivelling little turd! Poor Isla. I even feel sorry for her now."

Everyone looked at Jo.

"What?? I do. I really do." She said, "I'm not that heartless. It's not a wonder that she was so quiet on the drive home."

"Yes, but that's not the end of it." Said Phyllis.

"What do you mean?" asked Grace.

"Well, I'm afraid, I made matters even worse. You see, I was so sad for Isla. On Sunday, it was a gorgeous day and all she wanted to do was stay in the room, sobbing and crying. She had thrown the little boasting book with the fake Jessica in the waste bin. I took it out and had a look at the pictures. Such a lovely little baby with both Karen and Cameron pictured holding her so it was a cruel thing for Isla to discover she wasn't her granddaughter that way. But I also knew that they had been completely caught off guard by her visit. I decided I would go and see them myself to see if Cameron would come to talk to his mother and give her some kind of comfort."

"That's brave," put in Colin.

"So, what did you do?" asked Jo.

"I had a look at Isla's address book. She'd left it on the dressing table the day before when she'd copied out their address. I did the same thing and went to the bus station and caught the same number bus as she had the previous day. I found the villa easily; the Spanish are very kind, and they all seem to speak good English."

"Never mind all that. What happened?" Jo snapped.

"Well, I knocked on the door but there was no answer. Then I remembered that Karen was a Catholic, so she was probably at church or something, it being Sunday."

"Oh yes. There was a big kafuffle about them getting married in a registry office – don't you remember Jo?" Grace looked at her.

"Go on," insisted Jo, ignoring her friend.

"But the funny thing was, I could hear a lot of noise coming from the back garden, splashing and laughing. So, I found the back gate and let myself in. I could hardly believe my eyes."

"And?" the listeners said at once.

"The baby was asleep in her buggy in the shade, but Cameron was stark bollock naked and kissing that young personal trainer Karl, the one you were talking about Grace. The one with the David Beckham type tattoos all over the place and with all the muscles. He was naked too. And by the looks of them, they were both about to enjoy themselves...."

Silence. No-one said a word. Phyllis went on.

"Cameron begged me not to tell his mother. Of course, I said I wouldn't, but that *he* had to. I told him about how distressed she was over Jessica and how she had come all that way to see them and had been treated very shabbily. I insisted he come back with me to the hotel and talk to his mother, to explain everything to her. I mean, there is absolutely nothing wrong with being gay and there is no stigma or nonsense like that, is there? He took some persuading I can tell you. Cameron told me his mother would never accept his situation, but I told him that hiding from her wouldn't work as it was inevitable that she would have found out one day. In the end they both got dressed, put Jessica in her car seat and drove me back to the hotel. Once there, I went off to see a few more museums and left them to it. By the time I got back, Isla was sitting by the pool reading a book."

"Did she thank you?" asked Grace.

"No, not at all. She gave me a massive piece of her mind. She called me an interfering busy body and said that if I went back to Canterbury and a whisper about her son's sexuality after I had witnessed a fleeting fancy he'd had with another man, or any negative hints at his capabilities of fathering a child were to reach her ears, she would sue me. And then she told me never to try to get a part in her drama club again. Nor was I to go to her gym or attend any other meetings or quizzes or social events where she and her husband might be."

"Oh, I expect she was still in a state of shock. After all, it's not every day you have your own suspicions confirmed. And then again, she's lost the little granddaughter she thought she had. That is another blow," reasoned Grace.

"Well, actually the biggest thing she's got to face up to now is that Karen didn't give birth to Jessica. She only agreed to marry Cameron so that he could adopt a baby. Karen had been paid handsomely for that. The money was even probably provided by Isla selling some more of Hubert's shares as neither Cameron nor Karl has much money."

"Oh my God! That would really hurt her."

"Yes. So, after the divorce, Karl and Cameron are going to bring up Jessica. And that little cutie pie, and believe me, she really is a little beauty, far better looking than the one in the boasting book, will always be the living proof of her son's love for Karl. And unless Isla disowns them completely, Jessica will always be part of her perfect family."

After they had all gone home, Phyllis made a quick phone call to her friend Glynis, Karl's mother.

"Hi there Glyn. …yes, just got back. …Oh, it was lovely. Let's catch up over lunch tomorrow – I've got some great photos. You'll be seeing them all very soon….. Yes, they are coming back, so get the place ready. She is absolutely gorgeous, and you will love her. A chance to be a granny at last!…. See you tomorrow."

She opened her mail. She expected her credit card statement to be higher than normal, but then single supplements at hotels are very high so you might as well book a double room anyway. And she had been very lucky with the airfares. All in all, the weekend away hadn't cost her as much as she expected. Barry had been more than happy to draw her ticket when she'd told him her plan. He and Karl had been very close at one time. He knew how much Glynis missed her son and wanted him to come home so she could spend time with him and his husband-to-be, Cameron, and their little daughter, Jessica. And Barry was such a good sort. Despite being a professional, he made time to be part of the new drama group that Phyllis had joined. He was directing their latest production, which was where she had met Glynis and learned of all the subterfuge going on in Spain. All because of Isla.

Phyllis smiled quietly to herself. No-one suspected a thing. Revenge really is a dish better served ice cold.

Caroline

29.03.00

Aries: Highly creative yet often blind to the obvious.

Living in the city had been a massive shock for Caroline. She was a country girl, used to waking up in the morning to the sound of birds and the distant chug of a tractor in a field; her own little bedroom plastered with pictures she had done for one project or another, her old familiar duvet, and that smell, peculiar to her room, which meant she was home. She was safe.

But on that first day, she was woken with a start by a stranger singing loudly in the shower, so loudly that it felt that whoever it was, was right next door to her room. And then she remembered that it was exactly that. The small room smelt of paint and industrial carpet cleaner. Her clothes, usually littered on the carpet in the corner waiting to be picked up by her mother, laundered and then returned ironed and folded to her wardrobe, were lying across a chair because, despite the smell of the cleaner, the carpet had some very suspect stains. The chair was next to a desk upon which stood a laptop and a notepad, but the rest of the desk was covered with her toiletries as the shelves were already bulging with her art materials and books. The walls of the room had recently been painted a lurid orange, which made the room seem even smaller, and had a notice telling her that there was to be no smoking or candles lit and that no tape should be used to put up posters (Blu-Tack only, of which all traces must be removed on vacating the room). The back of her door, which had a single hook for her hoodie and coat, had a printed notice indicating the nearest fire exit and instructing her that it should be noted and used in case of fire or fire drill. She threw back her duvet and realised she was looking forward to the day. She had made it. She had managed to get a place at Canterbury University which meant that she was a student and she had to get on with growing up and being cool and having fun.

She had felt a bit lost when she'd waved goodbye to her father the evening before. The trip down from Yorkshire had taken longer than anticipated due to roadworks and other traffic jams that seemed to crop up on motorways for no apparent reason and then, miraculously, melt away. When they finally arrived, there had been queues of students, so it had taken ages to get her admitted and then a further queue for the key to her room and then at last, map in hand, they had wandered over the campus until they located the right hall to which she had been allocated. Meanwhile, she had seen loads of other students and lots of different stands encouraging the freshers to join this group or another. The place was buzzing. So was her head.

Her father helped carry all her stuff up the stairs to her room and then took her to the nearest supermarket where he bought her some bedding, some crockery and cooking pans and food for the week which they took back to the hall and stowed away in a cupboard in the kitchen. He wrote her name on her milk and on one of the shelves in the fridge where he put her butter and cheese. Then he took her back to her room, hugged her, told her how proud of her he was, slipped £50 into her hand "To keep you topped up for a bit!" and winking, gave her a last kiss before he headed back to his car and the Yorkshire Dales.

As she watched him head out of the campus car park, her mobile rang. It was her mother who told her yet again to remember that she had to eat properly now that she had to cook for herself and to do her laundry etc. etc., which was just the spur to get her to go over to the nearest stand and enrol in a club, not even realising that it was for badminton. When she filled in on the form that she was studying art at the Christchurch campus, one of the students called out to a particularly good-looking boy, "Hey, Jordan! You're doing art, aren't you? Can I introduce you to Caro here?" and Caroline blushed because he was so good looking and because her boring old name, Caroline, had suddenly become a very trendy Caro. He'd come over and kissed her on both cheeks like she had seen celebrities do on The Graham Norton Show.

"Welcome!" he said, "You're gonna fit in real well." And she blushed again, marvelling at his London accent and his dark eyes that contrasted starkly with his bleached white-blonde hair. He reminded her of Sick Boy in Trainspotting, a film she and her friends back home watched over and over so that it had become like a cult to them. She felt a little in love with him already.

She spent the evening with the badminton group, chatting with Jordan and Nadine who was doing psychology, had no intention of ever doing badminton and who chain smoked. Nadine was from Austria, was extremely tall and overweight with a rich throaty accent, some choice vocabulary that she hadn't learned in any school and a quick laugh which made her very likeable. Her father was a businessman, obviously wealthy as she had no student loan and her own car (left hand drive) and she told Caro not to mind asking her if she needed to go to the shops or anywhere. She and Jordan were in the same hall which was how they knew each other and the three shared pizza and red wine in her room until 1am at which time Jordan walked her back to her own hall and pecked her on the cheek.

"See you tomorrow," he called. "I'll take you down to the art campus. Meet at the car park at nine?" and he was gone.

So, although she had been half dreading her first day at university, she had actually enjoyed it and found herself singing in the shower as she got herself ready for the day.

When she looked at her phone as she was pouring herself a bowl of Shreddies, she saw three texts from her mother and a missed call from her sister.

'All good Mam. Eating well. Washed up. Got my laundry sorted. Don't worry. Love you xxx' and she included a smiling emoji and four thumbs up.

To her sister

'Hi Fliss! It's brilliant. Got classes so will phone you later. Love you xxx'

She looked out the window of the kitchen and saw how the other students were dressed, went back to her room and picked through her clothes until she found what she wanted to wear that day. She wanted to look arty without it appearing that she had tried too hard, so many of her clothes from New Look just wouldn't do. She settled on a plain tee-shirt and shorts with trainers – no socks, and arrived to see Jordan, who looked like he'd slept in his clothes, kicking a pine cone around the car park.

A morning hug and they started the walk across town to the art campus. Without the presence of Nadine, they were able to talk about the art they liked and found they had a lot to talk about. Jordan had been in Canterbury for three days already and had sussed out the places to go, the places to eat and the places to party. He'd already visited the art studios and managed to bag a space for himself with good light. He'd swapped stuff around so that he had an easel that didn't collapse and a workstation with drawers.

"Classes don't start 'til tomorrow so I think we should get your space sorted now or you'll end up in the corridor." And he took a piece of paper and wrote 'CARO' in very large letters, then selected what he considered to be the next best workspace for her, taping the paper to the easel and leaving a paint brush in a jam-jar on the desk.

"No-one moves brushes", he said. "Come on, let's look at the timetable. They told me they would be putting it up today."

The first-year timetable was displayed on the office door. Jordan took a photo of it and suggested they went for a coffee and decided what lectures and workshops they needed to sign up for. Caro was glad she'd met him because he seemed to know what to do. None of this preparation would have occurred to her had she been by herself, and she told him so.

"All very well being thought of as arty-farty, Caro, but when it comes down to it, we're paying a lot of money out for this so it's up to us to make sure we get what we want." And he pulled a notepad out of his bag and started writing in the units that they had to do and the options that were available to them. He then drew a freehand grid and slotted in the times of the core units, leaving it very clear as to what time they could fit in the workshops and studio time. He left some parts of the week free "To do whatever we like" he said and gave her a slow smile which made her insides melt.

They wandered down to the cathedral and he held her hand (she hoped it wasn't shaking) as he pointed out the Saints adorning the gate. He showed his student card (she had forgotten hers) and managed to get them both free entry so that he could show her the place where Thomas Beckett had been murdered, where The Black Prince lay and the gorgeous little Tudor Roses that had been painted on the walls in the crypt. They sat together on the grass in the autumn sunshine, and he told her a little about his family who seemed so much more glamorous and cosmopolitan than her own. His father was a designer who worked abroad and his mother, who did not work, spent a lot of time at the beauty salon or out with her friends. From references he made to their cleaner and the type of car his mother drove, she could tell he was used to having lots of money and she was aware that, unlike him, she'd had to take a large student loan to cover her tuition and living expenses. That £50 her dad had given her had already shrivelled down a lot and she knew the earnings she'd saved from her summer job wouldn't last all that long so she would be looking for a job. He looked at her with an almost reverent expression when she told him that.

"I thought I'd give myself a few weeks to find my feet and then get something, bar work or waitressing, just to help out. I can't expect my family to bail me out all the time."

And so began their friendship. It wasn't long before Caro got a job; she had to as Jordan and Nadine enjoyed doing things that she couldn't afford and the three were always together. She had far too much pride to accept Nadine's "Oh we can pay, don't worry" or Jordan's "But if you work that shift, we can't go out that night." And the money and tips she got from her job meant that she was able to cope better. She was often up all night finishing an assignment because of her hectic lifestyle, but she absolutely loved it. They were recognised on campus as being three best friends, but everyone thought that Caro and Jordan were an item. They were always together at workshops and studio time. Their artwork, although very different, was influenced by each other. He would always grab her hand when leaving a room and he would buy her little presents to cheer her up if her art wasn't working out the way she wanted. They did their research and assignments together in the library and went to student gigs together. By December, Caro's long blonde hair had been cut pixie short and bleached white, just like his and her nose had been pierced. Caro and Jordan - almost like twins.

When she got home at Christmas, her family were horrified but had to admit, the new hairstyle suited her very well. She had bought clothes from a charity shop and altered them, sometimes simply by ripping them here and there, so that she had a 'look' all of her own which she had completed with a small tattoo on her wrist and as winter had approached, she'd found a grey Crombie coat at a jumble sale (that Jordan would often try to steal from her) which completed the look she was aiming for. Caro arrived home as the art student that people in her home village in Yorkshire imagined an art student to be.

"I hope you're not taking ….stuff." murmured her mother on New Year's Eve as they got ready for the gathering at her Grandma's house that night.

"You're not sleeping around, Car, are you?" asked her sister as she drove her to the station for her journey back to Canterbury the next day. The family were disconcerted that she wanted to go back so soon after the festivities. It seemed like she couldn't wait to return. She told them she had to submit a body of work for assessment the following week and she had to get back to complete it as she was behind.

That was only half the truth. She needed to see Jordan again, but without Nadine, because she really did want their relationship to go further than hand holding and pecks on the cheek. She had never taken drugs; that wasn't her idea of fun. And she had never slept with Jordan; or anyone else for that matter. But she thought she might like to try. The text she got:

"Going mad here. Getting back to Canterbury for New Year. Coming back soon? No Nadine and I'm lonely. (Three heart emoji's and seven kisses)."

It was enough to make her cut her holiday short.

He met her at the train station and hugged her tight, kissing her on her cheek and her forehead but not on her mouth and she tried hard not to look disappointed as he grabbed hold of her backpack and took off, walking at such a fast pace that she could hardly keep up. Back in her room, he dumped the bag and headed for the kitchen. "I've bought you some milk and stuff so we don't have to go shopping. We can have something here and then head out if you like, but it's always dead on New Year's Day so we could just hang out and watch TV in your room?" and without waiting for her reply, started cooking some rice and microwaving a Thai Curry for two.

"There's no one else about so we have the place to ourselves! We can leave the dishes – nobody will moan. Do you want a coffee? Or tea? I've got so much to tell you. It's so good you're back." And he carried on calling to her from the kitchen as she stashed away her clothes, feeling a shred of hope that after they had eaten their relationship might develop.

It was already dark outside and very quiet. New Year's Day was a day for recovery for most people so there were a few good films to choose from that evening. They lay together side by side on her single bed which meant he had to put his arm around her, and she had to snuggle up to him as he surfed the channels looking for something for them to watch. She decided that if he wasn't going to do anything, then it was up to her to make the first move, so she lifted herself up and kissed him firmly on the cheek, she'd aimed for his mouth, but he moved at the last moment.

He stopped fiddling with the remote, looked at her and instead of going in for a full kiss like she hoped he would, he said, looking genuinely perplexed, "What was that for?"

Caro blushed and searched around for something to say.

"For asking me to come back early to be with you."

He looked confused.

"And for meeting me at the station."

"Of course, I would meet you. I've been looking forward to seeing you, you daft thing." And he started surfing the channels again.

"And for buying all that food and for cooking my dinner."

"Well, I know shops aren't always open after four on New Year's Day. Besides, Naddy is due back soon. I sent her a text too. She's catching a late ferry and should be here in about an hour. She's always hungry and eats like a horse. It won't last long." And he chuckled. "I had a hell of a job when the porter found me in your building though. Luckily, he recognised me and said he'd seen us around together. Had to show him all the stuff I bought and explain you were on your way back and in the end he was OK."

"Oh..."

"Oh, what?"

Caroline tried not to show her feelings. "Oh Jordan, go back to Film Four. They are showing Trainspotting in five minutes. It's old but it's good. One of my favourites."

She felt so let down. He was just her friend, her best friend. She knew she was a little in love with him, but he didn't think of her in that way. She hardly watched the film and was relieved to hear Nadine's, "Where the fook are you?" yelled outside her window, "Let me in; its fooking freezing out here."

He buzzed the outside door and Nadine came in, amid a cloud of smoke, laden with a large bag.

"Happy New Year!" she called and enveloped them both in a bear hug. "I haf missed you both. My fooking family were driving me fooking mad." And she flicked her ash onto the remains of the curry congealing on a plate on the floor. "Ant the drive was fooking terrible." She sank down on the bed. "Fooking snow all the way to Calais. Here." And she threw an exquisitely wrapped parcel at Caroline. "And this is for you, Jordan." He caught her gift as Nadine emptied the rest of the bag on the floor tumbling an array of expensive Christmas goodies onto the stained carpet. "And this lot of crap I am leafing at your place, Caro, because if I haf it in my room I will eat it all ant be a size 24. I will come round now ant then for a nibble!" and she chuckled heartily, which turned into a cough which ended up with Caro getting her water and Jordan giving her a swig from the bottle of brandy that had rolled out of her bag and landed under the bed.

Caro's gift was a book on Hundertwasser, one of her favourite artists who just so happened to be Austrian. Jordan's was a book on Hockney. It had 'We Two Boys Together Clinging' on the cover. He laughed out loud when he saw it and punched Nadine on the arm. She laughed too and lit another cigarette.

"Wasn't sure if you had it but it looked like your sort of stuff – so what the heck?"

Caro laughed too but felt uneasy. She didn't like to think too deeply about it.

The term started a week later, and the trio fell into their familiar routine. Caro found it hard to get back into her coursework. Her initial ideas were proving hard to get out in a visual form. She would start something and run it past Jordan and he would usually end up telling her that this or that was crass or mundane. Her tutors began to get concerned with her as they knew she spent a lot of time at the studio but was getting nowhere. Her time spent with Nadine and Jordan became expensive, so she looked around for a job again. This time she was lucky enough to land one in the student bar on campus.

"That's better," said Jordan "It means that even when you're working, we could hang out if we had nothing better to do."

One night Caro was serving a group of students who she could tell from all their talk were studying computer science. They were all very loud, probably as a result of the happy hour shots. A dark-haired student that she hadn't seen around campus before called her over and asked for her phone number. He was obviously drunk but wouldn't take her laughter or the shake of her head for an answer, insisting that she give it to him. "You are so hot," he slurred, pushing a beer mat towards her and asking everyone around him for a pen. "I've had to have a couple just to pluck up courage. You can't turn me down." She gave him the wrong number and told him to go home and be careful not to fall over. He was back the next day, this time very sober and told her that the number she had given him was for an art supply shop. She was just finishing a lunchtime shift and due at a lecture. She told him she had to rush to get to Christchurch.

"I thought you might be an art student."

Caro grabbed her bag and headed out the door. He followed.

"Oh, why is that?" she said as she hurried towards the bus stop. She didn't have time to walk.

"Well, you look different. Your clothes are completely unique, and you look a lot more interesting than the other girls around here."

She reached the bus stop and fumbled in her pocket for her pass. He was still there.

"You know Nadine, don't you? I've seen you with her and that blond guy."

The bus appeared over the hill.

"So, your number?"

"No time right now. Gotta go" and she got on the bus and swiped her pass. The doors shut. She looked back to see him staring after the bus and couldn't help smiling to herself. He was gorgeous.

The art history lecture was dragging, and Caro caught herself thinking about the dark eyed guy with the dimples. She didn't realise it had finished until Jordan dug her in the ribs and told her to get a move on. Propelling her towards his studio area and chattering away about how he was going to make an installation for his final project that year and could she just sit while he did some sketches of her and took some photos? He didn't seem to notice that she was in a world of her own. Caro was just sitting staring at the raindrops as they trickled down the windowpane when her phone started to vibrate. An unknown number.

"You shouldn't answer that," said Jordan. "It's probably PPI."

But Caro had a good idea who it might be, so she touched her screen.

"Hello?"

"It's me. Ross."

"Ross?"

"I got your number from Nadine. You didn't say no. You said you had no time right now, so that means you would have if the bus hadn't arrived. So, I told her that and she gave it to me."

"Oh."

"So, will you come out with me tonight?"

"Tonight?"

"Yes, let's get something to eat."

"I've got to do some work in the studio."

"That's ok. I'll meet you at campus whenever you finish."

"But I won't have time to change or clean up or anything. And I promised myself I'd be here 'til seven tonight."

"It doesn't matter to me. I just want to spend some time with you. Say you'll meet me."

She remembered the dimples and the dark eyes, so she did.

Jordan stopped drawing half-way through their conversation and looked intently at her.

"What are you up to? Who's Ross? And what are you doing tonight? Can I come?" he asked. But she just smiled and slid off the chair. She hugged him and told him she had better get on with her work or she would have to stay in Canterbury over Easter and then drifted off to her own studio space where she put in the best three hours she had done for a long time.

He was waiting for her in the pouring rain, sheltering under an umbrella by the entrance looking really happy when he saw her. Jordan wasn't far behind and introduced himself, almost pushing Caro to one side in his eagerness.

"You must be the elusive Ross?" Jordan put out his hand, "I'm Jordan. Where are we going?"

"Hello Jordan. Hi there Caro, come here." And Ross held the umbrella out towards her, "You're getting soaked."

Caro gratefully took shelter from the rain.

"Actually Jordan, really nice to meet you but I have to talk to Caro by herself tonight. I'm sure you understand. We'll catch up with you later perhaps. Student bar, about ten? OK?" and he put his arm round Caro's waist and walked off with her towards the underpass. Holding the umbrella over them both, he was quiet as they made their way to Nando's, and Caro didn't look back to see what Jordan was up to. Once inside, they both seemed to relax. He asked her all about herself, where she lived and her family and told her a little about himself. She suddenly realised that she had told him more in the short time she had known him than she had ever told Jordan or Nadine. And he seemed very interested in listening to her. On their walk back to Halls she did not mind that the rain forced them to huddle together under the umbrella. He took her to the door of her halls, and she went to her room feeling slightly lightheaded. Her phone pinged twice as she was draping her wet coat over her radiator. One was from Jordan, "Where are you? I've bought you both a shot." The other was from Ross; all it said was "xxxxx".

Jordan woke her early the next day. He was banging on her room door – he knew the code for her hall. She dragged herself out of bed and let him in. He pulled a face when he saw she was in her PJs. "Come on. Has lover boy made you forget?"

It was Saturday. No classes, but the studios were open so the students could work.

"We're going to Dungeness today. Nadine is taking us. I have to do some photography for my project."

"Oh, Jordan, do you mind if I give it a miss? I'm so behind with my work and I've got a shift tonight. I think I need to do studio time today."

"Well, I do mind actually. I need to place you in the landscape. I've been online and the place is seriously weird. It's quite barren and open. It will be the perfect backdrop to inspire my installation."

"Why can't Nadine be your figure? She has to be there to drive you."

"Don't be ridiculous. I need someone fragile, frail to contrast with that environment. Nadine's like a massive steamroller. She won't do at all."

"What the fook did you call me?" The cloud of smoke and throaty laugh preceded Nadine's entry into the tiny room that suddenly felt very overcrowded. "What is a steamroller?"

Between making coffee, showering, and pulling on some clothes that could actually have done with a wash, Caro grabbed a banana and was struggling to get into her boots when her phone pinged again. She glanced at the message and grinned.

"What's so funny Caro?" asked Jordan.

"At least put your cups over by the sink. I'll wash them later," she answered.

"Get a moof on why don't you?" Nadine lit up another cigarette, ignoring the "No smoking sign" that was displayed directly next to her. "I want to be back by four. I need a nap before I go out."

Once they were in the car, Caro, still holding her banana asked, "I can't remember you organising this at all."

"We agreed it last night. At the bar."

"I wasn't there last night."

"Oh yees, Jordan. Our Caro wasn't around last night. Look out you bastard!" and Nadine pulled a finger sign at a car that cut her up on the roundabout. A waste of time as she was left hand drive, and no one would see it.

"Never mind, you're here now," and Jordan turned to her and squeezed her knee. "Who are you texting?"

"Oh, just my mum. She's missing me." And Caro smiled to herself.

The day was bright and clear. The place was, indeed, very unusual. The contrast of the power station with all its steel and pipes and fences next to the beach, where birdwatchers were dotted around among the dunes, was acute. There was an old lighthouse and a miniature steam train that puffed in and out between there and Hythe. It was as though it was a place where nature and man collided. And man had made it look forbidding and ominous.

Caro let herself be posed and pushed about as Jordan clicked away. Nadine found a café where she sat outside and smoked while she ate another breakfast and complained that she had no signal on her phone. By twelve o' clock Jordan announced he had finished and that they could go.

Back in the car, they headed for Ashford because Nadine wanted to buy some designer gear at the centre there. As soon as her signal kicked in, Caro's phone pinged three times. She smiled as she looked at her messages and spent a lot of the journey texting back.

"Your mum must be missing you an awful lot," remarked Jordan. I've never known you so busy on the phone. Except to me of course."

"Just a little family thing," she answered, and carried on texting.

"You working tonight?" asked Jordan.

"Yes, I already told you earlier. I start at six."

"So you can't come to that film I want to see?"

"Sorry, no. But Nads might go with you? Nads?"

"Saturday night iss for drinking and enjoying. Not for sitting on my fat arse and looking at Botoxed people playing games on a screen. I haff other plans tonight."

"What are you doing, then?" asked Jordan.

"You are a nosy buggered. My brother is coming to visit, ant he is staying at The Abode. We are haffing dinner there which is why I needed something nice to wear."

"Well, can I come and meet him? I've got nothing else to do."

"OK, but you haff to wear something good. Not your usual shit."

And as they neared Canterbury, their conversation topic changed to clothes and places and people and Caro leaned back and shut her eyes. He would be there tonight; with his friends, but he would be there, and he was going to stay as she cleared up and he was going to walk her home.

Jordan had a huge repertoire of clothes to choose from and Nadine commented on how he looked OK which was a compliment from her. He had been over to Caro's to get her to sort his hair which was a little longer on top and sticking up 'Something About Mary' style.

"You look terrific, Jordan, really handsome. Have a good evening." And Caro kissed him on the cheek and watched as he sauntered over to the car park.

She took a little longer than usual to get ready for work; she wanted to look good for him. Surprisingly for a Saturday night, the bar was very quiet and her boss, who saw Ross waiting for her told her she could leave at ten o' clock. They didn't go to her hall, they went to his, where he made her hot buttered toast and tea and where she stayed for an hour just talking and kissing. He told her how he had only ever had one real girlfriend before. He hadn't gone out with anyone else on a regular basis since then. He'd always doubted himself and his judgement.

"But I knew as soon as I saw you. You're special." And he kissed her again.

"I'm not sure about that," she said, and she told him about how she had imagined that Jordan cared for her. "I know he loves me...in his way, but he doesn't want me at all. It really hurt. I'd built everything up in my head, but he didn't want to know."

"Oh, I have a feeling there's a reasonable explanation for that. But who cares? You don't still want him, do you?" and he gazed directly into her eyes.

At midnight, he walked her back. They took a short cut through the car park, passing a car which, Caro noticed, seemed to be misted up from inside and was rocking gently.

"Hmm. Looks like Nadine's having a good evening," murmured Caro.

"Huh?"

"That's Nadine's car. Look!"

"Wonder why she's not using her room. No-one would know this time of night." Ross nudged her. "No-one would know." And he kissed her again.

They went to her room. And no-one knew. Until they were woken up at ten o'clock by a hammering on her room door.

"Caro! Wake the fook up."

"It's Nadine." Caro looked startled. "What shall I do?"

"I can hear you Caro. You've got a man in there. Let me in."

Caro pulled on a tee shirt and pants and opened the door. Nadine came in with her usual blast of smoke. Her eyebrows shot up when she saw Ross. She laughed and coughed and said, "Why hello there, I'm Nadine. I've heard about you."

Caro felt embarrassed but Ross simply said, "Hi there Nadine. Heard a lot about you too. I'm Ross. What's the matter? You seem a bit flustered."

"Can't find Jordan. He's got my car keys. My brother came back to see the campus and Jordan said he'd run him back to the hotel as I had a fooking headache. My car's fooking missing and I thought Jordan was here, he's not in his room. I needed to see if he was with you. He probably didn't lock it. I'll have to phone the police."

"Don't do that Nadine." said Ross. "Where's your brother staying?"

Ross phoned the hotel and confirmed the car was in their car park.

"It's with your brother so relax," he said to Nadine.

"But where is Jordan? He's not answering his phone."

"I bet your brother isn't answering his either, Nadine," Said Ross, "Give him a call."

Klaud's phone went straight to voicemail too. Ross looked enquiringly at Nadine.

"Well?"

"Achh! I am so stupid. Klaud, he is, what do you say? A fast worker!" and she banged the side of her head with the palm of her hand. "But wait a minute, how did you know what kind of car I drive?" Nadine looked at him suspiciously.

"Oh, Caro mentioned it was red. There is only one red left hand drive car in their car park."

Nadine went off grumbling that she had to walk to the shops that morning. Ross got out of bed and put his arms round Caro who he could see had suddenly realised why Jordan acted the way he did with her.

"See Caro, everything in life has a reasonable explanation if you think about it."

And Caro laughed.

"Call me Caroline. I was named after a song, a lovely old song." And she picked up her towel and headed for the bathroom.

Nancy

19.02.52

Libra: Friendly and balanced.
Brings harmony and love.

We'd been lucky the summer of '76. It's forty odd years ago now, but I remember it as though it were yesterday. It started early and didn't finish until a thunderstorm in September brought us the much-needed rain and the feeling of relief that the drought had ended. We'd had soaring temperatures which kept us awake at night, and water shortages with hosepipe bans. The grass was burnt brown, newspapers were full of pictures of office workers sunbathing in London parks, beaches overflowing with people trying to keep cool and roads melting under the heat. The city was far too hot; the tiny flat above a souvenir shop in the High Street which, although cosy the previous winter, felt oppressive, and the park by the river was crowded with tourists. So, as often as I could I escaped. I would pack a bag and catch the number eight bus from Canterbury to go to a little beach at Westgate. It was less crowded than Margate and had much nicer sand for Ben, my little boy, to play on. I would sit at the same spot on the sand that the tide never reached and watch all the people come and go around me as each week passed. After he had finished work, my husband would come to the beach to swim and relax until we finally went home. It was a happy time, our skin turning to a golden brown and the sea air helping us all to sleep despite the heat in the flat and the sound of boisterous, drunken voices wafting through the open windows every night.

From the beginning of June, I noticed a woman. She brought her family to the beach every day and came to the same part where we sat. She was about ten to fifteen years older than me I supposed – guessing by the age of her eldest son. I heard her voice first. She spoke rapidly, loud and clear, with an accent that I couldn't quite place. That voice broke into my sunbather's doze, staccato-like and forced my eyes wide open. She had nine children, ranging from eighteen months to sixteen years, mostly girls, and orders to them were delivered like a metronome. And each was miraculously obeyed.

"Put your shoes together – I'll have my chair here – put up the umbrella - lay the rug under it – don't dig so near to the rug – no ice-creams until after lunch- take your sister to the toilet - don't forget to line the seat…"

"Mutti, can I go swimming?"

"Wait for your sister to come back with Libby and you can go together"

There was no whining or complaints from the children. The family worked together like a well-oiled machine with the mother issuing edicts from the deck chair from which she rarely rose. I couldn't help but look and even caught myself staring because it all seemed so odd. Behind me was a family with children demanding buckets and spades, Coca-Cola and snacks seemingly every five minutes and to my other side, another mother who was running around after her five-year-old like a headless chicken, threatening all sorts of diabolical consequences but never following through. I was lucky as Ben always had a morning and afternoon nap in his stroller and wasn't old enough for demands or wandering off when he was awake, but I studied these unusual neighbours as I wanted to discover the secret of their family co-operation.

Another oddity for me about this lady was how she looked. She wasn't old yet, her hair looked like it had been set on rollers like that of someone much older. It certainly didn't move in the sea breeze. She was the kind of person you would never forget because she didn't seem to 'fit' with the times. She never changed into a swimsuit but instead wore day dresses that looked too formal for the beach and more suited to the 1950's than the 70's. She also wore thick stockings, never taking them off to have a paddle or to let the sun get to her skin. The strange thing was that her two eldest daughters, probably fourteen and fifteen, were similarly dressed. Not a whisper of teenage fashion about their clothes. They wore headscarves tied over their hair and didn't seem to want to play in the sand, or swim, or wander off to find people of their own age. Neither they, nor the older boy, made any objection to taking the younger children to the sea or run errands for their mother. This behaviour was so unlike the other teenagers who appeared at the weekends with their parents, who spent all day listening to their portable radios, demanding food, or wandering around the promenade eyeing up the other boys or girls that were doing the same. The sun must have fried my brain a bit because

I didn't realise until I had been watching them for three days, that the boys were wearing skull caps and had long ringlets either side of their ears, which eventually informed me that this was a family of Hasidic Jews. I realised I must have appeared very rude and tried to curb my curiosity.

Yet the relationships operating within that family group continued to fascinate me, as all around me other families, who came and went through the many weeks, usually had one or two arguments each day. There was always a child crying and the phrase "Not Fair!" reached my ears with an appalling regularity. But the family whom I now named the clockwork one, because that's how it seemed to run, as smoothly as clockwork, just carried on being obedient and obviously not only enjoyed being at the seaside but enjoyed being with each other. There was a lot of laughter amongst those orders. By the end of July, the mother didn't have to say a word. The shoes were put together, the digging happened at a sensible distance from the rug, and the trips to the toilet happened without any fuss. When he was awake and scrabbling about in the sand, Ben would sometimes waddle over to them and try to play alongside the children. None of them spoke to him, which I thought unusual, but neither did they shoo him away or object if he used a spade they had left lying around. They would pack up and leave the beach by four o'clock and I noticed, on Fridays, they stayed only for the morning. They never appeared in their usual spot on a Saturday.

Occasionally the family was joined by friends; ladies who were similarly dressed and whose children were almost, but not quite, as obedient. But I was completely in awe of the original lady. I wanted to pick up tips on how to get my future children to behave as well as hers. I didn't want my young son to grow up to be a brat and whatever it was she was doing, I needed to learn. She seemed to command the respect not only of her children but also of the friends who joined her. In my head I called her The Voice as she was so easy to hear. So clear and precise. I kidded myself I wasn't being nosey. But I was.

"Gitty Lipschitz and I ...." She said one day to a gathering of two other ladies and their families who all immediately sat up straight and leaned in closer to hear every detail. The Voice went on to recount the saga of the re-opening of her summer house in Westgate and the transfer of her family to the coast for the season. It seems she had been received by the said Gitty for one Friday night dinner the previous week and this was a rare honour. Her companions were as engrossed in her story as I was, because as soon as the name Gitty Lipschitz was mentioned, it was as though a spell had been cast. The Voice continued all afternoon with brisk vigour, stopping only occasionally when she topped up her children with food and drink before they asked for it. The companions looked increasingly hot and uncomfortable in the heat, their day dresses clung to their sweaty bodies and their stockings wrinkled round their ankles and became clogged with sand dampened by their perspiration. Yet The Voice remained cool and efficient.

My curiosity embarrassed me. I tried not to be so interested – and yet - I turned over onto my back and propped a towel under my head so I could fit faces to voices as I pretended to be asleep. Every day I could hardly wait for Ben to take his naps so that I could give her my entire attention and watch and learn.

From June to August, I watched – surely she must have noticed me? By mid-August I had hoped to be on nodding terms, but it was obvious that she had everything she needed with her family and the friends she already knew. Ben's sand-pies stood next to those of her youngest, but it seemed that the little boys had no conversation either; they just played alongside each other as toddlers do. New companions replaced the old, but none could take the purgatory of the seaside like she whose composure and hairstyle remained untouched by soaring temperatures. It gradually became apparent to me that The Voice was a close confidante of Gitty Lipschitz, a woman of some standing, a mentor and leader in their community and the tale of the Friday dinner was repeated again and again.

One day in August, she caught me fully gazing at her. I felt myself blushing but by then I was so brown I don't expect she could have seen it.

"Sorry," I stammered, "Please don't think me rude. I have seen you and your family practically every time I come here since June. You seem such a happy family."

"You think?" she answered.

"Well, yes. I mean, your children are so good. They never squabble or make demands."

As I spoke, a father behind me was yelling at his child to NEVER go in the sea without a grown up. And did he hear him? And if he EVER did that again he wouldn't be able to sit down for a week.

She glanced at the man and then looked back at me.

"God has lent us these children. Why should they not be loved and happy?"

"Oh, I agree. I expect a lot of other people would agree too. It's just that….I don't know. You seem to have cracked it."

She sniffed.

"Well, for example. See that group of teenagers over there," and I nodded towards some French students who were staying in Westgate for a few weeks at the foreign language school nearby. They were larking about in the sand and scattering it all over families who were sitting on rugs and in deck chairs, and who were complaining loudly at their antics. They answered the families back in French, saying they did not understand what they were saying, but laughed as they said it. One man stood up and said he'd had enough and was going to see the deck chair attendant to get them to clear off. It was all loud and unpleasant.

"Paaa! That one there," she pointed to a young boy, "He is probably not old enough to have a Bar Mitzvah. He should not be here alone. His parents should be with him to show him how to behave. And those older ones, they have not been taught respect. They have not been shown respect. Respect must be taught. Taught by example. It is the parents who have caused this behaviour. Not the children."

And she waggled her head to and fro.

Just then, her five-year old son came to her, crying. Sand kicked at him by the French students had got into his eyes. She turned her full attention to him and spoke to him in Yiddish. She did not tell the French kids off. She did not rise from her seat. Her little boy was kissed, and the speck removed from his eye with a startling white handkerchief. She then held his head in her hands and spoke quietly to him, smoothing his hair and pointing to an area of the beach that was away from the boisterous teenagers. She sent him back to play. No drama.

She didn't speak to me again, nor I to her which I suppose in itself was strange, although we did nod to each other every evening when she left. She had reacted to her son's problem in the same way that I would have, so in some ways we were quite alike. I would never have complained to kids who I knew would laugh at me. But unlike her, I had no real community in which to have a reputation. I had no real deep religious beliefs either. I was just a young mother living in a stuffy city flat who would soon have to go back to work and juggle my child, work and home like so many countless others. And I would just have to do the best I could.

I went on to have two more children who I used to take to the beach on hot days in the summer. As we could afford it, we bought a small house on the outskirts of Canterbury and as the children and our income grew, we moved yet again until we too had a home near the sea. Our children grew up happily and I hope had a sense of their own worth. We weren't that different, that Jewish mother and me. I never had brats who kicked sand around or who made constant demands for this or that, who caused scenes in public or hurt others and laughed about it.

But, for all that, deep inside, although I had a great deal of respect for her, I still felt a little sympathy as I realised nobody has all the answers. She had to conform to a set of rules she had been born into and I didn't. Yet she had a strong community around her which I lacked. The days were hot and long that year, an uncommon treat for the British. By the end of it I had a lovely tan and had enjoyed the freshness the seaside offered me. She must have enjoyed the seaside too, but never once did she remove those stockings or change into a sundress. By the last week of August, I noticed a third daughter wasn't wearing her swimming costume but was sitting in a deck chair next to her mother, watching the other children having fun on the beach.

Jon

03.01.89

Capricorn: Intractable, austere.
No belief in horoscopes, Chinese or otherwise.

He stared at the script and tried to visualise how he would stand and wait as Tessa delivered her line. The audience had to see how incredulous he should appear without him having to ham it up. He had to pause for just enough time for them to see his reaction before Jimmy, their buffoon of a prompt, hurled the words across the stage for everyone to hear and then think he didn't know his part.

"The man's an idiot" he muttered to himself as he stirred his coffee, dunking his third chocolate hobnob and ramming it into his mouth before it disintegrated and was lost at the bottom of the cup.

His mobile vibrated in his pocket, and he fished it out with chocolate covered fingers, so sticky that he couldn't swipe the screen to answer the call before the caller rang off. He wiped his hands on a nearby tea-towel and looked at the screen. It was Tessa, an actress that Jon did not think would be able to carry the part she had been given. He could see that he would have to coach her a lot so that his own brilliance was able to shine. He wiped the screen of his phone and then rang her back.

"Sorry, missed your call. Was on my work phone."

"Oh, that's OK, it wasn't important. You'd soon find out from Merve."

"Find out what?"

"I just rang to give you the heads up really – seeing as you couldn't make our last rehearsal."

Jon bristled. He didn't like having his absences pointed out to him.

"There was no way that could have been avoided. Merve knew that" he could hear Tessa puffing on that vape thing she was using since she gave up cigarettes.

"Yeh, well…anyway. Tonight's rehearsals are at his house, and he's doing photos as well. So, he wants you to bring the clothes you think your character would wear and, as you are supposed to be my husband, I thought I would tell you what I am wearing so that we could, you know, sort of gel"

"Gel?"

"You know what I mean. It's no good me wearing a bikini with a beach cover-up type thing if you come in chinos and a tie. It *is* supposed to be set at a barbecue. So, have you got a flowery Hawaiian style shirt and some shorts and maybe a sombrero? Or do you need me to get Gus to dig his out? You are about the same size and its hard getting hold of that sort of stuff in January. Even the charity shops don't carry….."

Jon didn't hear anything else she said. He was horrified. He didn't know what upset him more – the idea of appearing on stage dressed like a yob or wearing Tessa's boyfriend's clothes or anyone else's come to that.

He was equally furious that in his absence, his interpretation of the party in the play (sophisticated cocktail), had once again been overruled in favour of this outdoor fiasco.

"So, I'll bring them along anyways just in case then, OK? I think I need to get a spray tan too before we finally hit the stage – the dimples on my legs look much better when they're brown!! Gotta go, kids are screaming for their tea. See you at 7.30." The screen on his phone went blank and Jon reached for another hobnob.

At exactly 7.30, Jon parked outside Merve's rather imposing house in Old Wives Lees. He didn't like leaving the car on the road as there were no streetlights nearby, but as it looked that he was the last to arrive, he had no option; the drive was already full. He yanked his proposed costume out of the boot and strode to the front door. In his head he was rehearsing his objection to the barbecue. He wanted Mervin to see that the gravitas of the entire play would be lost if the setting was not in a dining room, around a table with the characters in full evening dress so that the audience could appreciate the drama that was taking place. He pressed the doorbell and waited. It started to rain.

"Ah, Jon, me old mate" It was Gus. "Just in time. We were about to re-cast you! It's good you aren't on 'til the second act." and with a deep chuckle, Gus held the door open to let him in. Jon tried not to let Gus see that he was not happy about being called a 'mate'. He tried to adopt a neutral facial expression that did not expose his disapproval at the sight that hit him as he walked into the lounge.

It was a beautiful room, large enough to hold a baby grand piano and lavishly carpeted. The sofas were of excellent quality, in fact everything about the room screamed luxury. Everything, that is, except for the gaggle of people scattered around drinking beer from cans and dropping ash onto coffee tables instead of into the ashtrays provided. The fug of tobacco smoke hung heavily in the air and, even to Jon's untrained nose, it was not the kind that should be smoked by decent law-abiding folk, but reserved, in his way of thinking, for students from the university.

"Where've you been?" Merve made his way unsteadily towards Jon, "We've been here ages. You've missed supper."

"Yes, it was lovely. Didn't Tess tell you? Merve laid on Chinese from the local and we had to use chopsticks – but then I expect you can guess that by the noodles decorating my chest!" and Vicky laughed as she pushed her voluminous bosom towards Jon which, indeed had a bean sprout and a few strands of egg noodle nestling in her capacious cleavage.

"Oh, don't waste that," laughed Merve, "I expect you've kept them nice and warm." And to his horror, Jon watched aghast as Merve winked lasciviously at him, bent over, and ate the said food stuff from her chest, holding her by the waist with one hand and tweaking her bottom with the other.

"Very tasty," he said as he emerged sucking the beansprout through his teeth, "Always better when it's served on such a pretty platter" and the couple burst into laughter.

"Tess just told me she would see me here at 7.30" said Jon who wasn't quite sure what to say or do at that juncture.

"Oh, that's because she thought she couldn't get here earlier – babysitting problems. Well, as it was Sunday, I thought we could make it into a little party, and we've been here all afternoon. I tried your mobile but couldn't get through." Merve showed him his phone. Sure enough, he had rung him that morning, but he had rung his work phone and Jon made it a point never to answer that at the weekends.

"But never mind, you're here now. I think there's some sweet and sour left in the kitchen and a bit of chicken. Go and help yourself." And Merve wandered over to another group of women and was received with a loud burst of unseemly laughter as he proceeded to touch one of them inappropriately.

Jon didn't bother with the Chinese food – he was sure it was full of MSG, and he had heard a rumour that someone had been seen netting seagulls at Herne Bay, which they had then sold to the local Chinese restaurant for them to serve as chicken. His mother had laughed at him when he had told her about it at his last visit with her the previous Sunday.

"Don't be so daft!" she had said as she'd ruffled his hair (he hated that) and continued placing her order for chilli chicken and rice with the local take away.

"If you don't want chicken, you could have beef," she went on, holding her hand over the mouthpiece "'Cos I'm not cooking today. I've got my Bridge evening tonight and, as you're here, you can go and fetch this for me."

"But we always had a roast on Sundays," he almost whined.

"Those days are gone, Jon. I've done enough cooking in my life and now it's time for me to enjoy myself." She returned to the phone. "And I'll have a portion of curried beef, some sesame toast and two pancake rolls… Fortune cookies? Oh yes, lovely…How long? …Great. My son will pay when he gets there. Thank you. Zai yan." and she replaced the receiver.

"Zai yan?" asked Jon.

"It's Chinese for see you again or something. I'm not quite sure, but the girl there always smiles at me when I say it. It's their New Year soon so I think it's nice to make the effort to be welcoming. She's a long way from home."

"That girl went to school with me and was born in Canterbury. She's probably completely confused and too polite to point out that a simple 'goodbye' would do." Muttered Jon as he was ushered out the front door for the short walk to the take-away.

He hadn't touched the chicken that day but hadn't been able to resist the curry. Besides, he had been hungry, and it had cost him quite a bit as his mother hadn't paid him back. She made him open a fortune cookie.

"Absolute bunkum," he sniped. "Ridiculous! Anyone could have had this cookie. They churn them out in a sweat shop somewhere in China."

"Oh Jon, go on. What does it say?"

After some cajoling, he read aloud, "Silence is golden."

"I wonder what secrets you're keeping my boy," twinkled his mother. "No, don't tell me. Not until you're ready." And she beamed at him, "Will I need to buy a hat?"

After convincing his mother that he wasn't keeping quiet about some imaginary romantic partner, he went on to lecture her on believing any type of horoscope or fortune telling.

"It's all codswallop," he had told her. "Silence is golden indeed! I'm in a play for God's sake. I have a star part. I have to be far from silent"

And here he was, a week later, being offered Chinese food again, but he really didn't fancy the drama group's leftovers because he had inadvertently polished off the entire packet of Chocolate Hob Nobs earlier. In fact, he was feeling a little sick. But he did have to tell his idea to the prompt, so Jon put his carrier bag of rehearsal clothes in a corner by the piano and walked over to talk to Jimmy.

"Hi there," boomed Jimmy, "Didn't think you were coming today, Jon. We've already done act one. Luckily you aren't in it. Didn't have to prompt once either. Hope you've learned your lines!"

"I wanted to talk to you about the party scene actually," said Jon, ignoring Jimmy's last remark despite the urge to tackle him on it. "I want you to let me pause before I react to Tessa's line about my being late."

"Oh yes?" said Jimmy, scratching behind his left ear, "Blooming hearing aid's giving me hell. I'm going to take it off if it's all right with you, so speak up." And without waiting for a response, he pulled his hearing aid from behind his ear and with a "That's better, I'm all yours" which rang out across the room, so everyone turned to listen to what was being said.

"I've already told you, Jimmy, and it's a bit delicate so I don't want to shout."

"Sorry, you're dedicating something?"

"No, it's a bit *delicate.*"

Jimmy looked at him blankly. The rest of the room had all turned, eager to listen to Jon's delicate problem. Jon shrugged his shoulders and mouthed "Don't worry" to Jimmy and walked as nonchalantly as he was able towards the kitchen, just wanting to get away but knowing every eye in the room was on him.

It was in the kitchen that he discovered Tessa, smoking a cigarette.

"Greetings husband number two" she giggled, waving a fork, and scattering fried rice over the floor. "I've got the munchies big time."

"I thought you told me 7.30"

"Oooh, did I – sorry. That was the time I thought I could get here because my mum was playing up about babysitting, but as it turned out, I got here earlier. Do you like my costume?" and she twirled around, scattering even more rice as she turned and then, reaching out with the fork to steady herself as she lost her footing, she put her hand in what remained of a container of pork dumplings sending them rolling across the work surface, eventually dropping in a congealed heap onto the floor to join the rice.

"Steady!" said Jon, reaching out to help her before she trod on the mess and ended up amongst it herself, "Watch what you're doing. Why are you smoking and eating at the same time? That's really disgusting. And I thought you'd given up smoking anyway."

"Oh, I have," giggled Tessa "I've given up cigarettes. But THIS isn't a cigarette. Want some?" and she pushed the stump of the spliff in his face. "Anyway, whatcha think of my cossie?" She waggled her hips seductively at him causing her beach wrap to fall open. He was struck dumb as he saw her full breasts almost enclosed by a tiny bikini top and her large, stretch-marked stomach wobble in time with her waving arm.

Jon leapt back as though he had been burned. He'd never been good with handling women. He was always embarrassed when they showed any kind of interest in him. It wasn't that he didn't like women or that he preferred men. It was just he couldn't cope too well with any hint of a relationship. He didn't really have friends as such either. He'd joined the drama group at the advice of his mother after she moaned that he needed to get a hobby, to get out more and mix with people. She had said that amateur dramatics would mean he didn't have to be himself – he could pretend to be another character and that would help him with his shyness.

"Very nice, but I think an evening dress would have been more appropriate."

"Can't wait to see you in your outfit, Jonno. Go and try it on – I've left it by the piano. Isn't the view just beautiful from here?" and she turned her gaze towards the kitchen window, through which nothing but the reflection of the kitchen lights and rain running down the pane could be seen. "It's like an abstract painting."

Jon sidled backwards into the lounge and made his way towards the piano where he had left his bag. He picked up both carriers as he could see his sophisticated dinner party idea wasn't an option; the whole cast were dressed as though they were on the Costa del Sol. Even Jimmy, who, although always clearly heard, was not actually ever seen on stage (unless Phil had a mix up with the curtain), was in costume. He was wearing thigh length shorts with his socks and sandals, a bright pink tee shirt (stained with black bean sauce) and a hat he had brought back from a recent trip to visit his daughter in Melbourne, the corks of which were clearly the cause for his hearing aid discomfort as they kept brushing against his ears.

"Is it ok if I pop upstairs and change, Merve?" asked Jon, lifting the bags up to show his intentions to the director, who was now sitting with his (much younger) wife on his lap on one of the sofas as she dabbed at him with a tissue to remove curry sauce from his cheeks.

"Go for it" he called back. "We are going to do the photos first, so you need to get a lick on. Use the room at the top of the stairs on your left. Talking of licks," and he turned his attention back to his wife, "why don't you just lick it off my love – much quicker!" and he nuzzled his face into hers as he groped her bottom in full view of the assembled cast. Jon heard her shriek with delight.

He escaped up the stairs and found the assigned room which was full of a variety of discarded clothes draped over chairs and the bed. There was no lock on the door which made Jon uneasy, so he went into the ensuite and, using the clothes from his own and the bag provided by Tessa, managed to assemble an outfit in which he felt comparatively comfortable – fitting the barbecue scene but also retaining a semblance of dignity for his character. He put the unused items back into their relative bags and opened the door to go back downstairs.

He quickly shut the door again and leaned against it, his heart pounding. He knew that what he had just witnessed would be imprinted on his brain for ever. The sight of Phil's hairy, spotty backside moving up and down with a grace he never exuded when shifting the scenery and the sound of Tessa's squeals would haunt him for the rest of his days. He was so glad that he hadn't left his coat on that bed and pitied those who had. He spent ten more minutes in the bathroom praying they would be finished soon and didn't need the loo afterwards. What would he say if they did? The embarrassment was unbearable.

He pressed his ear to the door to see if he could hear any more noises and then tentatively opened it a fraction. The room was empty. Breathing a sigh of relief, Jon went downstairs and joined the cast who were lined up in front of Merve's bi-folding patio doors which now had its blinds lowered and to which someone – obviously not Phil as it was straight – had pinned a large poster of a tropical rainforest borrowed from the local Save the Planet group. Jimmy was positioning an expensive looking camera so that it could capture all the cast in one shot and Merve, who was now strangely business-like, was ordering his cast to stand in certain places.

Jon could see that despite having drunk too much Prosecco, Merve had a good eye for detail, so he was happy to stand where he was directed and put his arm around Tessa. He knew he had to play the part of a deceived husband but that at the start of the play, he was supposed to have doted on her. He put on his doting face and placed his arm across Tessa's shoulders. He felt her sway and realised she needed to be held around the waist so that she didn't fall over.

"Try to smile, Jonno" called Merve, "You look like a codfish with that expression…. that's better. Phil, lovely as you are, you aren't cast so bugger off. Mick, could you hold those barbecue tongs a little higher? Great, that's great. Now Vicky, could you stand closer to Mick – you are supposed to be married after all, and you don't know yet that he's screwing around"

"But we are married," called back Vicky, "and he is screwing around!" and she moved closer to her husband.

Everyone laughed. Except Jon.

"Right. Dave. Can you squat down in front of Tessa and Jon, and Karen can you put your foot on his knee like you're a big game hunter? Terrific! That's terrific. Ok Jimmy. Try that one.

"What?" said Jimmy.

Merve went over to him. "Put your bloody hearing aid in for fuck's sake. And take that daft hat off. You'll get corks in the frame.

"Pardon?" Said Jimmy.

Merve pushed him out the way and looked through the lens.

"That's good!" He proceeded to take the pictures. He moved them around a little more, changing an expression here and a limb or two there until he had a bank of pictures to choose from. Jon marvelled at his ability and realised that Merve must be an excellent advertising executive. He certainly knew his stuff.

"Right. Now, Mick, go and swap the tongs for the large fork and give it to Vicky. Vicky, I want you to hold the fork towards him as though you are threatening him with it. Tessa, put on a lot of lipstick and then kiss Mick on his cheek so we get a good impression of your lips. Dave, grab a seat, sit on it, and put Karen across your knee as though you are going to spank her.

"She'd like that!" voiced Dave with a twinkle in his eye and rubbing his knees as he had been squatting for too long.

"Cheeky bugger." came back Karen, who happily spread herself across Dave's knees, "Ooo, couldn't you empty your pockets first, something's digging into me!"

"Nothing in my pockets love," smirked Dave and he tapped her lightly on the bum.

"Jimmy wouldn't like that," said Karen.

"Jimmy wouldn't feel it!" replied Dave. "No, don't tell me to shh. He can't hear it anyway." And he and Karen both broke into a fit of giggles.

"Enough, you two," called Merve and they immediately stopped. "Karen, I need you to scowl and Dave, you are triumphant. That's better... Now, Jon and Vicky. Jon, turn your back on Tessa and Tessa, lean your cheek on Jon's back and hold him around the neck. Jon, fold your arms and look indignant. No indignant, not angry...No that's not right. Jon you are a complete, anal fuckwit."

Jon glared at him.

"That's what I want! Perfect!" and Merve snapped away. "These are great" and he continued to make small changes until he felt he had another bank to choose from.

"Now I want singles for the programme. Sarah, get some make up remover to Mick's cheek please" and his young wife bustled around immediately while Merve carried on lining up each character one by one until all the cast had a picture for their profile.

Jon was still smarting at his insult when Merve called for his cast to take their places for act two. He was not on stage at the time as his 'wife' was propositioning

Mick, so he took this opportunity to approach Merve and make his suggestion about the dramatic pause he had been planning all afternoon.

"For fuck's sake, Jonno, I need to concentrate on the actors. Can't you see me about it later? No, no Mick. Don't give her what she wants straight away…Walk over to the barbecue and look like you're turning the sausages. Make her wait. The audience knows you are already screwing Karen, so a man who can have any woman he likes makes them wait. Ain't that right Sarah?" and his young wife who was busy applying more make up on Vicky's face laughed out loud and called back, "Oh, stop!"

"Go from Tessa's line, 'He wouldn't notice what I was doing. He's too interested in making money.' Start to move as she is speaking and then let her dangle."

Jon slunk back to the offstage part of the room and stood next to Jimmy who was following the script and cleaning a piece of food from his teeth with a toothpick.

The play continued with its storyline following the twists and turns as written. The cast seemed to be word perfect, Jimmy only having to prompt once when Dave forgot his line – he had been knocked to the floor by Mick and was trying to get on his feet at the time, but Jimmy had been anxious to be seen doing his job. Instead of carrying on graciously, Dave shouted at him to give him a bloody chance and then carried on with his lines.

At last, Jon was to have his entrance. He turned to Jimmy, "Don't forget to let me have that pause." He mouthed each word so that, in the event of his hearing aid break down, Jimmy could see what he was saying.

As he entered, he could see Fiona (Tessa) his wife in a romantic hold with Andrew (Mick). Jon stopped in his tracks and waited. He counted silently to himself as he had in his own kitchen that afternoon. He only got to three.

"So that's why you arranged for me to be late!" boomed Jimmy.

Jon hit his forehead with the palm of his hand. "Merve, I just think that I would be shocked to see my wife in a clinch like that with one of my friends, so I wanted a pause there so the audience could appreciate my reaction and give Tessa time to look upset.

"Ok, sounds good – Jimmy?"

"What's up Merve?"

"Give Jon time when he comes in."

"Will do Merve." replied Jimmy.

"Ok, let's go from Tessa's line: *he thinks I'm perfect in every way.*"

Jon went back to the place where the door would be.

"He thinks I'm perfect in every way…" murmured Tessa as she moved to snuggle into Mick's shoulder.

Jon entered and started to count: one, two, three, four…

"So that's why you…" shouted Jimmy

"For God's sake Jimmy, I was ACTING" screamed back Jon, unable to control himself. "I asked you to let me have a pause before spoke. Why don't you ever listen?" and Jon threw the prop, a bottle of wine he was bringing to the party at Jimmy and flounced off. Luckily, the bottle was empty, so it was only broken glass that had to be cleared up. There was a mumble from the rest of the cast and Merve called for them to carry on..

At the end of the scene. Jimmy came up to Jon.

"Sorry, old mate. Merve's had a word with me, and I'll give you the time you need in future. Having a bit of trouble with the old hearing aid today. Think I need new batteries." And he tapped Jon on the shoulder and smiled at him sheepishly.

"I'm sorry for behaving like that, Jimmy. It won't happen again." And Jon smiled back though inside he still wanted to smash Jimmy in his stupid face, not just for prompting him unnecessarily, but also for causing him to look like a spoilt child in front of everyone else.

The cast would have liked to run through the play a second time, but everyone had had enough, and they were glad when Merve told them to meet for the technical rehearsal at the Church Hall the following Wednesday.

The play was to run for three nights and was booked out for the Saturday. Jon was excited as one of Merve's clients, who had once produced a play on Shaftesbury Avenue, was going to attend that night. He was hoping to be 'discovered' and he spent a lot of time that day ensuring that he was word perfect. The technical rehearsal and Thursday and Friday night's performances had gone well and although the audience was not so large, they had laughed and clapped at the right moments. The locals had come to support their friends on stage and to take advantage of the very reasonable prices charged at the bar there, so each night had been most enjoyable. It was expected that Saturday would be just as good and the laughter even louder from a bigger audience.

Act one went well. The intrigues of the couples in the play were well established and when Merve popped backstage in the interval, he was full of compliments.

He brought a case of champagne with him and told them that after the play, he and his client would be joining them backstage to toast their success. Jon could hardly contain his delight. Act two was called and everyone went to their places.

Jon waited in the wings next to Jimmy who gave him the thumbs up just before he heard his cue.

"He thinks I'm perfect in every way." Said Tessa.

Jon entered through the French windows. He was holding his bottle of wine. He started to count in his head; one, two, three, four, five. He altered the expression on his face so that the audience could see his reaction; six, seven, eight. He opened his mouth but just couldn't remember his line. He glanced nervously at Jimmy who gave him the thumbs up and nodded madly. Tessa, now turned completely to him and gave him a look to urge him to speak, nine, ten, eleven. The audience shuffled audibly. Twelve, thirteen. Jon looked at Jimmy again, but he was gazing at the script and did not see him.

"I suppose you think that this is why she arranged for you to be late?" said Mick, saving the day. The audience erupted into laughter.

Jon dropped the bottle as he was supposed to and exited back through the French windows.

At the post-production party, Merve commented at the brilliance of Jon not to saying his line at all. "It made the play even funnier!" he remarked as he filled Jon's glass for a third time. "I don't know why we didn't think of it before! And the timing! Perfect. Just Perfect. Good on you, Jonno. Giving up your only line in the play like that for the better good of us all. Who would have thought it? That silence of yours, it was absolutely golden!"

"My silence was golden?" thought Jon as he watched with envy the Shaftesbury Avenue producer chatting with Tessa and Mick, putting their numbers in his phone and congratulating them on their amazing performance.

And he remembered his mother and the fortune cookie he'd sneered at.

"My silence was sodding golden!"

Josephine

18.12.79

Sagittarius: Joyful, creative.
Family orientated. Loves life.

When I was a little girl, my parents moved to Australia. I didn't want to go. I remember seeing our home being packed up and bits and pieces sold off. It made me very unhappy. I refused to part with any of my toys and hid under the stairs on the day we were supposed to fly to Perth. But when you're a child, there's not a lot you can do when grown-ups have made up their mind about something, even though you might cry and yell that you didn't want to go. You didn't want to leave your home or your nan who you loved so very much.

Our new home was beautiful, and I had my own bedroom as did my brothers, and a swimming pool. But I missed my old life so much. I missed my friends and most of all I missed my nan. Phone calls were okay, but they weren't the same as dropping in to see her, visiting her biscuit tin where she always had the ones she knew I loved, and climbing onto her lap for a cuddle whenever I felt low. There was nothing like a nanny cuddle to make me feel better.

I made friends with the boys who lived over the road from us and one day, one of them asked me why I was so sad.

'I really miss my nan,' I told him, 'She's so far away and I don't know when I'll see her again.'

Julian was Australian and had lots of relatives nearby who he could go and see whenever he wanted. We were sitting in his back garden in the cubby we had made there in the tree, throwing honky nuts at his cat Tigger who was completely ignoring us as he stretched out in the sun.

'That sucks,' he said. 'Perhaps you need to adopt a granny? Rowan from school, he's from England. He adopted Maria who sells the veggies from her garden. On the corner. You know the one?'

I nodded.

'But she's Italian and doesn't know a lot of English. He thinks she likes him best because she ruffles his hair and gives him a plum whenever he calls there to get his mum's tomatoes. But she does that to all the kids. He just doesn't realise it.'

'I don't want to adopt Maria.' I said.' I don't like plums.'

'Well, what about Mrs Pepper? She's always good for a glass of juice and a cake.'

I had seen Mrs Pepper. She was a very posh lady who lived in the granny annex of the big house next door to Julian. She was always dressed immaculately and whenever she went shopping or out with her friends, she used a taxi as she didn't drive.

'Does she like kids?' I asked. I had never seen any children my age visiting the Pepper house.

'I expect so,' answered Julian, 'She hasn't got a husband and she only had Mr Pepper and he's married now. And he's only got Lucy. Lucy is weird, she has different coloured hair and rings through her nose and only wears black Dr Martins even if its 40 degrees, so she will never have kids. Mrs Pepper is English, so I expect she'll like you. Give her a try and see how you go.'

So that afternoon, I took some of the cookies I had made with my mum the day before – they were a bit burnt but Nan's don't usually mind that kind of thing – and went over to Mrs Pepper's house. It was really hot, and she was sitting on her veranda. I said hello, told her my name, gave her the cookies, and asked her if she would be interested in doing some grandma duties as I was missing my nan.

Mrs Pepper was fascinating. She was a tiny woman with thick glasses and gunmetal grey hair and much older than my real nan who was big and bouncy and had boobies you could bury your head in. Mrs Pepper wasn't that kind of nan. She insisted our relationship should remain on a Mrs Pepper and Josephine basis (not Jo or Josie as my family and friends called me) and that when I visited, I would water her plants in the house with a dainty watering can with roses painted on the side. For that she would tell me tales of her life and give me afternoon tea and cakes once a week and let me take her little dog for a walk in the bush. She was ever the lady and when she farted, which she did quite a lot, especially when she bent over, she carried on as if nothing had happened. So did I.

Mrs Pepper and I became good friends. She was a good talker, and I was always ready to listen. She had led an amazing life. Her husband had been a stockbroker in the city in London and they had been very rich. She had sailed on the first voyage of the Queen Mary, first to Cherbourg and then on to New York. She showed me photos of that ship and I could not even imagine the lifestyle she'd had. Mrs Pepper had travelled the world. She had photos of India and Egypt, South America, and Russia. Everywhere she went, she bought something from that place to remind her. And they filled her little lounge with colours and textures that should not have gone together. But that didn't matter. Mrs Pepper smoked quite a lot and would put her cigarette into a black holder so that it looked very long. 'It stops your fingers going yellow; very unladylike', and she flicked her ash into an ash tray that sat on a pedestal and whirled around when you pushed a button down. We had nothing as exciting in our house. My parents didn't even smoke. But the best thing in her house that I really loved was a tiny Impressionist painting by Pissarro. She took it off the wall and let me take it to show my mother who was an art teacher, not worrying that I might drop it or forget to bring it back. She knew I would be careful. Mrs Pepper had real class. My mother freaked when she saw it and hastened it back to her, carrying the little gem as though it were made of crystal.

On special days, like the Melbourne Cup, Mrs Pepper asked me to help her get ready to go to lunch with her friends. Mrs Pepper had a hat with a real dead blackbird on the top. It's feathers still glistened as did its eyes. And she wore matching black button gloves that came up to her elbows. I helped her button them up. They were made of the softest material. She said they were calfskin. She had a scarf made of fur with a fox head on the end. When Mrs Pepper got herself dolled up it looked like she was taking her pets out to lunch with her. She gave me a pair of her gloves. She told me she'd had all her gloves hand stitched especially for her in Paris. They were cream coloured, but she didn't wear them any longer as they were stained at the fingers. I was so proud of those gloves but after a year or two, I couldn't wear them as they were so tiny, and I was growing fast.

By 1986, Mrs Pepper had been my surrogate grandmother (she didn't like the term granny or nan) for two years and she had become a firm favourite with the rest of my family. She even managed to tame my brothers when they came to visit, lured by my tales of cucumber sandwiches and fairy cakes. Young Mr and Mrs Pepper asked us to keep an eye on their mother that autumn as they had to go to the Eastern States for Lucy to go into rehab. We didn't ask questions; it must have been painful enough for them and we were happy to oblige. It was April and all over the news that Halley's Comet was to be seen in the skies for the first time since 1910. My father got out some chairs and we set them up in the road alongside our other neighbours. My mother and I went to fetch Mrs Pepper so that she could see it too. My dad said it was a once in a lifetime thing and that we should all remember it. Mrs Pepper took great joy in telling him, and everybody else assembled there, that she'd already seen it in 1910 when she was a girl. The whole street cheered.

As I grew older, I noticed Mrs Pepper didn't go out so much and I was the one who had to make the tea in the teapot (never mugs) and pour it into the bone-china teacups, while she sat in her special chair which lifted her up when she had to stand. She had one of those walking frames that you could put things on and push around the house and a contraption like a cage appeared around her toilet. My mum said it was to help her get up from a sitting position, but from the smell of her house, I think Mrs Pepper was having rather a lot of accidents and not making it to the toilet in time. She was already small, but she seemed to shrink even more and started looking like the bird that was on her hat.

I suppose it was inevitable that I would be the one to find her. It was a very hot day in early January and my mother asked me to take some guava juice to Mrs Pepper and ask her if she would like to come over for a paddle in our pool. By then, she had a wheelchair and as she was so tiny, it was easy to push her about. I went straight away and knocked. There was no answer, but her dog was whining and scratching at the door inside. I knew young Mr and Mrs Pepper were at work, so I looked for the key she kept hidden beneath a loose brick. The smell hit me as I went through the door. Mrs Pepper was lying on the floor, very still. I leant over her, scared that she might be dead, but she looked up at me. I breathed a sigh of relief. She had fallen and had messed herself with shock. Her eyes pleaded with me. She couldn't talk. But I knew what she wanted. Above all else, she needed her dignity.

'Don't worry,' I said, 'I'll sort all this. No one will know.'

I cleaned her up, changed her, made her comfortable and scrubbed the carpet. I opened all the windows and doors to help clear the smell of disinfectant and rinsed her soiled clothes through before putting them on to wash.

Then I rang her daughter in law and told her that Mrs Pepper had had a fall, and could she please come home as she was also unable to talk. I waited with Mrs Pepper and held her hand.

She'd had a stroke. Her son arranged for her to go into a nursing home and my visits to Mrs Pepper became scarce until eventually, they stopped altogether. I didn't go to her funeral.

By the time I turned twenty-one, my family had returned to live in the UK. It was so lovely to be able to see my nan again and as often as I wanted. But isn't it funny how the grass is always greener sometimes? Once back in Canterbury, I missed the sun and my swimming pool. I missed the friends I had there who I had grown up with and the easy way of the Australians.

My twenty-first birthday was spent at university with my new friends; it was the last day of term. I had a great time. At least, I think I did as I can't remember all that much about it. It felt strange having a birthday in the winter as I was used to being in the pool or on the beach in December. I woke up the next day with a bad headache to the sound of my phone ringing. By the time I got to it, it had gone to voicemail. It was my mother. I had run out of credit so couldn't ring her back, but as I was travelling home for Christmas that day I knew it wouldn't be long before we could have a proper chat.

'A parcel has arrived for you. It looks exciting. It's from Australia. Have a good trip. See you soon. Love you.'

I finally got home around sixish. Lots of hugs and kisses. Plans to celebrate my birthday again, this time with the family. Opening cards that had come to my home instead of to halls. Catching up on gossip and telling them all my news.

'Goodness,' said my mother,' Almost forgot. This came for you. I had to sign for it.'

It was a small wooden crate. Sent from Australia.

My father got a claw hammer and eased the wood apart. Inside, packed in so many layers of straw and paper lay the tiny Pissarro I had so admired. And a letter written by Mr Pepper to me lay beneath it.

Dear Josephine,

My mother dictated the following to me and requested that this be sent to you on your twenty-first birthday. Many happy returns from us all here. I hope you like her gift to you. She was adamant that you should have it. And can I thank you for all you did for my mother. Your visits meant the world to her and kept her young at heart.

With fondest regards,

Donald Pepper.

This is to be given to Josephine on her twenty-first birthday in recognition of the fine young woman I know she is to become. Always remember, Josephine, that a lady's dignity is worth more than anything else in life and your love and kindness helped me retain mine. Always value yourself because you have a beauty far deeper than your skin. You have a beauty of the soul. Never lose it.

With love from your surrogate grandmother.

Mrs Pepper xx

I have learned to treasure those things I have in my life and not pine for things beyond my control. I have passed what Mrs Pepper taught me on to my daughters. And whenever I look at that little painting, I remember her and her gloves and her hat, but most of all I remember her incredible dignity.

Charlotte

05.06.90

Gemini: Deep thinking, unforgiving.
Darkness lurks beneath the surface.

The first time I realised that Katy told 'stories' was when we were six.

It was the Christmas holidays and she had come to stay while her mum was having a baby. I remember feeling very unhappy as she kept on about how Father Christmas thought she was special and that she was to have an extra present because she was better than all the other children. It made me feel bad. I already felt bad as Katy had the blonde curls and blue eyes that I had always wanted, and her mother allowed her to have black patent shoes and socks with frills and bows on the cuff, which my mother never bought me. This extra present was a little brother, another source of envy for me, and she preened as she showed me the gift she had bought for him. It was the Barbie doll I had been given that Christmas. It was Sporty Barbie. I had wanted it ever since I had seen her advertised on the TV in September. She had sunglasses and a tight-fitting ski suit in bright pink and her skis attached to the car that my grandad had bought for me after three months of very heavy hint dropping. I loved that doll. I knew it was mine as I had added a scarf from Shopping Barbie to her outfit to keep her extra warm.

She knew I knew. She just looked at me with that 'what you going to do about it' look. But I was furious and tried to take my Barbie back.

'If you dare say anything, I'll say you gave her to me. And I'll cry.'

When Katy cried, you could hear her from the bottom of the street. The noise was awful.

"I'm going to tell" I said and got up to go to the kitchen.

Katy slapped herself around the face, leaving a red mark.

Then she cried. And my mother came running.

And the mark on her face made them believe the story she told. They believed that I had slapped her. And they made me give the doll back to her.

And I swore never to talk to her again.

She got away with murder.

But of course, as she was my cousin, I had to talk to her again. Even worse, we had to take her on holiday with us when I was fifteen because her mum and dad were divorcing. They had never got over their little son's death when he was only six weeks old. My uncle had been devastated as he had found the baby when he and my dad had come home from golf. He had moved the pillow to pick up the basket and discovered that little Nathan wasn't breathing. The doctors said it was SIDS. Poor little Nathan. But I heard my father tell my mother that no baby needs a pillow at six weeks, so why was one found by the Moses basket and why had it been left on the floor? Neither my uncle nor his wife could forgive each other; they both became very depressed and argued about it for years. Their divorce was inevitable. Once they agreed that their marriage was over, Uncle Jack asked us to include Katy on our summer holiday to Cornwall that year as she had been through so much and needed a break. And of course, my parents, who doted on Katy, agreed immediately. 'She can share your bedroom, can't she Charlie?' I had to nod my agreement. I had no choice.

We had a little holiday home in St. Ives, and I knew a lot of the locals there as we went as often as we could. I had practically grown up with Jason who lived next door. Tall, always bronzed and very handsome, Jason was two years older than me, and I loved him with all my fifteen-year-old heart. But as soon as Katy saw him, she told me she was the one he would love. Not me. And as we went to the beach as a threesome and surfed and swam together, she was there, with her milky, smooth complexion, showing off her bikini in her perfect figure. We always left our phones and money and Jason's asthma pump in a secret place under the boardwalk so we could enjoy each day and have fun. Which, that first week, we certainly did. But on the Saturday, Katy showed me a text she'd had from Jason; he wanted to see her by herself.

"So would you please go shopping with your mum today, or just do something else and give us some space?"

I was heartbroken. She went off by herself early and called at his house. I saw them leave together. He looked back at my window, and I dodged back behind the curtains. I didn't want him to see me crying. I spent the morning helping my dad in the garden and didn't make a fuss when my mother asked me to gather all the clothes that needed washing from my bedroom. Katy just dropped her things where she took them off but the shorts she'd worn yesterday had made their way under her bed. They clonked against the floor as I pulled them out and Jason's phone dropped from the pocket. I knew Jason. He'd used 1234 as his passcode on everything since he was first allowed a phone. There were six missed calls from his landline number the night before; he must have spent ages looking for it. I looked at the text he'd supposedly sent and wasn't surprised to see that it had been written this morning. But obviously not by him. I was furious.

When Katy got back that evening, I confronted her with what I'd found. She took the phone and simply deleted the text. "Don't know what you're talking about," she smirked. "I found that phone last night and I'd take it to him now, but he's gone to hospital."

I went cold. I ran next door. Jason's parents weren't there, but his sister Ruth was. She looked pale and frightened. She was furious when I gave her Jason's phone. It seemed, Katy had strolled up to the house on her way home and told them that Jason had had an asthma attack and had collapsed as he couldn't find his puffer. Ruth said Katy told them she couldn't phone for help as I'd taken both their phones the day before because I was jealous.

"So, if he doesn't pull through, it'll be down to you, you evil little cow."

And she slammed the door in my face.

It was touch and go with Jason, but he gradually recovered. My parents cut our holiday short in embarrassment. They refused to believe me when I told them I hadn't taken his phone, or Katy's.

"I really can't blame you for convincing yourself that you had nothing to do with this, Charlotte," said my mother, "But as Katy told me she found her phone in your dressing table drawer, it's obvious you are lying. And if there's one thing I detest more than anything else, it's a liar." And she pushed me into the back of the car and ignored me all the way to the Watford Gap. Katy just sat there, that smirk I knew so well, plastered over her face.

She had got away with murder.

It took me three weeks to pluck up the courage to contact Jason. He was surprised to hear from me as Katy had told him that I found him boring and that I only put up with him when I came to St. Ives because I pitied him.

"That's absolute crap!"

I told Jason about finding the phone; that it was obvious she had written the text to me telling me to back off, and that everyone thought it was me who had behaved badly.

"I told Katy I wasn't interested when she came on to me and she went all funny. When I said it was you I liked, she went ballistic, grabbed my inhaler, and screamed that if I ever said anything about it, she would tell everyone I had tried to touch her up. Then she just took off up the hill. I tried to run after her and that's when I had my asthma attack. It was bad Charlie. I couldn't breathe."

I thought he'd had a lucky escape. He could have been up in court on an assault charge. Or dead.

"She always gets away with murder." I told him.

Anyway, his parents had already decided they didn't want to chance living next door to people like us, and they were moving to Newquay. It was too late to clear it with them; their house was sold.

I never saw my old friend again.

And now this.

I'd had to ask her to my wedding, but I absolutely refused to have her as a bridesmaid despite my mother nagging me. I'd heard her on the phone to Katy.

"No, Katy my dear, I'm sure it's not because she's frightened you'll outshine her…"

I was livid.

I told my mother that perhaps it would be better for everyone concerned if I had a Las Vegas wedding. That shut her up. She wasn't going to miss out on being the 'mother of the bride'.

In the end I managed to get married and have two children without encountering Katy too much. I heard that she had married herself but was going through a divorce. That's when she came to Canterbury for a 'short break' with my parents.

Who visit me and my little family every Sunday.

For lunch.

"Of course, she must come too." said my husband.

"It's rude not to include her." said my father.

"You need to get over your jealousy, Charlie," said my mother as she bounced my two-year-old daughter on her knee. "You're so lucky. Look at what you've got. A lovely home, two gorgeous kiddies and a doting husband. Katy can't have children, you know. That's why her marriage is over. She would die to have what you've got. Some men are so shallow."

I knew why she couldn't conceive. She'd had a messy abortion after her last affair. Her reputation had even reached us here. She might have moved to London after her baby brother had died, but she had kept in touch as her parents had inflicted her on us every Easter, 'for a little change of scene'. How I'd hated those holidays. She always had more eggs than me.

I watched that bitch like a hawk when she arrived. I watched her worm her way even further into my parent's affections. She charmed my kids and flirted outrageously with my husband. But I never let my guard down with her.

Her 'short' visit with my parents got extended each week and the excuses they gave me for why she had to stay got more and more complicated. She had money troubles as her husband was being difficult, and no, she couldn't work as she was too emotionally traumatised. And, of course she wasn't a financial drain on them as she hardly ate anything, and her clothes didn't cost very much.

And every Sunday she turned up for a roast and never offered to wash up.

But then one weekend, about three weeks after she had arrived, I had shingles. The doctor asked me if I was under any extra stress. If only he knew. He gave me medication and I was generally very drowsy as well as uncomfortable. So, I was in bed when our Sunday guests arrived. My mother took over cooking lunch from my husband who was caught up in a work problem. My father played football in the garden with my son. When he brought me a cup of tea, I asked my husband where Chloe was. I was horrified to learn that Katy had taken her down to the river.

To look at the ducks.

"She said to tell you her little brother loved looking at the ducks."

He thought I was mad as I dragged myself out of bed and hurtled down the street in my pyjamas. The people at the riverside thought I had lost my mind when I charged along the bank screaming her name at the top of my voice. The men fishing quietly thought I was crazy when I snatched my daughter from Katy's arms and pushed her with all my might into the filthy water. I put Chloe down and screamed like a maniac as I held Katy's head under. I had to be restrained. Katy had to be resuscitated.

And that's why I'm here. And the nurse has just given me that pill which makes me feel so tired, like I have felt for quite a few months now. I think.

And she's at my house. With my husband. With my kids.

And when I get out of here.

I'm going to have to find somehow to get away with murder.

Acknowledgements

Like a child, a book is often the product of a village.

My heartfelt gratitude goes to Bex from Grosvenor House, whose belief and encouragement has jolted me into doing something with my writing. Without her advice and input this book would never have happened. My thanks must also go to my daughter, Abby whose support, when my self-confidence flagged kept me on course and who also, along with the lovely Jane Daulman, undertook the onerous task of proofreading my entire manuscript. Thanks also to my clever son, Duncan who took my paintings of the cathedral and some of my characters and digitally produced the cover-design.

Finally, I must thank my late husband, Bill, possibly the most outrageous and exciting character I have ever known. Many of his experiences and the people who I met because of him have influenced and brought colour to my stories.

About the Author

Barb Dobson emigrated with her family to Western Australia in 1983, where she gained a degree in Art Education at Curtin University and taught art in various High Schools around Perth.

Returning to the UK in the late nineties, she continued teaching in East Kent and became familiar with the areas around Canterbury.

Exhibiting artwork in both Australia and the UK she has also co-written and directed three plays as well as some short sketches for the virtual Edinburgh Festival in 2020.

Now widowed, Barb lives in Birchington-on-Sea, close to her three children.

www.ingramcontent.com/pod-product-compliance
Ingram Content Group UK Ltd.
Pitfield, Milton Keynes, MK11 3LW, UK
UKHW031030161224
452563UK00001BA/17

9 781803 811031